THE Mariposa HOTEL

A **tangerine street** ROMANCE
A NOVEL IN THREE PARTS

THE *Mariposa* HOTEL

A **tangerine street** ROMANCE
A NOVEL IN THREE PARTS

Julie Wright
Melanie Jacobson
Heather B. Moore

Mirror Press

Copyright © 2016 by Mirror Press, LLC
Paperback edition
All rights reserved

No part of this book may be reproduced in any form whatsoever without prior written permission of the publisher, except in the case of brief passages embodied in critical reviews and articles. This is a work of fiction. The characters, names, incidents, places, and dialog are products of the authors' imaginations and are not to be construed as real.

Cover Design by Rachael Anderson
Interior Design by Heather Justesen
Edited by Cassidy Wadsworth & Kelsey Down
Published by Mirror Press, LLC
E-book edition released November 2015

ISBN-10: 1-941145-81-7
ISBN-13: 978-1-94114581-4

Welcome to tangerine street

Tangerine Street is a must-see tourist stop with a colorful mix of one-of-a-kind boutiques, unique restaurants, eclectic museums, quaint bookstores, and exclusive bed-and-breakfasts. The Fortune Café, situated in the middle of this charming collection of shops and cafés, is a Chinese restaurant unlike any other because, well, to be honest, the fortunes found in the cookies all come true . . .

OTHER WORKS BY JULIE WRIGHT
Spell Check
Death Thieves
The Newport Ladies Book Club Series
My Not-So-Fairy-Tale Life
Cross My Heart
Loved Like That
Four Chambers
The Fortune Café
The Boardwalk Antiques Shop

OTHER WORKS BY MELANIE JACOBSON
Not My Type
Second Chances
Twitterpated
Smart Move
The List
Painted Kisses
Always Will
The Fortune Café
The Boardwalk Antiques Shop

OTHER WORKS BY HEATHER B. MOORE
The Aliso Creek Novella series
A Timeless Romance Anthology Series
The Newport Ladies Book Club Series
Heart of the Ocean
Love is Come
Finding Sheba
Lost King
Slave Queen
The Fortune Café
Boardwalk Antiques Shop

Part One

Ghost of 913

One

"Watch out for room 421," Taryn whispered, her eyes focused over the housekeeping cart to the offending door.

Mari Niles glanced in the same direction, saw nothing but the closed door, and turned her attention back to the cart as she pulled out a new tissue box and several lotion bottles. Room 423 requested extra lotion. The guest was a regular at The Mariposa Hotel and insisted she only kept coming back because the hotel boasted the best lotion in all of California. Mari slid her gaze back to door 421 to see if anything changed. It hadn't. "Why? Are they vampires?"

"Worse. Cart pickers."

"Ah. I see." Cart pickers were *like cactus under the bare foot*, as Mari's grandma would have said. Mari didn't ever mind when a room called down and made requests for extra items, but it really bristled her sensibilities when people stole stuff off the cart. "I don't understand those people," she told Taryn. "Seriously? Like it's worth your soul and humanity to nick a roll of toilet paper?"

Taryn tightened her dark hair back into her ponytail holder. "Who cares about souls? It means I have to go all the way back down to the basement to restock a cart I've already stocked."

Mari vocalized her agreement with a sigh.

Taryn fixed the glare she'd been giving door 421 on Mari. "You *are* going to the party tonight at Blake's, right?"

Mari blew a raspberry at her friend, who had been trying to set her up with Blake pretty much since the day Mari punched her time card for the first time. Blake, who worked in grounds, didn't have one original thought in his head and felt the compulsive need to ask Mari out every few weeks. "Not a chance. Blake's a tool. Not even a nice expensive tool. He's a dollar-store-hammer kind of tool. I've never seen anyone jump to do management's bidding as fast as he does."

Taryn's glare deepened. "You need to get out there, start dating again."

"What? And give up the glamour of wiping dribbled-on toilet seats? Never!"

"Seriously, that guy ruined you." Taryn finally turned her attention back to her own cart.

"How is getting my degree and finally having space that belongs to me being ruined?"

"You're ruined because you're so worried about getting Virginia Woolf's *room of your own* that you forgot you need a life of your own."

When Taryn and Mari first met, Mari constantly found herself shocked by Taryn's literary references. The girl had a quote from a famous author for just about every situation. Mari still felt pretty stupid over being judgmental and making assumptions that hotel maids must be illiterate. Almost everyone at The Mariposa had some kind of education. And even the ones who didn't have formal education were still intelligent and interesting. "I have a life," Mari said, feeling sullen.

Taryn snorted. "Oh honey, being alive and having a life are not the same thing at all. You're almost thirty-one. You aren't getting any younger. Having a life requires relationships with *humans*, not relationships with school books."

Mari opened her mouth to explain that the relationship Taryn insisted had ruined her had done so precisely because it denied her the relationship with school books. It had also denied her other relationships. She'd given everything she had to her ex-husband, and he'd readily taken. She'd pick her books and her solitude any day over that train wreck. The chance to explain all this disappeared when the door to room 421 opened. Taryn glowered at the old man who peeked out through the crack. She pushed her cart with energy down the hall as if to give him visual proof that her cart was, and always would be, out of his reach.

Mari didn't bother tossing snappish stares at the accused cart-picker, but she did push her cart to the opposite end of the hall from her friend. She did not want to make an extra trip to the supply room just because some guy wanted to thieve a dozen single-use shampoo bottles. The door to 421 closed with a click. Mari focused her attention on her cart. She checked her roster, scanned through the day's schedule, and went to work.

After a pretty grueling day of cleaning after, fetching for, and listening to the myriad guests who were with the fashion expo being held at The Mariposa, Mari discovered that sometime throughout the day, room 421 must have found her cart unattended and made off with three tissue boxes, two rolls of toilet paper, and four lotion bottles. The

Mariposa Hotel really did have the best lotion around, but the thief could have at least *asked* rather than pillaged.

She took the service elevator to supply and congratulated herself on concluding her workday early. That meant she would have time to finish her criminal law homework, eat dinner, and make it to bed at an hour that bordered on reasonable. As she began unbuttoning the tunic, a female voice called out to her. "Mari, do you have a minute?"

"Sure," Mari said as she turned and buttoned her tunic back up. Deanne was like that mouse the picture books warned children to not give a cookie; when someone gave her a minute, she would want an hour.

But she was the manager. Mari valued her job at The Mariposa Hotel. The pay was more than fair, and everyone respected her for going back to school and tried hard to work around her new schedule though most of her classes were online.

Deanne had a clipboard in her hands and a smile on her face as she looked up and saw she had Mari's full attention. "I'd like to congratulate you, Mari!"

"Congratulate me, ma'am?" Deanne was maybe only a decade older than Mari, not old enough to require a "ma'am" title, but she expected to be addressed with what she considered to be respect. Mari thought of "ma'am" as something you called someone so elderly they were likely to be a corpse soon, but she used the title her boss expected.

"Yes. Your incredible work ethic made you eligible for a special assignment."

That was code for *you're too much of a sap to say no, so we've given you extra tasks, Mari.*

Mari pasted on her very best and most obedient smile, the one she had learned to use when dealing with her ex-husband, and said, "Wonderful. What would you like me to do?"

"Room 913; you cleaned it yesterday to prepare for our guest and did such an impeccable job, he has now requested you as a permanent situation for the duration of his stay. His room requires special care and discretion. Discretion as in you're not to discuss his room with anyone who may ask, and you are not to mention any oddities you find in the room to any of the other staff or refer to the room in any way to the staff."

Wasn't that pretty much the policy for every room? Mari wondered, but she smiled and bit back her snarky response while Deanne continued.

"We were wondering if you would be willing to take sole charge of that room until alerted otherwise."

"Of course, ma'am." Mari widened her smile and tried to look grateful to have the responsibility of this assignment even if it meant she would *not* be leaving early and would *not* be in bed at a reasonable hour. "I'll get to it right away."

Deanne beamed. "It's so good to count on you, Mari."

"Thank you, ma'am." Mari didn't drop her smile until the elevator doors closed on Deanne's face.

At least she now had a good excuse not to go to Blake-the-Tool's party. Not that she didn't have a good excuse before. Of course she did. Homework counted as one of the best excuses. But this was one that would keep Taryn from hitting the repeat button on the you-need-to-get-a-life conversation.

Mari stocked the minimums—just enough to get her through one more room—on her cart and headed to the ninth floor. She sighed as she thought about her homework. Her professor worked hard to keep the class real and interesting because state codes were pretty boring at first glance. Dr. Morgan used Disney classics and *Seinfeld* episodes to teach, and Mari found that she loved it. Tonight's homework was to discover all the different laws that were violated in the Disney classic *Cinderella* during the scene when the sisters ripped the dress the mice had sewn into shreds. Mari had to give her professor credit; Dr. Morgan took the state code book and made it something memorable.

The elevator announced the floor, and the doors dinged open.

Mari tapped her key card against the door and called out, "Housekeeping!" She keyed open the door when she received no answer and entered the room while putting in her earbuds and tapping the iPod screen to her playlist.

She went to the bed first, as that was where she always started when cleaning a room, and stopped short, frowned at the smooth white duvet, and gave the room a quick once-over. Everything was spotless, as in pass-the-most-rigorous-Deanne-inspection-ever spotless. The bed appeared untouched. She flipped up a corner of the duvet and peered at the way the sheet corners had been folded and tucked under the mattress. Those corner folds were her signature in a room. None of the other maids bothered with clean corner folds because they took too much time, but Mari found she couldn't cut the corners, literal and otherwise, that a few of the other maids did to shave off time.

The perfect corners meant no one had slept in the bed. The way the hotel stationery and pen sat at the exact angle hotel management specified and the way the chair was pushed into the desk meant no one had sat at that desk or touched the paper.

Mari peered into the bathroom and grinned. "Looks like I'm getting home early after all," she murmured. The lotion, soap, shampoo, and everything else remained untouched.

She hoped the special "care and discretion" meant that the room's occupant was staying at a mistress's house instead of the hotel because that meant she'd be getting off early every night until further notice.

She reached out to flip off the light, but her fingers hovered over the switch. She cocked her head to the side and squinted at the dark recesses of the counter cubby. A small overnight bag had been tucked deep inside as if the owner wanted it to remain unseen. She breathed in deep and felt the muggy remnants of a recent shower in the air. Her fingers stretched farther and found the towel closest to the shower door.

Damp.

Huh. So someone *had* been in the room.

But what sort of person folded the towel exactly in thirds and hung it back on the towel rack? Curious, she opened the closet. Every hanger hung exactly in place. The only difference was the fact that a nondescript black carry-on had been tucked into a corner.

More curious, she checked the bed again and let out a triumphant "Ah ha!" The ghost of room 913 had accidentally placed a feather pillow under the synthetic instead of the other way around.

She circled the room several times, not sure what to do. The room was a smidge off from being as perfect as if she'd been the one to clean it. Sheets wouldn't be changed until the guest's third day of occupying the room, towels would be switched out at the same time as long as the guest hung them back up, which her ghost had clearly done. She went back to her clipboard to read the notes.

No. The guest wanted a fresh towel every day. Okay. But why take the trouble of hanging up the used one if you wanted a fresh one? Regardless, she did as asked. She probably should have vacuumed, but the floor was spotless. The vacuum marks from the day previous were still mostly visible.

"So do I call it a day?" she asked the room, almost expecting the walls to answer. When it didn't, she shrugged. "Happy birthday to me?"

It wasn't her birthday, but she'd picked up the phrase from her mom, who always said it whenever something unexpectedly delightful landed in her lap. Mari couldn't remember the last time she'd had a cause to say the phrase and smiled at getting the chance to do so now.

"Thank you, ghost," she said, hoping that every day was just a towel change. She smiled as she left the room exactly as she'd found it. Well, not *exactly* . . . She had left a fresh towel and switched the pillow order.

Two

Grant pretended to buy a drink from the pop machine while he waited for the maid to leave his room. He didn't know why he hadn't introduced himself and thanked her for taking care of his room like he always had with the housekeeping attendants from the hundreds of hotels he'd visited in the past. He just hadn't expected her to make him blink and look again—only look a lot harder and a lot longer—when he saw her. Time slowed and his mouth dried up when he saw her, and he couldn't stop himself from staring.

The last time he stared at a pretty girl for that long had been in the ninth grade when Jennie Hill had stood up to introduce herself. That was, of course, before he embarrassed himself by trying to talk to her and ended up revealing himself as the socially awkward kid he was.

Not that he didn't like looking at pretty women; he wasn't stupid. But with Mari, he recognized immediately that he gazed on something different.

He appreciated her dark hair up in a bun with loose bits falling over her long, tanned neck, and the way her eyebrows arched over her dark eyes. He genuinely appreciated that even the maid's bulky uniform couldn't hide her shape because it would be positively criminal to hide a shape like hers. But none of that was what stopped him cold. It was the way she moved.

She had a strength to her walk.

Which didn't really make sense, not even to him, and he was the one thinking it. But watching her walk was enough to make his breath stutter in his throat, and he couldn't find the words of greeting he had intended to offer when she cleaned his room. He liked meeting the staff who had access to his room because it helped build a rapport and kept them from asking questions about the quirks of his room and the sometimes-guests who appeared there. But instead of greeting her, he'd gone and hid in the alcove with the ice and pop machines.

Professional. Real professional, Grant.

The way his mouth had dried up and his tongue seemed too tied to work, he felt like the time he'd eaten pine nuts and discovered he was allergic. But who ever heard of allergic reactions to a beautiful woman?

She'd gone inside, propping the door open. He heard her humming along to whatever she listened to on her iPod and strained to catch the tune well enough to identify it. When he finally did, he grinned.

She was listening to the overture of "The Marriage of Figaro" by Mozart. He'd expected something different and felt judgmental for the assumption. Just because she worked as a maid didn't mean she'd have crude street rap blaring from her playlist. Though, if she had been listening to street rap, he knew all those songs too. His work required him to know whatever was young, hip, and usually not his style. He sometimes wondered if he'd like that kind of music better if

he hadn't been forced to memorize the lyrics and bob his head to a beat that never felt anything more than foreign.
Probably not.
Maybe not.
He sometimes wondered if he wouldn't be so judgmental of maids, waiters and waitresses, and C-store employees if he hadn't had to bribe so many to look the other way.
Maybe.
Probably.
There was no denying that helping criminals hide from other criminals had jaded him against society in general.

But then, here was this woman with her dark hair pulled back in a bun that was anything but tidy, and with her long, thin frame that seemed to glide over the floor as she moved, and with her faint hum to the movements of Mozart and her occasional wave of an arm as if she was conducting an orchestra in a way that suddenly made society look good.

She wasn't in the room long, not that he'd expected her to be. There wasn't much for her to do. If he ended up with another guest in his room, she'd have a ton of work cut out for her, but he didn't really expect that outcome with the case he currently worked. When she exited the room, Grant felt indescribably stupid as he ducked his head, slid a five into the machine, and actually touched the button to release a drink. He wasn't even sure which button he'd pressed; he just didn't want to get caught staking her out.

He reached down to retrieve the bottle that fell out of the machine into the receptacle and couldn't help it; he looked up as she passed him and smiled.

When she absently smiled back, he had to put his hand against the machine to steady himself. Had any woman ever struck him that way?

No.

Not ever.

Which had always been just fine with him, because his job discouraged relationships. Maybe not discouraged but more like his job made anyone he'd been in a relationship with want to never talk to him again. Women didn't enjoy boyfriends who disappeared for sometimes months at a time without any explanation of where they'd gone off to.

Not that he thought that his maid smiling at him made for the beginnings of a relationship. He wasn't a total amateur.

When she'd disappeared behind elevator doors, he looked down and saw the drink he'd inadvertently purchased.

Diet root beer.

"Guess I deserve that," he muttered to the machine.

Maybe he was an amateur after all, losing his focus like that.

"Idiot," he said, but he felt more peevish toward the machine than to himself. How many soda vendors sold diet root beer? The hotel manager must have had some kind of freakish childish food preferences. The guy probably dunked his Oreos in his ramen noodles.

With the woman gone, Grant left the unwanted drink on top of the machine for the next person and made his way back to the room to get his paperwork in order. It wasn't until hours later, when he turned down his bed to go to sleep, that he realized she'd caught his pillow alteration. He'd switched them because of his personal preference, and he didn't want to fall into bed too tired to make the change and end up with a sore neck.

He felt the grin come back in full force and was glad to not have witnesses. Not one in a thousand people would have noticed such an insignificant detail. But in his line of work, he knew there were no insignificant details. And a woman who noticed the little things was a person who could never go unnoticed.

Three

Mari spent the night pressing charges against the cast of *Cinderella*. She charged Cinderella's stepsisters and stepmother for assault with gang enhancement because it was three against one, Cinderella with the theft of a pumpkin, and the godmother with trespassing. A productive evening for certain, as far as homework went. And because her ghost had required so little in the way of maintenance, she even made it to bed almost at a decent hour. She was ready for her morning class and felt a degree of gratitude that she had the next day off work, even if it did mean she'd be working the weekend.

A day off meant more time to study. Mari wrung every second out of that day and actually caught up with her schoolwork. She rewarded herself with a long hot bubble bath that grew tepid, then cold, while she pored over her books.

The following morning, Taryn waited for her at the bus stop. As soon as Mari stepped off the bus, Taryn shoved off the low retaining wall that led out to the beach off of Tangerine Street and threw her hands up in the air. "Honestly, Mari! Why weren't you at Blake's party?"

It took Mari a few moments to figure out what Taryn meant. "I thought we already had the tool conversation."

"He was looking for you! How are you ever going to get a man when you act like you're an island surrounded by sharks?"

"I'm not trying to get a man. I'm trying to get an education, remember? Law school as soon as I get my degree in criminal justice? Besides, I had to work late the other night. Deanne gave me an extra room." She shook off the twinge of guilt for not mentioning that the extra room took less than five minutes.

"Oh." Even Taryn, with all her great plans of remarrying Mari off, couldn't argue with more work. "I just worry about you being alone."

Mari smiled at her then gave her a quick hug. "I'm not alone, you crazy lady. I have you."

"I'm a poor replacement for a husband because, as cute as I think you are, I just don't think of you like that. And what about kids?"

She'd hit a sore spot. Mari covered her pain by saying lightly, "I'll just play with your kids when you and Armando get your act together and make the world a cuter place by adding your blended genetics to it. Until then, I'll play with your dogs."

"What dogs? I don't even like dogs."

Mari laughed. "And you say I have issues?"

Taryn shrugged and fell into step beside Mari, who decided it would be best to get moving so she wasn't late for work. "Slow down!" Taryn insisted.

"Can't. I know exactly how many minutes it takes to get

from the bus stop to the hotel without being late. And we've already used up two more minutes than we have to spare."

"Tell me again why you won't buy a car like every other human."

"You know I can't afford it."

Taryn grabbed Mari's arm and tugged until she slowed down a little. "And you know I think that's a crock of crap. You have all that alimony money you never touch. What's the point of making him pay every month if you never spend it?"

"Because it hurts him to pay, and because it would hurt me to spend it."

"You're so lost, Mari. So, so lost. If I had that money, I'd have a closet full of so many dresses that Cinderella's godmother could have outfitted an entire kingdom of peasant girls." Mari smiled at the Cinderella reference, since she'd made Taryn help her study during their lunch break several days prior. Taryn shot a stern look that wiped the smile from Mari's face. "You're still letting him control you by keeping your life deliberately hard just to spite him."

Mari picked up the pace and was glad when Taryn followed along. "My life isn't deliberately hard. It's deliberately mine. I *will* use that money someday. On a terrific charity that he doesn't believe in."

"That statement smacks of bitterness." Taryn's step hesitated at the front window of Delilah's Desserts to look at the display of baked heaven, but Mari tugged her arm to keep the momentum.

Mari didn't respond to her friend's observation. She wasn't bitter. Not anymore. So she put him through medical school without so much as a thank you. So she put off her own education so they could afford to eat and have shelter without piling up any student debt. So she put off the idea of having children until "they were ready" and "could focus," and she went to baby shower after baby shower for her friends with her heart breaking a little more each time.

Yeah. So maybe she was a little bitter. That was why she sued him for alimony right after he left her. But the thing was . . . she didn't feel bitter anymore. Not really. She felt sorry for the premed student he hooked up with who never finished her college education either. Mari often wondered what it was about him that made women give up their own identities to shelter in his cold shadow.

She also felt insecure about the money deposited automatically into her account every month. Mari's mother, Taryn, and the handful of others who knew Mari well enough to know about the monthly income told Mari she'd earned it by paying his way through school. But she knew it for what it really was: a last-minute act of spite. Suing him had been done in anger—enough to make her feel confused about the money.

Not confused enough to cancel the court order, but enough to not touch the accumulation in her savings account. Besides, if she could put that waste of human skin through school, she could certainly do it for herself.

They approached the revolving doors of The Mariposa Hotel in contemplative silence and skirted around to a service entrance, where they carded in and changed into their work clothes for the day. The locker room was already empty by the time Mari closed her locker and buttoned up her housekeeping tunic. She checked her roster and saw that she still had the ghost room on the ninth floor. She decided to save it for last just in case it was like before.

A room that only needed fresh towels and the most basic maintenance would be a nice way to end her day. Of course, with her luck, the ghost probably decided to throw a party in his room and she'd have to clean up beer bottles and vomit, the idea of which made her groan.

Taryn misinterpreted the noise and, without looking up from her own roster, said, "Okay, okay. I'll stop trying to hook you up with Blake. He's a nice guy though. He really is. Maybe a bit of a suck-up and maybe a bit of a yes-man, but nice just the same. And he's got some very traditional ideas. He's the kind of guy who sticks, you know?"

"I've had my share of sticky guys."

"You know what I mean, Mari."

"I know what you mean. I just know that *I* mean to drop it."

Taryn sighed, grumbled something Mari felt certain she was glad not to hear, and pushed her cart onto the service elevator to start her day.

Mari echoed that sigh and followed. Time to work.

The day went by quickly. Mari listened to one of her law books that was available on audio while she cleaned instead of her normal music. She worked more slowly that way, but with a test coming up, she needed the extra time with her schoolwork. She turned off her audio when she keyed open the door to the ghost room.

She smiled when she checked the sheets to find the corners folded and tucked and the damp towels hanging in a perfect trifold from the towel bar. "Why aren't all my rooms as well-behaved as you?" she asked.

The ghost staying in room 913 was absolutely gifted if he could tuck in sheets exactly the way she did. It seemed a pity to waste his perfect mimicry if he really was sleeping in the bed and making it up in the morning, but with no way of knowing if he'd slept in the bed or not, on wash-the-sheets day, she had to strip it and start fresh. She gave the bed a bow of acknowledgement and immediately went to work stripping it to the mattress. After replacing the linens, doing an unneeded vacuuming, and sanitizing the bathroom she suspected had been already sanitized by the room's occupant, she stood in the center of the room and surveyed her surroundings for several long moments.

Everything looked exactly as it did when she first showed up, except the shampoo bottle and the conditioner bottle were now back in their proper order. The ghost had not used the items but switched the order, as if testing her.

She wasn't sure if that was funny, interesting, or annoying.

Was the ghost messing with her? Was he trying to say he could clean a room better than she could? Was he some hyper-obsessive-compulsive who wore one of those face masks to avoid breathing the same oxygen as everyone else? Or was he playing a game and glad to have a willing participant?

And she must have been a willing participant, because when she discovered the out-of-order-bottles, she smirked as she put them back into place and felt like she'd just made a valuable move in a chess match.

Mari had never had a guest who didn't leave some sort of identity in the room when they went out for the day. The young families had toys littering the floor and packages of diapers shoved in a corner; the single girl had an elaborate arsenal of makeup, jewelry, and clothing. The business man had cufflinks, a watch, papers left on the desk or nightstand depending on where he plugged in his laptop, and white shirts lining the closet. The business woman had power suits hanging in the closet and an assortment of heels to add variety to her wardrobe. If guests went to the beach, sand grit lined the bathtub. If they went to a movie, ticket stubs and the remnants in bottoms of popcorn buckets were left on the dresser for her to throw away.

This guest left no sand, no ticket stubs, no identifying clothing. He only left a generic black bag in the closet, zipped up and unknowable.

She'd never felt such a curiosity before regarding any of The Mariposa Hotel's guests. She had never before felt a desperation to know what brand of shampoo they used or whether or not they went to the beach. But she wanted to know everything about *this* guest. Was he old, young, married, single? Was he even really a he?

She couldn't say why she believed she could be friends with the room's occupant. She was usually right about things like that. It was the reason she decided to go into law. Mari's intuition, or whatever it could be called, had been referred to as her superpower by many of her friends. If something was missing, she could usually find it. If a person was lying, she usually knew. And it wasn't that Mari believed in voodoo or witchcraft or magic, but she trusted herself and this gift of gut feeling. The one time she'd been stupid and ignored her intuition had ended in a messy divorce from a messy man.

Whoever her ghost was, he wasn't anything like her ex. She'd been away from her bad decision, as she called him, for well over two years. She felt a freedom in being her own person on her own terms, and she liked being alone. So why was she now thinking about this mystery and wanting him to show himself?

She gave herself a hard shake of reality. With only a semester left in school, she had no intention of losing her momentum to any other bad decisions. No matter how hard Taryn pressed her to date, Mari had every intention of going solo for a long, long time.

Four

Grant saw Mari Niles again standing at the bus stop while he was coming back to the hotel from a walk on the beach after a long day working with the witness under his protection. Mari no longer wore her maid's uniform, but he recognized her long, lean lines and the adorable slight upturn of her nose that gave her the look of a woodland pixie. Her jeans were tight enough to show off her figure without being trashy about it, and the simple blouse accented her thin frame. She'd loosed her hair from her maid's bun, letting her long tresses flow free and wild in a way that made him wish he could run his fingers through them, the way she was doing at that exact moment.

His step faltered at the sight of her.

She'd switched the shampoo and conditioner bottles.

He recognized the stupidity of switching them in the first place as soon as he'd done it. What were the chances of her noticing when the bottles were almost identical? He bet most of the hotel's guests messed them up regularly and accidentally used conditioner when they'd meant to use shampoo.

But she *had* noticed.

He caught himself grinning again just thinking about that moment of discovery. He tried to make his face passive but found himself not up to the task of lying to himself. In front of him stood a woman who intrigued him. He would be a fool not to go up to her and start a conversation.

Yes. A fool. So why wouldn't his legs move forward? *C'mon, you amateur, go talk to the girl.* But his legs still refused to carry him toward her. Where had this paralysis come from?

He could take down a drug lord and minions equipped with weaponry far superior to anything ever assigned to a U.S. Marshal, and he couldn't talk to a pretty woman?

Pathetic.

With that thought, he forced himself into action but had only taken a step when a yellow sports car pulled up to the curb and the driver started talking to the woman. Grant's muscles tightened against his forward momentum, and he only just managed to keep from falling off the steps leading back to the hotel's revolving doors. From the animated way the guy in the car spoke to her, he must know her. He was probably a boyfriend or something.

He wasn't a husband. Grant had run background checks on the hotel employees before he singled out Mari Niles. She wasn't married but had been previously, had no children, had no criminal record of any kind or associations with those involved in criminal activity. Those background checks suddenly seemed wholly inadequate. Why didn't those checks mention any intimate relationships so he would know what the next move should be?

Ah well. The game had been fun while it had lasted, and he was glad he hadn't made a fool of himself by asking her out for dinner. The rejection that followed would have been awkward for both of them.

Grant pivoted with the intent to head back down Tangerine Street to find a restaurant when he halted again and turned back to the maid and the man in the car. She was frowning and speaking louder than someone in a casual conversation. Grant cocked his head as he watched her look both up and down the street as if searching for help. The guy got out of the car and rounded the front rapidly. Just as rapidly, Mari Niles retreated.

Her coiled, tensed body betrayed her fear, and Grant realized he'd misinterpreted the situation before. Whatever was going on wasn't good. He rushed to reach Mari before the man could.

The man hadn't touched Mari yet, but he stood dangerously close and maneuvered himself around her to cut off any escape with an agility Grant found impressive considering the man's slurred speech as he said, "C'mon. You know you're flattered. I bet you've never even seen a car like that, huh? You want a ride in my fancy car?"

"Get away!" Mari yelled. "What I want is for you to leave me alone before I force-feed you pepper spray!" Her hand dove into her purse, and she was just pulling something out when Grant stepped between them.

"Why don't you get back in your Hyundai and drive home so you can sleep this off?" Grant said. The guy flinched at having his car brand named out loud.

Not that there was anything wrong with the Hyundai Genesis. The car was respectable enough, but it lacked the luster that brands like Mustang and Miata had. It certainly didn't deserve the title of "fancy car" the guy had given it. Grant grimaced at the guy's rumpled yellow Hawaiian shirt visible under his faux leather jacket and hair that, at a distance, looked to be the moussed-messy style but on closer inspection was actually just greasy and unkempt.

"Who do you think you are? Telling me what to do? The lady and I were just talking."

"Doesn't look like the lady is really all that interested in anything you might have to say. Move along."

"No." The guy braced himself as if readying to fight.

Grant narrowed his eyes. "I'd really rethink that choice you're about to make if I were you." He knew he shouldn't do it, but he put his hands on his hips, which pulled back his suit coat and revealed the gun holster cradling his Glock. It wasn't *exactly* brandishing a weapon. He was just casually putting his hands on his hips.

But it did give the desired effect.

The guy retreated several steps at the sight of Grant's weapon. "You can't carry that without a permit." The word *permit* ended on a high, squeaked-out note.

"I *have* a permit," Grant said and smiled wide enough to show all his teeth. "You should probably go now."

The guy bolted backward, running into the fender of his own car before skirting around it and back to the driver's side. The zipper from his jacket scratched along the hood before he was able to yank open his door, stuff himself inside, and tear off down the road.

Grant pulled out his phone. "You okay?" He started swiping out a message when he glanced up. Mari still gripped her pepper spray in her hand, only now she had it aimed at him.

He startled. "Whoa there!" He put up his hands and phone to placate her and to block a direct stream of the spray should she actually use it. "You can put that down. I just saved you."

"By flashing a *gun*! I'm supposed to feel safe now that I'm alone with a stranger and a gun?"

For some reason, her calling him a stranger hurt his

feelings. He had sort of felt like they were old friends after he'd run the background check, handpicked her from the staff to be the one with his room access, hid in an ice machine alcove to watch her work, and then all that . . . what could he call what had been taking place the last few days with her? Flirting via organization? Regardless, of course she didn't know him. *She* hadn't run any background checks. She hadn't been spying on him. She had no idea he was the same guy whose room she'd been assigned to clean.

Thinking about the situation from her point of view, he had to admit, he would have come off as a total stalker if he confessed to knowing her as well as he did. No wonder she had yet to put away her one line of defense. "I'm sorry if I scared you. I didn't mean to. I just wanted to help. I'm a law enforcement officer. That's why I carry a gun. And so we're clear, I *didn't* flash my weapon at anyone. I just put my hands on my hips to look stern. Didn't your mother ever do that?"

Mari smiled faintly at his attempt at a joke.

"So, we're okay? You going to put away your spray?"

She lowered it but didn't put it away.

He gave her credit for that. Smart to keep a weapon in hand when the situation seemed unstable. If he was her, he would have done the same. She looked beautiful, even with her back rigid and her eyes probing—almost glaring at him. Would asking her to dinner now be a bad idea?

Yes. Definitely a bad idea. Asking out a glaring girl was certain to end in pepper spray to the eyes. So instead he carried on with the one thing he could no longer put off. He looked down at his phone again, checked the street the driver of the car had turned down and hit send on the message.

"What are you doing?" she asked.

"Alerting the local police that there is a drunk driver in

a yellow Hyundai with the license plate of 256 DAR eastbound on Grove Street."

"Oh." Her fingers lost their white-knuckled grip on her pepper spray canister. She still didn't put it away, but at least she'd relaxed. "You really are a cop."

"Something like that."

"What does 'something like that' mean?"

He hesitated. His job of transporting important witnesses until the trials they needed to testify at was complicated. Most of the time, the witnesses he transported were no big deal. But sometimes he had custody of witnesses who were pivotal to making or breaking a case against high-profile criminals. Those witnesses needed to be alive to testify, and it was his job to make sure they stayed that way. His occupation wasn't something he advertised, for obvious reasons. Part of keeping a witness safe was keeping an extremely low profile, which didn't include flashing his gun at people, as Mari had described it. He rolled his eyes at himself. A pretty girl, and he jeopardizes a case?

But he knew Mari wasn't just a pretty girl. She was a girl who conducted imaginary orchestras and was as OCD as him.

He took too long to answer; Mari's bus pulled up. She turned toward it without hesitation, seeming glad to find safety behind the bus doors instead of being out on the street with him. The doors opened with a whoosh of hydraulics that kicked up the smell of diesel exhaust coming from the bus's undercarriage.

Mari climbed the stairs while he fumbled for something to say. She turned at the last moment and called out, "Thanks for helping." Then she ascended the last stair, and the doors closed on any chance he had to respond.

Five

Mari collapsed onto her bus seat. Well . . . *that* had certainly been the most interesting thing to happen to her in a while: forcefully propositioned by a drunk and saved by *something like* a cop.

She glanced back as the bus pulled away from the curb and out onto the street. The cop still stood there, looking a little rejected. She didn't know why that made her feel bad, but it did. He was a good-looking man, the kind she would have fallen all over herself to force a meeting with back in her pre-husband days.

Very good-looking.

Through the bus window, could he see her watching him watching her bus pull away?

She hoped he could, because maybe then he would see that she finally decided to offer him a friendly smile. Maybe then he would see that she thought he might be interesting. Maybe then, if fate designed such things, they would meet again at the bus stop, and he would think she might be interesting too, and they could start their meeting over again—without the awkward moment of guns and pepper spray and loud-mouthed males.

The bus turned off of Tangerine Street in the direction of her home. Mari leaned her head against the window and found she didn't have the energy to pop in her ear buds to listen to even music, let alone law books. Red and blue flashing at the side of the road made her lift her head. As the bus neared the yellow car pulled over and the driver walking a shaky line for the sobriety test, she smiled. Her something-like-a-cop had made the world a safer place.

It wasn't until she was home and daydreaming about meeting him again that she realized she'd very much come to consider him as *hers*.

She must really be living in a make-believe world if taking ownership of strangers didn't feel abnormal. Maybe she should have been studying psychology instead of criminal justice so she could self-diagnose her delusions.

"What's with you?" Taryn asked as they prepared their carts the next morning.

"What do you mean what's with me?" Mari asked.

"She means you look happy," Christina said.

Mari turned an indignant glare on her friends and then smiled when she realized she'd put her hands on her hips. *Yes,* she thought, *my mother did do this when she scolded me.* "I always look happy."

Christina shook her gray head of curly hair and hitched up her polyester pants. "No, honey, what you do is pretend to look happy so that no one knows you're miserable."

"I do not!" Mari insisted.

But Taryn was nodding. "Yes, you do. This is why I keep trying to set you up so you can be as happy as I am."

Mari tossed a hand towel at her friend. "A woman does not need a man to make her happy."

Taryn conceded the point while folding the hand towel and settling it onto her own cart. "You're right. But *humans* need real human contact and connection. You never go hang out with me when I ask. You don't go out with anyone else either. You never come to dinners, parties, and get-togethers." Taryn looked at Christina. "Did I forget anything?"

"She never calls her mother," Christina offered.

"Right." Taryn turned back to Mari. "You go to a job where the majority of your interactions are with empty rooms. You go to a school that is mostly online. You go home where there are only your plants and your TV. So no, you don't need a man, but you do need a human. You need some connection. And bantering with me in the morning and a few times throughout the day isn't enough. Can you blame me if I feel like you need an intervention?"

Mari leaned back into the stack of folded towels and narrowed her eyes at her friend. She wanted to feel angry at the words that cut into her core, but Taryn really was her best friend and lately had become one of her only friends as she silently slipped into the shadows of other people's lives.

I'm like my ghost in 913, she thought.

But she couldn't let Taryn believe she had become the hermit she really was. "I don't need an intervention because I do have connections—more than just you two. I talk to Raegan—the event coordinator."

"Wait. She's the event coordinator? I thought she was the florist," Christina said.

"She just likes arranging flowers," Mari corrected

Christina. "And not only do I talk to her, I'll have you know I've met someone."

That got both Taryn's and Christina's attention.

"Who?" Taryn wanted to know.

"Where?" Christina asked.

Mari shrugged and placed the stack of white towels she'd been leaning against in the under-bin of her cart. "At the bus stop."

Taryn's lifted eyebrows proved her disapproval of the meeting place. Taryn believed in the magic of romantic encounters. She obviously didn't see anything magical in bus-stop meetings.

But maybe she'd change her mind when Mari explained the whole situation. So Mari did, right down to the guy coming to her rescue by showing his gun to the drunk. Taryn and Christina both leaned their elbows on their carts while Mari recounted all that had happened. Taryn loved the story enough to sigh, but she straightened up from her cart and smoothed out her tunic. "If he's a cop, you'd think he'd be more careful about flashing his gun to people. Doesn't he watch the news? Doesn't he know about the riots in the streets due to improper police procedure?"

"There was going to be rioting on Tangerine Street if that drunk had laid a hand on me!" Mari said, wanting to defend the cop who'd defended her.

"I don't know," Christina said with a nod of agreement at Taryn. "He sounds like a control freak."

"That's right." Taryn hurried to add in her own advice. "You watch out for him. He might be Bad Decision: The Sequel."

Mari watched in disbelief as Taryn and Christina hurried to finish packing their carts and view their rosters. "Are you two serious?" Mari finally asked. "You go on and on and on about me needing human contact and relationships and then immediately find fault when I tell you I've met someone?"

Taryn made a hushing motion as if Mari's protest was nothing more than an irritating fly. "This guy doesn't count. Do you even know his name?"

She had Mari on that one. Mari didn't know his name. But she wanted to know. Didn't that count? He was nice. And nice-looking. A combination a girl didn't get very often. Though how nice was he really? What did Mari know about him?

Nothing.

A "something like" a cop was hardly enough to go on. "Fine. I'll try to get out more," Mari said, feeling sullen with the agreement. "Does that make you happy?"

Taryn gave her a long, hard look. "It won't if it doesn't make you happy, school-girl."

Then Mari felt bad for being sullen. She reached out and wrapped her arms around her friend. "The fact that you care about me makes me happy. Thank you. Seriously. Thank you." Taryn hugged her back.

Christina rolled her eyes at the two of them. "I hate to break up this love-fest, but we have rooms to clean, and Deanne is sure to come down here and find us not even started yet."

With that, they wrestled carts on to the service elevator. Mari saved room 913 for last again, and toward the end of her day, she found herself looking forward to seeing what new puzzle he might have for her to solve.

When she got inside the room, she blinked in surprise. The bed was unmade.

"What the?" An unmade bed in a normally pristine

room made her ghost seem like he'd turned into a poltergeist.

His toiletry case was zipped up tight but had been left on the counter, as if he'd been in a terrible hurry. She wondered what would have caused him to be in such a hurry. A sick mother? A sick child? An emergency at the office that would get him fired?

She settled in to do her job as per usual, feeling disappointed in not having a puzzle to solve. Her adventure with this room was at an end and it was now just like every other room.

Sort of.

She still didn't know anything about the occupant. An unmade bed and a toiletry case in the wrong place hardly gave any clues beyond a rushed morning. His towel wasn't damp, so he was in too big of a hurry to shower.

Maybe he was a criminal running from the police. Maybe that was why the undercover something-like-a-cop had been hanging around Tangerine Street. Mari smiled to herself, liking the idea of linking the two oddities in her life. Who would she be loyal to, the cop or the criminal-ghost?

Those thoughts occupied her while she finished up her work day and moved toward the elevator with her cart.

"Oh Mari!" a voice called from behind her.

Mari recognized Deanne's voice immediately and briefly fantasized ignoring it, jumping on the elevator, and slamming her finger into the doors-closed button, but she instead turned and faced the woman who was sure to give her more work.

Deanne did not disappoint. Someone didn't show up in laundry, and since Mari was so good and quick with folding, would she mind very much going and giving a helping hand?

Mari did mind but didn't say so. She hated how much

Deanne intimidated her. She tried giving herself a pep-talk about being a strong woman who could stand up for herself as she stowed her cart and went to laundry, though the "helping" Deanne had asked for ended up meaning "doing alone" since the laundress took a ten-minute smoke break three times during the hour. Mari really needed to work harder on her self-pep-talks.

By the time she'd finished the laundry and clocked out, Mari had missed her bus and the bus that followed by only a few minutes. That late at night, the buses were sparse, and it would be an hour and a half before another one came. Mari changed out of her work clothes and tried not to grumble out loud about her overbearing boss.

It's more hours, she thought. *More hours means more money. More money means no student loans.*

Mari's friends had already left for the day, so Mari hefted her school bag and walked in the direction of the atrium. She met up with Raegan, the event coordinator/florist, at the main floor lobby.

"Working late?" Raegan asked.

"It's who we are, isn't it?"

Raegan laughed. "I guess it is. Though today has been a little much. I could really use some sleep. Do you ever feel tempted to take a nap when you're cleaning rooms? I mean, there's a bed right there."

It was Mari's turn to laugh. "I think about it all the time, but then I'd either be sleeping in someone else's sheets or I'd be messing up a bed I just made and have to redo it."

Raegan nodded her understanding. "I see. A temptation avoided with logic."

"Most temptations can be avoided with logic." Mari hitched up her school bag again.

"What do you do about the ones that can't?"

Mari gave her best serious look as if she was about to impart some incredible wisdom, and then whispered, "Run."

Raegan laughed. "Seems like a sound strategy." Her phone buzzed in her hand, and she gave Mari an apologetic look before mouthing a goodbye and answering it. Raegan worked harder than anyone else at the hotel. Mari wondered what Taryn would think about Raegan's work habits. Surely they were worse than Mari's, right?

She turned away from the main lobby and down the corridor to the atrium. The smell and feel of the atrium made her take a deep breath. The moist air and scent of varying flowers relaxed Mari instantly. She wound through the atrium to The Mariposa Hotel's secret garden, beyond the archway of rose bushes thick with pink and red blossoms. Though the garden was clearly marked on all the placards, so few guests ever actually went there that it may as well have been a secret. It was the perfect place to study until it came time to meet her bus. She'd crammed for numerous tests and written many papers among the greenery and exotic flowers and found she actually looked forward to using it again today.

This was the perk of Deanne making her stay later.

She took a deep breath of the potted plumerias and hibiscus and tucked herself into the private corner she'd claimed as hers shortly after being hired on with the hotel. The corner's true perfection was that she wouldn't be readily visible to anyone who might wander in. The last thing she needed was for Deanne to find her and give her more work. Even though Mari had already clocked out, Deanne was capable of that kind of thing. The corner gave Mari a wall to lean against and was actually quite comfortable. The soothing sound of the water continually pouring into the well that had been imported from Mexico when the owners built the hotel allowed Mari a moment to close her eyes and feel peace.

She snapped her eyes open again when she heard footsteps on the garden's paving stones. A man's voice uttered a quiet oath, which seemed odd enough she leaned a little forward to see who dared enter her sanctuary.

Her eyes widened when she recognized the dark brown hair trimmed short and feathered to the side in such a way that she almost wondered if he flashed his gun at his hair in order to intimidate it to behave. The something-like-a-cop stood near the well and scanned in all directions before determining that whatever he'd expected to find wasn't there. He must have been looking for someone, but whoever it was, they hadn't come this way; Mari would've seen them.

He wiped his hand down his face in frustration. "Where did she go?"

She? Mari felt a little bugged by the idea of him looking for a woman, and then it occurred to her . . . What if he'd seen her in the lobby and followed her into the gardens? What if she was the *she* he was looking for?

She hated how much she wanted to be found but knew that she couldn't just step out from the foliage and surprise him. The guy was a cop—or something like one, anyway—and her startling him might end with a bullet in her forehead.

The idea of him wanting to find her as much as she wanted to be found made her blush enough that she was glad the greenery had her hidden. The man's shoulders slumped as if in defeat, and then he took a real look around as if noticing his surroundings for the first time. He inspected the well, his fingers playing lightly over the intricate tiled-mosaics of butterflies. He peeked over the edge, and then his right shoulder lifted as if he was telling himself, "Why not?"

Mari inched toward the entrance, glad she could escape while remaining hidden through the plants if she kept along the wall. Since he seemed intent on staying, she figured she'd find somewhere else to study. Part of her wished this had worked out differently. If she hadn't been lurking in the bushes, he would have come upon her naturally and they could have talked—exchanged names and maybe phone numbers.

But her being located where she was made everything too weird. Maybe she could . . .

She stopped and watched him as he fished a coin from his pockets.

He closed his eyes, turned away from where she could view his face, and dropped the coin into the well with a splash.

Turned away from her as he was, she felt like she could move again. Mari silently, but swiftly, picked her way over the bark mulch toward the exit. She'd made it to the rose arch and was about to slip out when, with his back still to her, he said, "I know you're there."

She froze where she stood, her toes so close to the paving stones she felt she only need wriggle them to make contact. Her fingers were already wrapped around the antiqued silver railing that separated the garden from the walkway. How did he know she was there? She'd been completely silent, and he had his back to her.

She didn't answer. Nothing could be more awkward than this moment of silence while he waited for her to reply and she had lost any words that made sense.

"I only wanted to talk to you for a moment," he said when it became painfully obvious she had every intention of remaining as mute as one of the garden statues. "I hope I'm not coming off as a stalker by following you, but I wanted to apologize for yesterday. I didn't mean to alarm you."

When she still didn't answer, he said, "You have to show yourself, you know."

That was an intriguing statement, and she couldn't keep herself from asking, "Why?"

He nodded to the well. "I made a wish. I paid a full penny for the chance to speak to you."

Mari really did have no choice. She had to show herself or she would look like a ridiculous child for continuing to hide when she'd already asked him a question that he'd answered. She stepped out from the bushes, feeling shy and stupid and grateful he still faced the well so her reappearance from within the hotel's greenery would seem less weird.

"I wasn't hiding from you." She decided she needed him to understand this fact first and foremost. "I only came here to study," she reaffirmed. "Not to hide."

Only then did he turn. Mari felt gratitude that she'd already composed herself, or seeing him up close and face to face would have been her undoing. Had she called him good-looking before?

Good-looking had been an understatement. He was beautiful—not in any Hollywood pretty-boy way, but something else entirely. His blue eyes made for a nice contrast against his tan skin and his dark hair and dark eyebrows. She knew from experience that those eyes didn't miss much and that they understood all that they took in.

The way he smiled at her without any hint of judgment for the fact that she'd been hiding in a garden corner revealed compassion mingled with competence. She didn't know many cops who had compassion . . . okay, she didn't know *any* cops besides this one, who had already identified himself as merely something-like-and-not-actually a cop. She had some ex-law enforcement professors, and none of them could be described as compassionate, though maybe her view was skewed because they handed out an overabundance of homework. Maybe she was stereotyping from what she saw on the news, but it seemed that law enforcement was filled with hard-nosed, jaded people who cared more about the crime than the people committing the crime.

That was part of why Mari wanted to go into law school. She wanted to be a defense attorney. She wanted to make sure everyone's voice had a chance to be heard. But for as much as she believed everyone had a voice and a right to speak, she sure couldn't figure out where her own voice had gone once their eyes locked.

He put his hand out. "My name is Grant Venturi."

Ha! Take that, Taryn. I've got a name now. She took the proffered hand and felt a thrill zing through her at the contact. "Mari Niles."

"I no-noticed you have a state code book in your hand. Is that what you're studying?"

He didn't seem like the sort of guy to stutter, so that caught her by surprise, but the bigger surprise was that he kept her hand a second longer than would be considered normal professional-greeting-time and that he gave her hand a slight squeeze upon releasing it.

"Yes. Code book. I'm in school right now getting my bachelor's, and then I'm going to law school in San Diego."

"Oh. Nice. California Western School of Law?"

"Yes, actually."

"It's a good school. What kind of lawyer? Estate? Intellectual property?"

"Defense," she said and didn't know why she felt defensive saying it and then decided that rather than feeling hurt by his assumption, she'd have a conversation with him about it. "Why do you automatically assume I'd be a desk lawyer? Women are just as capable in a court room as men."

"I didn't mean that to be insulting. You just seem so organized."

Organized? How did exiting the foliage like some sort of animal make her seem organized? And even though she was organized, it still sort of felt like an insult. Before she could retort, she caught the flustered look on his face that said he wasn't at all trying to be insulting. She let him off. "I'm betting my future clients will be glad I'm organized. Messy defense attorneys lose cases."

He grinned and leaned against the wishing well. "Touché, Mari Niles, Esquire. How soon before you get your bachelor's degree?"

His grin put her back at ease. "I'm on my last semester."

"Wow. You're almost there. The last semester is where I felt like I might never be done even though I was so close."

She nodded her understanding. That was exactly how she felt. "So what did you study in school?"

"Criminology."

"Huh. I suppose that would be useful in becoming 'something like a cop'?"

He laughed in a way that made her insides tingle with happiness. He thought she was funny. Once she'd made him laugh, she found she wanted to do it again and again and again.

"You'll make an excellent defense attorney. Not a single detail escapes your notice, not even the order of pillows." He startled as if he'd said something that maybe he hadn't meant to say. Mari narrowed her eyes at him.

"What's that supposed to mean?" And then she glanced around, remembering they were in a hotel and how the first time she'd run into him, they'd been within a close proximity to the hotel. "Are you a guest here at The Mariposa?"

He looked like he might lie for a moment. Mari knew that look from when the Bad-Decision started seeing the pre-med student. But Grant changed his mind and nodded in acknowledgment of the fact. "I am."

She felt enormous relief that he hadn't lied. She did not want this guy to disappoint her. "What room?"

He smiled widely, working hard on his appearance of innocence. "That's kind of a forward question to be asking a guy you only met."

"You flashed a gun at me. We're way past too-forward, don't you think?"

He dropped his feigned-innocent look and fixed her with a different look, one so intent she almost felt the need to reach out to the well to steady herself. "Room 913."

"So you're my ghost." She hadn't meant to say it out loud like that. Such a statement had to sound ridiculous.

"Ghost?"

Mari's face went hot when she realized she'd called a guest a ghost. What would Deanne say to that? "I mean, your room . . . it's very tidy, almost like no one's there. I'm the maid for your room." She hurried to add that last part to make sure he understood what in the world she was doing in his hotel room. How was it possible that her ghost and her cop were the same person? She had daydreamed that they could be connected, but she imagined them to be on two opposing teams. She hadn't imagined them to be the same guy.

"Is it really so unusual to be tidy?" he asked.

She answered his question with a question. "Do you not sleep in your bed at night, or do you really remake it up the exact same way I do?"

He lifted his shoulder in a shrug. "Your way seems like the best way."

"Yes, then, your level of tidiness is unusual. I started calling you a ghost because it appeared that no one ever entered the room besides me. You even hang the towel the same way I do. A closet containing a few orderly belongings that look so generic it seems on purpose hardly makes the room feel occupied by a breathing human. I'm sorry. My explanation sounds worse than the original words, so I'm just going to stop here. And I should probably go . . ." She meant to finish by saying *catch my bus* but knew her bus wouldn't come for a good long time, and she didn't feel like lying to her ghost from 913.

So instead, she turned to make a hasty retreat, but he laughed, straightened from where he'd been leaning against the well, and placed a hand on her arm—so gently, the touch could have been the single beat of a butterfly's wings. "Don't go," he said.

"I'm not really supposed to bother the guests. And I'm definitely not supposed to insult them, so—"

"You're not bothering me. Not at all. I came here to find you, remember? Besides, how many people humor a ghost by keeping his shampoo bottles straight?"

Mari grabbed his hand and laughed. "You *did* do that on purpose! Did you do the pillow on purpose too?"

"No, the pillow was on accident. But when you caught the switch and changed it back, I wondered how observant you really were."

It was at that moment that Mari realized she had a hold of his hand. How observant was she? Maybe too much, because she did *not* want to let go. She did let go, of course. But instead of releasing his hand with a casual indifference, she dropped it as though he'd burned her.

She gave a nervous laugh that sounded like the kind a high school girl might have given. And then she decided a person might actually be capable of dying from embarrassment. At least she wished a person could, because maybe then she would die instead of having to face this bizarre moment where her fingers still tingled from a touch that she had no right to steal from him.

Instead of looking away and pretending not to notice her overfamiliarity and then her hot burn of shame, he smiled and watched her as if he was studying for a test later and she was the subject matter.

"What?" she finally said.

"I have a few questions."

"Okay. Ask."

"Tell me about this well."

Questions. Right. About the well. Not about getting her phone number. Dang. But he had entered the garden to find her. That meant maybe he felt some of the same zing she felt. Maybe. Hopefully.

They both turned to face the wishing well. Mari had no idea if turning away from each other had been as hard for Grant—she loved knowing his name—as it had been for her. She had an intense desire to simply look at him and nothing else.

"What did you want to know about the well?" She prompted him when it looked like he had gotten lost in the act of turning. Maybe it *had* been as hard for him as it had been for her.

"It's got a very antique look to it, not just crafted to look old but like it has an authenticity to it."

"It was built in Mexico, and the man who bought the property here in Seashell Beach decided to have it transplanted to the hotel. The well is actually the reason the hotel has its name. 'Mariposa' means 'butterfly' in Spanish."

He probably already knew that detail, but he didn't try to preempt her knowledge with his own. That small act of respect won her over entirely. If he asked her to dinner, she'd say yes.

"The fact that it's a wishing well with butterflies on it was the reason the owner took such a liking to it," she continued. "He's part American Indian. I can't remember which tribe, but it has an oral tradition where butterflies carry wishes to the Great Spirit in the sky to be granted."

"I believe it. I already got my wish."

She smirked at him and rested against the very well they discussed. "You, my friend, are a wish-waster. A whole penny could have gotten you anything."

He edged closer to her and leaned down so they were almost eye to eye. "I don't see how that makes me a wish-waster. A whole penny got me everything."

That decided it. *She* was going to ask *him* to dinner. But before she could, he said, "Would you like some help studying? I know a lot about California State Code. How about I buy you dinner and help you study? We could start our meeting over again without the pepper spray this time."

"And without the gun."

"Yeah, we definitely don't want that happening again. What do you say? Dinner?"

"In a public place?" Mari asked, just in case she was wrong about this guy being the nicest human she'd ever met.

"Of course a public place. A guy like me needs to be careful of girls who make a habit of going into my hotel room whenever they feel like it."

She smiled at how easily he made her feel secure and safe without making her feel dumb or paranoid over it. She smiled because she was doing something totally crazy. Going out? Her? Mari Niles didn't go out, because she had school to finish and no more Bad Decisions to make. But . . . if she went, maybe Taryn could stop lecturing once and for all. Besides all that, she felt that this was a guy worth knowing. And she was also going to get her homework done.

Could it get any better than that?

When Grant-the-Ghost and Something-Like-a-Cop offered her his arm like a real gentleman would do for a real lady, Mari felt the entire monarch migration take flight in her stomach.

Yes, apparently it could get better. And she wondered if those butterflies would carry her wishes to the Great Spirit in the sky.

Six

Grant couldn't believe she'd said yes. He knew he was throwing a Hail Mary when he offered to help with her homework and take her to dinner. And sure, he *hoped* she'd say yes. But the fact that she actually did was something he hadn't really seen coming.

His wish really had come true. He'd wished for Mari to talk to him and to like him and find him interesting enough to go to dinner with him.

And now that she had her hand in the crook of his arm while he led her out of the gardens and onto Tangerine Street, he felt—for the first time in a long time—entirely uncertain of what to do next.

Grant was the kind of guy who always had a plan. And behind that plan lay two or three contingency plans just in case. Variables were always considered. They had to be. The truth was always at stake, and lives were almost always at stake.

But at that moment, though no lives were at stake, the urgency he felt to get this one thing right was far more important than anything he'd felt in the past. How could he exist in such a terribly key moment without a backup plan?

Why would you need a backup plan? He wondered to himself. What did he think was going to happen? Did he believe she was going to bolt and leave him without a way to contact her again?

No.

Especially since she was his maid, and he had a lot more information on her than she could guess at.

But he didn't think she'd appreciate knowing he'd run a background check on her. He'd even almost slipped up and told her as much when she'd introduced herself with her name. He'd said, "I know." Sure, he changed it to "I noticed" to cover up for the mistake, but the fact that he'd made any such kind of blunder made him feel terribly insecure.

He really liked that Mari was studying law. That kind of common ground could not be ignored. The fact that she smelled like his hotel sheets—clean and fresh—made him take a deep breath just to smell her again. She surprised him with everything that made her so uniquely her.

Law school. He totally hadn't seen that coming.

"Where would you like to go for dinner?" he asked.

She gave him a sidelong look and pulled away a little, leaving her hand only barely in the crook of his arm as she said, "I assume you aren't from here, or you wouldn't be staying at the hotel, so should I also assume you are unfamiliar with Tangerine Street and don't know what's available?"

He didn't like the idea of her putting distance between them. Would it be too forward for him to put his arm around her and snug her in close? Probably. Instead, he answered her question by informing her she was right about him not knowing the area very well and tried not to pay attention to the fact that she let her hand drop entirely as she pivoted in order to get a good look down both sides of the street.

"There's Just North, where you'll get great Mexican food. I'm giving you that option first because they're my favorite: live music, great food, nice beach views out the back windows, which are open when the weather is good. There's the Fortune Café for Chinese—though they serve a few non-Chinese dishes as well. They're kind of quirky. There's Geppeto's—pizza. We also have a few sandwich shops, a few sushi places, and Nathaniel's Crab Shack."

He really wanted to try the crab shack but opted to go with her first choice since she'd already declared it to be her favorite. What guy heard something like that and then chose differently?

Not any guy looking to make any kind of good impressions. And if Grant was any kind of guy today, he was one who wanted to make a good impression. He wanted to make a *great* impression.

"The Mexican place sounds great."

She fixed him with a look that said she'd caught something, understood something. "Nathaniel's Crab Shack is a favorite of mine too. Want to try that instead?"

"Really, whatever you want is good with me."

She smiled, showing off the straightest, whitest teeth he'd ever seen. "You'd seriously go to Mexican when you obviously prefer the Crab Shack just because you think I want it?"

She caught him. The woman didn't miss anything, did she? He shrugged in response.

"Do you even like Mexican food?" she asked.

"Absolutely."

"And you like seafood?"

"Absolutely."

"So, let's compromise. We can go to Just North today, and if we like the company . . . maybe we can try again tomorrow and go to Nathaniel's Crab Shack, at least, that is, if you'll be around tomorrow."

"I will definitely be around tomorrow." Grant couldn't believe how easy she was making this on him. He wouldn't have to ask for a second date opportunity. She had handed it to him like a present wrapped in shiny foil paper. Now all he needed to do was be good company. He could handle that, couldn't he?

Sure he could. That was the backup plan. Be charming, fun, communicative. *And totally forget the fact that you're leaving Seashell Beach immediately after the trial and you don't know when you'll ever—if ever—be back.*

Because if he allowed himself to think of that problem, the logic would overcome this intense need to get to know this woman better. If he allowed the logic to take over as it did every time he came to an emotional opportunity, would he ultimately lose his humanity altogether?

Maybe.

Probably.

And Grant knew he needed his humanity. He'd seen plenty of others harden themselves because of the type of people they were forced to work with every day. But he also saw others who were only hard when they had to be and also soft when they needed to be. Most of the time those people were the ones who had solid relationships outside work. The others . . . well, the others usually turned into isolated drunks.

Grant recognized the relationship factor missing in his life but hadn't concerned himself with it until he saw Mari and found himself wanting to know her better. Only then did the hole in his life marked "failed relationships" seem to be darker and deeper than ever. It was a hole he needed to fill.

Another date tomorrow.

Perfect.

"Just North it is," he said and started to lead her to the right.

She laughed and put her hand on his arm again to stop him. "It's the other way," she said, and this time, she kept her hand on his arm as they walked. He'd never been so grateful for a wrong turn.

Seven

"I went on a date!" Mari exclaimed when Taryn finally came into work.

"Are you making that up just because you want me to get off your case?" Taryn asked.

"Probably," Christina said, looking put out that Mari had waited for Taryn to share her good news.

To make up for it, Mari filled Christina's cart's under-bin with freshly folded towels while she talked. "I'm not making it up and I have actually been on three dates."

"What?" Taryn squealed.

"When?" Christina lifted a gray eyebrow in skepticism.

"Over the weekend. His name is Grant. He's the cop I told you about." Mari frowned inwardly at this information she shared with her friends. He hadn't ever really explained what branch of law enforcement he occupied. He was really good at evading the question—to the point that she didn't ever realize he hadn't answered the question until she was home and thinking about all they'd talked about when they'd been together.

In spite of not knowing the details of his employment, Mari felt she knew everything about Grant Venturi. And when she sighed, Taryn squealed again.

"Girl! It sounds like you've found love at last!"

Christina snorted, even though she eyed the towels in her cart with appreciation. "Mari is not in love. Three dates is not enough time to get to know anything about a stranger."

"I know lots of things about him," Mari insisted and almost felt spiteful enough to put the towels back on the shelf.

"Yeah," Taryn agreed. "Mari knows all sorts of things about him."

Christina snorted even louder, making her sound like some old-woman version of a fog horn. "Oh yeah? What does Mari know about him?"

Both women turned to Mari. And then Mari noticed that what had been a private conversation had turned into a group conversation, because it seemed everyone was packing their carts a little more slowly so they had a good excuse to stay in the basement and listen to Mari's news.

Mari swallowed hard, hating that her mind suddenly went blank. "Well . . . I know he has one younger brother he calls Spike even though his brother's name is really Spencer. His brother lives in Chicago." She smiled at everyone as if she'd completed her assignment and wanted praise for a job well done, except everyone seemed to be waiting for her to continue. So she did. "He's a sucker for food of any kind except fortune cookies." She'd discovered that when they'd ordered take-out from the Fortune Café for a beach picnic. He'd fed them to the seagulls. "He likes fine art but really gets into funky art. He likes the surrealists and modern artists." She based this fact on his reactions when Tangerine

Street had hosted a sidewalk art festival the day before. "He doesn't cuss." A lot of heads nodded approvingly at this tidbit, which she based entirely off when he accidentally caught his hand in the door of the Fortune Café and didn't say anything worse than "ouch."

"A man who doesn't cuss is likely to have a cool head and an even temper," Christina said, though she seemed grudging about having to pay any kind of compliment.

So Mari topped off her information with the one thing she knew everyone would approve Grant on. "He loves dogs," she said. "I know because he fed half his dinner last night to Sandy."

With that, Mari had them all convinced. There were several coos and clucks of adoration. Everyone loved Tangerine Street's rogue hound. Sandy was a hound dog/Labrador mix, and he belonged to no one and to everyone all at the same time. Sandy was the ultimate beach bum. He lounged on the boardwalk most of the time but also kept an eye on things. He'd even alerted a tourist mom that her child was choking on a hotdog. If a Seashell Beach local saw anyone hurting or harassing Sandy, there would be the vengeance of an entire neighborhood to contend with. The harasser might not make it out of Seashell Beach alive. Everyone loved Sandy. And if Grant had been good to Sandy, then Grant was good people.

Mari knew a lot more about Grant Venturi than she'd shared with everyone. But some of the other things felt private—like they belonged to her alone. She certainly didn't tell anyone he was a guest at the hotel. Not that there were any rules about that sort of thing, but it felt weird, and she didn't want to find herself the center of a sticky situation. She knew his parents lived in Michigan in a town that was located on the thumb part of the hand shape that made up the state. He had grown up in Michigan but now lived in San Francisco.

San Francisco was at least in the same state as Mari. Yet, the words *San Francisco* gave Mari a sort of anxiety. That was his home, his home that was not Seashell Beach. It was a good seven-hour drive from Seashell Beach. Was seven hours too far?

Mari wasn't sure. Maybe it didn't matter? Maybe just her getting *out there* again and taking part in the dating scene was good enough. Only it didn't feel good enough to Mari. She really liked Grant. Maybe she wasn't exactly in love with him yet like Taryn had implied, but she liked the way he made her feel competent and capable. Even when helping her with concepts she didn't understand in her homework, he'd managed to make her feel like she *could* understand if she managed to be patient with herself.

And though she hated comparing Grant to the Bad Decision, she couldn't help but see all Grant's superiorities. Grant owned the upper hand, not just in relation to the Bad Decision, but in relation to every other boyfriend and date experience Mari had ever known.

Over the last several days Mari felt like she *could* be in love or was at least hanging out in Love's neighborhood and doorbell-ditching Love's address.

And it scared her to death.

Finding the right guy was great and all, but why couldn't it be at the right time—like after she graduated from school and had a law degree already? And why couldn't it be the right place, where the guy in question lived within a twenty-mile radius?

As Mari entered the elevator and pushed the button for floor four, she sighed again.

Taryn mistook the noise for something else. "So you seeing him again soon?" she asked.

Mari smiled in spite of all her worries and misgivings. "Tonight," she said. The elevator doors slid open. The cart-picker from room 421 stood in the hallway with his luggage and a frown on his face, saying, "We'll miss our flight if you go any slower than that. Seriously, Alison! Leave it for the maid. That's what they're paid to do."

"Not paid enough," Taryn grumbled under her breath as she muscled her cart out into the hallway.

Suddenly Mr. Room 421 looked less anxious about his wife's expediency and more interested in whether or not Taryn or Mari might leave a cart unattended. Both women hovered near their carts and mused over their rosters as if they planned on looking at their clipboards for the rest of the day.

Room 421's wife finally exited the room. She strong-armed a bulging suitcase while her husband had a single small duffle over his shoulder. He *tsked* as he passed Mari's cart with a deep regret that she hadn't yet vacated her post. Once he and his wife were safely tucked into the elevator going down, Mari went to work. She started with room 421.

Nope. Not paid nearly enough at all. The room was thrashed. Blankets and pillows and towels were everywhere and on top, among, and under them were dozens and dozens of various brochures. They must have gone to a trade show for general merchandise if the brochures could be counted on for valid information. Pizza boxes with moldering remnants made the room smell like something had died in it. And the wife had apparently lost a war with her makeup case since broken compact blush powder had been smeared all over the vanity counter. The greasy smears were probably what she'd been trying to clean when her husband had been yelling at her.

Mari centered herself and found calm by thinking of Grant. So what if someone ground cheap makeup all over the counter and on the floor? She had thoughts of Grant to keep her company while she cleaned it.

Thinking of him was the best company she could find when he wasn't directly in front of her—company she didn't mind keeping.

Eight

"You should have told her what you do for a living from the beginning," Grant said to his mirror as he shaved off the stubble that had grown since the previous morning. But how had he known she would become so important in his life?

Grant had been seeing Mari for over a week, and every moment made him that much more certain he never wanted to leave Seashell Beach. Yet, his job overseeing the star witness's safety was almost finished. Over a week of seeing Mari and only just over a week left to be able to see her.

Dominic's trial was only nine days away.

He frowned at his reflection. Hope, the star witness, grew more fidgety as the trial loomed closer. Grant had spent the better part of a year coaxing Hope to testify against her boyfriend—the heroin dealer who ran a billion-dollar operation in the Santa Monica area. How much longer would he be able to keep her convinced she was doing the right thing? Dominic's girlfriend didn't live up to her name. The young woman groused about everything under the sun.

The sheets were too scratchy, the food was too bland, Grant wasn't nice enough or helpful enough or fun enough.

As if being fun was a U.S. Marshal requirement. Last time he checked his job description, *fun* hadn't been anywhere on the list. As long as the witness still breathed and wasn't bleeding, he was doing his job. If she felt bored, she had only herself to blame, because Grant was a fun guy, no matter what she said.

Mari thought he was fun. At least he hoped so.

Grant finished his getting-ready routine, tucked everything back into his toiletry case, and stowed the case into the cubby under the counter. He gave the room one last glance and tilted the lampshade slightly toward the wall.

He grinned, knowing he'd handed Mari an easy one. She'd likely make fun of him over it later when they went to dinner, but with Hope waiting on him more and more impatiently each day, he needed to hurry.

Needing to hurry and wanting to hurry were not the same thing at all.

After he finally arrived at the safe house where they kept Hope secured until the trial, her first words to Grant were, "It's about time you showed up."

Grant didn't respond but looked to his partner, Joanne, to see if she had any insight as to why Hope grew more disagreeable each day. Joanne gave a slight shake of her head to say that, no, she didn't have any idea why the girl was becoming a bad houseguest either.

"Sleep well, Hope?"

She glared through her over-mascaraed eyes. "Not at all. I might as well be sleeping on straw. Did you buy my bedding at the local barn?"

He didn't respond to that either. In not too many days, Grant would no longer be Hope's babysitter. Joanne would stay to mop up details, and Grant would be back in San Francisco. That thought didn't fill him with the relief it used to.

When Hope ran from Dominic, she brought evidence against him with her and, in a decision fueled by both fear and the desire to get even with him for cheating on her, called the authorities to rat him out. Grant had hid her in Louisiana before the trial date came up. During the time in Louisiana, Hope had become close to Joanne, and Grant stepped aside to let that friendship blossom. He'd made the right choice, since Hope trusted Joanne far more than she trusted Grant. Keeping the witness comfortable and making sure she felt safe was the top priority—not just making sure she felt safe but that she *stayed* safe.

Grant stayed close by but in an alternate location in case Hope had to be moved during the trial. He checked with her daily, verified the marshals around her were doing more than playing cards, and went back to the second location at night. The situation allowed Joanne greater responsibility, since she was up for promotion, while also keeping Grant close enough for emergencies.

When Hope realized she hadn't gotten a rise out of him, she said, "Another body floated up this morning."

That got his attention. He turned to Joanne. "What happened?"

"The woman who used to be Hope's hairdresser turned up dead. They think Dominic's goon was grilling her for information about where Hope might be and got carried away."

Grant turned back to Hope. "Do we have any reason to believe the hairdresser has any clue about your whereabouts?"

"She's my hairdresser, not my mother."

"You hate your mother," Grant reminded her.

"Yes, well, I'm not all that fond of my hairdresser either. She totally messed up my highlights on my last visit. And to rub lemon juice in the wound, you haven't let me out to get it redone."

Grant wanted to remind her that if he let her out for a hair appointment, she'd better like the hairstyle enough to be buried in it, since she possibly wouldn't live long enough to have another one.

"When were you going to tell me?" he asked Joanne.

"We only received the news a few minutes before you showed up. The message is probab—"

His phone buzzed. He glanced at the incoming message relaying the information Joanne was just in the middle of telling him he probably already had.

He sucked in a deep breath of air and stalked to the window to look out. He hated this—hated that another person was dead. How could a guy behind bars still have the power to have another person interrogated to death? How did the justice system fail so tremendously?

"Do you think he wants to find me because he misses me?" Hope asked.

Grant turned around to face her, certain his face had to betray the shock and disgust he felt at such a concept. Did she want to be missed by such a monster?

"Don't look at me like that, Grant. He was usually really sweet to me. He told me he loved me all the time."

"Especially after he gave you that black eye?" Grant asked. "I bet he told you he loved you a lot after that, right?"

She shuddered, letting Grant know he'd hit the mark. "He said . . ." But she didn't finish whatever it was that he'd said. Instead she stiffened and squared her shoulders. "It's not all his fault, you know. He had a crummy childhood, bad parents, abusive nannies . . . he said he wanted to be different from all that—that he wanted to change." She squinted as if trying to see something in the distance better. For once, she didn't look combative and annoyed with Grant. Instead, she looked sad. "What do you think? Do you think someone like Dominic can change?"

Grant almost said no, but one look at Hope's face made him stop and wonder if she meant the question sincerely. Was it possible she still loved the guy—even after the news she'd just received?

He let the question pass unanswered and spent his day with Hope trying to be friendly and fun. He told her the story about The Mariposa well and the legend of butterflies carrying wishes to the Great Spirit in the sky. She liked the story but seemed distracted.

"What if he gets off scot-free?"

"You'll make sure that doesn't happen," Grant said.

"Can you help me? Help me like we were in a courtroom and you were the defendant's attorney asking me questions. I don't think I'm ready for this. I want to be ready."

So Grant and Joanne spent the rest of the time going over possible scenarios of the trial. They grilled her on the questions the defense attorney would use to trip her up, and Grant couldn't help but think of Mari and her desire to be a defense attorney.

He wondered what questions a lawyer like Mari would ask, and it helped him fine-tune his questions.

But even with all that, Hope proved difficult, questioning the way the system worked and tossing back his questions with impatient retorts that it didn't matter if she answered the questions right, because Dominic could still kill people from behind bars.

Hope had worn Grant down to a pile of exhaustion by the end of the day. The only thing keeping him from absolute mental breakdown was the knowledge that he would be with Mari soon.

Mari was quickly becoming Grant's only sanity.

Nine

Mari walked with Grant along the shoreline and then cut a path to the boardwalk so they could enter Just North from the back. She watched the waves pressing forward and curling in on themselves as they broke against the shore. Was she doing that? Was she rushing in to a moment of futility? Beating her head against the same shore again and again and again?

She peeked at Grant through her hair. He'd paused to look at the sea, poised in a position of perfect ease and contentment.

And she felt something wash over her, like the waves washing the beach. This was an entirely different shore from anything she'd encountered before. Standing with him felt right all the way down to her toes buried in the sand. She tugged on his hand to indicate she was done looking at the water.

Why look at water when she could be staring across a table at him?

"Are you sure I'm not distracting you from homework?"

Grant asked after they'd been seated and served drinks. Mari had seen Grant every single night since their first date. She was glad he took her home every night after they spent time together instead of saying goodbye to her at the hotel. She hated the idea of anyone seeing her fraternizing with the guests. It raised too many questions, and all of the answers awkward. Besides, his taking her home meant she didn't have to take the bus. Mari really liked not taking the bus.

And she liked the extra few minutes it gave her with him.

They walked on the beach a lot. He helped her study a lot. Being with Grant felt like a needle pulling tight stitches to the places where her soul had ripped at the seams. She felt safe with him.

The restaurant choice had been his, and she felt a thrill of pleasure over the fact that he loved her favorite restaurant as much as she did. The music tonight was low key and rich. The new girl who bought the antique shop down the street was playing her saxophone, which gave a very sexy backdrop to Mari's dinner with Grant. "No. You're not distracting me."

Grant grinned and gave a look that said he caught the lie but didn't care enough to do anything about it.

To be fair, she hadn't exactly lied. It wasn't *him* who distracted her. It was his mouth and all the things he said, and his mouth and all the things she wished it was doing. All this time, and no kiss goodnight?

At their age, the idea of such platonic dating seemed weird. Mari wasn't about to go another night with no kiss. If she had to threaten him with her pepper mace, he *would* kiss her goodnight.

"Is there a particular law firm you're interested in working for, or will you set up your own office?"

Mari wondered if they were worried about the same thing: distance. Was his work coming to an end? How long could she count on him being her ghost in room 913? "I don't know. I figured I'd stay close to Seashell Beach. I've been here for a few years, and it's close to my folks and my sisters. But I'm not married to the idea of sticking around if other opportunities present themselves."

She gave herself an inward eye roll. *Married, Mari? Why do you always pick the wrong words when Grant is around?*

But Grant didn't seem to notice. He had his hand over hers in the middle of the table, which was a little too small to comfortably fit two people. Mari now saw the wisdom in such table arrangements. She almost felt like leaving a special tip for the intimacy the tables offered, even if the waitress didn't have anything to do with it.

His hand was warm and calloused. Her grandmother used to always say a man without callouses wasn't good for anything. Based on his hands alone, Mari knew her grandmother would approve.

"It really doesn't matter where I go as long as I'm doing some good, you know?" she continued.

"Good as in getting the bad guy off, scot-free?"

"Was that cynicism I heard just now?" she asked.

Instead of getting defensive like the Bad Decision would have, Grant tightened his fingers around hers. "Sorry. It's been a long day."

"Want to tell me about it?" The sax-playing antique store owner went into a long soulful solo that sent shivers down Mari's spine.

He gave his head a jiggle that landed somewhere between a shake and a nod. "Sometimes the justice system fails, that's all."

"And that's what a good defense attorney will prevent."

He blinked at her as if seeing her for the first time. "And here I thought a good defense attorney helped criminals navigate the plea bargains offered by the prosecutor."

She knew he was baiting her, making her defend herself the way she would defend a criminal. He challenged her to be her very best and to trust her own instincts. "A good defense attorney would only do that if it was in the best interests of a truly guilty client."

"What if you don't know? What if you think you might have a guilty client but you just don't know?"

"We believe people are innocent until proven guilty."

"Are they? Really?"

Mari wondered if he was still trying to challenge her or if he was trying to work something out in his own mind. "Yes," she said.

"What if you have doubts? If you believe a client is guilty, do you still work your hardest to prove their innocence?"

"Absolutely," she said.

"Why? Why not work a little less and let justice prevail for once?" He swirled his drink around in its glass, letting it slide over and around the ice cubes. He looked into his glass and seemed to see past it.

"Because a lazy defense creates a lazy prosecution. A lazy prosecution ends in the wrong people doing time for crimes they didn't commit. Innocent people go to prison, and the guilty are free to commit more crimes. Every system of any value has a check and a balance. A good defense attorney is the check that keeps the balance."

"What if . . . even after all that, there still isn't balance? Do you still believe in it?" He gave his glass another swirl. The waitress came over and offered him a refill, probably thinking his swirling was a hint that his glass was nearly empty.

"I have to believe in it. It's the only system we have."

"What if a person made mistakes? What if they're guilty, but they want to be innocent? How is there anything balanced in that?"

"If he wants to be innocent, he won't mind paying society back for his crimes. It isn't perfect, but it isn't broken. Not really. It works . . . most of the time. Are you okay?" She squeezed his hand and bent her own head to meet his downward gaze.

He took a cleansing breath. "Yeah. I'm fine. Just a long day."

"Long day where? I've been wondering where you go during the day," she asked him. "I keep thinking you might be in your room when I go to clean, but you're never there. Are you in town for a cop convention or something?" A convention being held in Seashell Beach and not being held at The Mariposa was unlikely. Raegan, the event coordinator, had turned the hotel into a convention hotspot.

"Just in town for work." He looked down at his menu. "Have you tried the fajitas?"

She squared her shoulders, refusing to allow her questions regarding his work to be put off any further. "Yes. They're fabulous. What work brought you to Seashell Beach?"

"You know . . . I'm a cop."

"Sort of, you mean."

"What?"

"You're sort of a cop. Or *something like*, according to what you told me the first time we met. Pretend this is one of my homework questions, and give me a straight, clear, homework-type answer—the kind that gets an A+ and not a C. What type of cop are you?"

Grant opened his mouth in what might have been a genuine response, but his phone rang. His eyes went wide with alarm when he saw the number and he hurried to answer. "Grant here." He sounded serious and a little bit angry.

His eyes fluttered closed briefly, and he let out a huge breath as though someone had punched him in the gut. "Right. I'll be right there . . . No. Wait for me." He jabbed his finger against his telephone screen as if the device was to blame for whatever trouble befell him.

"Grant?" Mari asked as he pushed his chair back and pulled out his wallet.

He dropped two twenties on the table even though they hadn't ordered anything but drinks and an appetizer to tide them over while they decided what they wanted.

"Grant?"

His eyes sagged as if his already long day had just promised him it would never end. "I'm sorry I won't be able to get you home. Here." He handed her another twenty. "Call a taxi, and text me when you get inside so I know you made it okay."

"Grant!"

He finally really looked at her, not at the table, not at the wallet or the money in his hand, but *her*. "I know. I know you want to know where I'm going and why and who I'm with, but I can't . . . explain right now. It's all complicated, and another person makes it more complicated. I'll tell you as soon as I can."

And then he did something that dazed Mari too much to ask anything more of him. He bent down and kissed her full on the mouth. It wasn't the slow, long, lingering kiss she'd been imagining for this particular goodnight, but neither was it a quick peck of friendship. This felt like something more than either of those. It was familiar and intimate and achingly sincere. When he pulled away, she jolted at the hole his absence created.

"I'll call you soon. Love you."

And then he was gone.

A kiss and a "love you" and then gone. *He kissed me,* Mari thought. The saxophone crooned in rhythm to her internal chant: *He kissed me. He kissed me. He said he loved me, and he kissed me.*

"What?" Mari said and shook herself and blinked several times as she tried to get her bearing.

The waitress tapped her pen against her order pad. "Are you ready to order, yet?"

Mari glanced around the dimly-lit restaurant filled with couples engrossed in intimate conversations. "Um, no. Something came up, and we have to leave." Mari said *we* as if she and Grant were one person.

She felt fuzzy and frazzled inside. Grant had been preoccupied and intense all night. Then he'd gone off on the justice system, asking questions so strange she hardly knew what to make of them.

What if a person made mistakes?

Had Grant been talking about someone he knew? Or was all of that hypothetical? Just homework stuff?

Or . . . was Grant talking about himself?

Mari gasped and shoved her chair back to stand, nearly knocking the waitress over in her rush to be moving, doing something besides sitting there.

"Thanks," Mari said to the waitress. She stumbled to the front door and to the twilight settling over Seashell Beach.

She felt lost—even on Tangerine Street, a place she

knew better than anywhere in the world. She walked and before long was in front of the revolving doors of The Mariposa Hotel. She slipped inside, ducked into the elevator, and hit the button for the ninth floor.

What if a person made mistakes?

What kind of mistakes could Grant have possibly been talking about?

What if they're guilty but they want to be innocent?

She pulled her maid key out of her purse and slid it over the pad to room 913. She let herself into the room before she could stop herself, all the while asking, "Oh, Grant . . . what are we doing?"

Ten

"What do you mean she vanished?" Grant felt sick inside. The girl in their protection, the witness who was so pivotal to the case that they had no case without her, had walked.

With the trial only a week away, he'd thought they were home free.

Apparently, he'd been grossly wrong.

She was afraid, understandably so. Dominic picked girlfriends who were at least half his age. Their youth helped him in making them feel small and powerless. But Hope wasn't like the others. She had iron under her over-moisturized skin.

All indicators had showed she was ready for this step, ready to walk away from the life she'd lived before, paid for by the depraved acts of her boyfriend, and do the right thing by putting him in prison forever. When he'd asked Mari about the guilty who wanted to become innocent, he was asking about Hope.

But she had walked away from her chance to do the

right thing, snuck out at some weak point Grant hadn't seen and still couldn't see.

He should've known something was wrong by all the questions Hope asked when he'd visited her earlier. She kept talking about Dominic as if he was simply a guy in the wrong place at the wrong time, as if he was a guy who could be reformed, be made better.

And then she would shiver and talk about how guilty her boyfriend really was. She talked about people he'd killed because they were inconvenient. The hairdresser's death had really rattled her. Hope had exhausted him by waffling back and forth regarding Dominic's guilt. *He might reform,* she said. *He should get the chair,* she said. *I'm afraid of him,* she said. *I still love him,* she said.

"I'm missing something," he muttered as he turned and inspected the room Hope had been sleeping in. He wished Mari could have seen this room before this moment. If she had seen it before and then been allowed to walk in later, she'd find the clue—that missing detail that might help guide Grant to where Hope was hiding.

Mari.

He felt sick that he'd let the L-word slip out. What kind of stupid stress-induced fog had done that to him?

But he didn't have time to think about what he'd said and shouldn't have said. He couldn't have let Mari see the room. And he still couldn't. If Dominic found out Hope was free and walking, he'd make sure she never saw another sunrise. The more people who knew about Hope, the more likely it was Grant would end up identifying her body at the morgue.

Grant checked Hope's room thoroughly, and then he checked it again. She'd left no indicators, no clues as to what she might have been thinking when she left.

"Was she agitated the last time you saw her?" he asked Joanne, who looked miserable beyond belief at having lost her charge.

"Not more than usual. She talked about how much she had loved Dominic and that he had treated her well most of the time and that maybe she needed to give him a chance to be a better man. You know, same stuff she's been doing since we took her into protection. She kept going over the things she believed the defense attorney would ask her and then shook her head and complained that you were staying too far away to be of any use."

"What? But she was the one who wanted me to keep my distance because she didn't trust me!"

"I guess she changed her mind."

Grant honed in on the one bit of information that didn't fit. "No. She didn't change her mind about me. That's just an excuse. She changed her mind about something else." Hope had always been so sure she had everything she needed. Grant had been sure too. What changed?

"I don't know. She wouldn't say anything besides she didn't feel safe and that if she said she was sorry, maybe he'd take her back."

"She said that? That if she apologized, he'd take her back?"

Joanne nodded, and understanding dawned on her face. Hope had never said that before.

Grant's heart felt like it skipped several beats. "She's going back to Dominic. Time to go." Grant turned to one of the other house-sitters. "Keep this room clean. I don't want anyone in here, understood?"

He turned back to Joanne. "Let's move."

He thought of Mari as he slid in behind the wheel of his car. He wondered if she was angry that he'd left her with no explanation and a freakish show of over-emotion. He thought of all the things people forgave and overlooked in relationships. If someone like Hope could forgive someone like Dominic and choose to go back to him, surely Mari would forgive him for not being able to tell her the whole truth. And for also telling too much of a truth.

But he wondered if that was really true. As much as Mari believed in being innocent until proven guilty, Grant knew Mari had experienced far too much of the guilty in her life. Her ex-husband had given her all kinds of trouble—though she didn't talk much about it. Prying the little information Mari was willing to share about that part of her life had not been easy for Grant. She seemed to want to move past it, not dwell on it.

Mari had said something that had deeply affected Grant. She'd said she allowed herself to be tied to the memory of what her ex did to her for far too long and that tying herself to that memory had kept her from progressing on the river of her own life. In fact, instead of progressing, she said, clinging to that memory was drowning her a little every day. Mari was a get-over-it-and-move-on-with-life kind of girl, but was she a forgive-and-allow-him-to-be-in-her-life girl?

He rolled his lips together and relived his one moment of bravery that day: he'd kissed Mari. If nothing else, he would at least have that. Telling her he loved her had been a bit of an accident. Not that he didn't actually think he might be falling hard, but that the words had slipped out before he knew they even existed. What did Mari think of such a thing? Way too much, way too soon?

Probably.

Either way, he couldn't allow himself to think about it. He had to find Hope.

He had to get her to choose her own innocence over her boyfriend's guilt.

Eleven

Mari awoke with a start. She'd fallen asleep on Grant's bed in his hotel room. She rubbed the sleep out of her eyes and pulled out her phone to check the time: 6:38 am.

And Grant hadn't come back to his room.

She swung her legs over the side of the pristine white bed covers and stood on shaky legs. She'd waited for his return until she'd finally succumbed to her own exhaustion. Where had he gone? Where was he now? She checked her phone again. No messages. No missed calls. No sign that he had tried to contact her and tell her what was going on.

But he'd kissed her—a kiss that seemed to hold the depth of promises he intended to keep. He'd left her with the declaration of his love.

What if they're guilty, but they want to be innocent?

Had she really been so stupid as to fall for a Bad Decision again? Gah! Would she never be able to trust her own instincts where men were concerned? And he'd left her with a declaration of love? After just under two weeks?

Who did that sort of thing? No one could know how they felt about another person in so short a time. Was his kiss and love-confession a diversion tactic?

What if Grant was guilty of something? What would Mari do then? He might be involved in something dangerous. Was he really on the law's side of things, or had she just wanted to believe him because the nice-looking and looking-nice combination had thrown her off and because Taryn had just given her the lecture of a century over letting people into her life?

What if Mari had been right when she'd assumed her ghost of 913 was a criminal running from the cops? And if he was, whose side would Mari be on?

She didn't know.

What she did know was that her shift started in one hour and twenty-one minutes.

She glanced around the room and decided she might as well use it to get ready for the day. What difference did it make if she made a bit of a mess when she'd be the one cleaning it up later? Mari crossed to the bathroom, snatching The Mariposa shampoo, conditioner, and body wash on her way past, locked the door in case Grant returned, quickly unclothed, and stepped into the shower. She tried not to think about how there would be no game for her today. There would be no item out of place for her to discover. Grant had kept up the game even after he'd started taking her to dinner every night. But not today. There might not even be a Grant today.

Mari couldn't let herself think that way; she couldn't let herself think at all. Instead she let the hot water run over her while she chanted out various state codes for her upcoming final.

But each code had Grant's voice behind it. Each

mnemonic had Grant's smile hidden somewhere within. How was she ever supposed to take her final when it was a painful stab at the person she thought she knew, but didn't know at all?

She couldn't let herself worry about finals and Grant when the more pressing matter was getting to work. Mari wasn't the sort of woman who carried a beauty arsenal in her purse. She had a single lip gloss, no brush or comb, no mascara, nothing that would help her really get ready for the day. At the very least she had to comb her hair out.

She spied the dark toiletry kit hidden in the recesses of the vanity cabinet. Surely Grant had a comb . . .

"No," she said aloud. It was against all the rules. The Mariposa staff were absolutely, under no circumstances, supposed to be opening the guests' luggage. But Grant wasn't just a guest, he was also her . . . her . . . what?

What title did Grant own? Study partner? Friend? Boyfriend? Her stomach did a pathetic flip-flop when she thought the word *boyfriend*, even if it was a juvenile term.

Regardless, Grant wasn't just a guest. He was the man who had met her lips with his own and told her he loved her. Surely opening his toiletry case to borrow a comb was justified in those circumstances, wasn't it? Borrowing wasn't the same thing as spying, was it?

She pulled out the soft black leather case and unzipped it before she could change her mind. The contents were vastly disappointing: a comb, razor, travel-sized shaving cream, shampoo, and body wash, deodorant, toothbrush, toothpaste, and floss. The case could have been packed by a clerk at a drug store for all the personality that went into it. The generic contents matched that of the bag.

Feeling disgruntled, Mari used the comb to rake through her hair and do it up into a bun. Once she was cleaned, dressed, and basically ready to go downstairs and change into her uniform, Mari realized she still had forty-eight minutes before she needed to clock in. She thought about the zipped-up black bag in the closet.

She didn't need anything that could possibly be found in the bag, nothing that could keep borrowing from turning into spying. But she also couldn't stop herself. She wanted to know if Grant was who she believed him to be. She could not allow herself to get into another Bad Decision situation. And if she had to spy a little to keep herself safe, well then . . .

She crossed the floor to the closet, swept open the closet door, and carried the bag out into the middle of the room. With a prayer for forgiveness and a barrage of guilt, she unzipped the top and threw it back so she could clearly view its contents.

On one side of the case were three pairs of khaki pants, rolled up to prevent folding creases, and three button-up shirts: two blue, one white. There were boxer shorts and socks—typical generic man clothes. The other side was occupied by a cloth shoe bag with a pair of dress shoes inside. Nothing special or identifying there either.

"You really are a ghost, Grant Venturi."

As she folded it back up to stow it into the closet, Mari spied a smaller second case, one she hadn't seen before. It wasn't in the closet, but between the door to the hotel room and the closet. She knew she hadn't simply missed seeing the suitcase before; it wasn't there before.

It hadn't been there when Mari had entered the room the night before.

It hadn't been there when Mari had gone to take a shower.

"Grant?" she called out, knowing he wouldn't answer

because there was nowhere he could hide in the room without her seeing him.

It unnerved her to think someone had been in the room while she'd been in the shower. She was the maid in charge of the room, so none of her coworkers would have entered. The bellhop always knocked loudly. He'd learned the valuable lesson of a loud knock after walking in on guests in less-than-proper moments. The poor kid almost quit after that.

Mari opened the room door and peeked into the hallway. Empty. She closed it back up again and double-latched it.

With nothing to lose now that she'd already committed more crimes than any Disney show could offer, Mari glared at the newcomer's suitcase and unzipped it, throwing back the top immediately. Mari shook her head in confusion at what she saw. Women's clothing. Mari tried to wrap her mind around all the reasons Grant might have for packing women's clothing in a suitcase but couldn't come up with any that made sense. She pulled out the top silky garment and found that it was a very pretty, very pricey Vera Wang sundress. The one beneath it was a Kenneth Cole—not nearly as pricey but still out of Mari's current budget. She drilled through the rest of the contents: sandals, two lacy bras, several pairs of lacy panties, thongs, and swimsuits. There was a pair of yoga pants, a set of heels, and a third dress that looked much classier than the two sundresses. Several tattered regency romance paperbacks were in a side pocket. At the bottom of the suitcase was a little handbag.

"What do I think I'm doing?" She shivered as the manic craze of violating a guest's privacy finally left her with nothing but her guilt and horror at her own actions.

Mari drew the line at the handbag.

As she repacked the suitcase, careful to leave it all in perfect order, and aching with a guilt she never imagined she'd be in a position to feel, a note fluttered out of one paperback books.

She picked it up to return it to the book, even though she had no idea which page it had been tucked into so there was no way for her to return it exactly, and spied Grant's name written at the bottom of the page. She couldn't help it. There weren't that many words, and she couldn't un-see them if she'd had the willpower to try.

Hope,
You are a strong woman and have all my faith. You will do great things, I just know it. Believe in yourself, and you got this. I will keep you safe. We'll get through this together. You can trust me. I promise.
Grant

Mari felt her cheeks burn with shame.

Again!

Had it happened again? Had she allowed herself to become infatuated with a man who declared faith and trust and then broke that same faith and trust as soon as her back is turned?

What had Christina called it? Bad Decision—The Sequel?

And where was this Hope woman now? How did her suitcase just show up in his hotel room? Why was he traveling with her things but without her? Mari frowned. That didn't make sense. After having a moment of total meltdown, Mari focused and tried to think rationally. She didn't believe he was cheating, not on her, and not on this Hope person, no matter what it looked like on the surface.

Innocent until proven guilty. She didn't look at any of the other notes or letters. She wasn't sure she could stomach what she found. Besides, she wasn't sure she could live with herself for giving in to the entire mess of the night.

A guy told her he loved her, and she took a dive off the cliff of ethics? Who was she angrier with? Grant or herself?

Herself.

Which meant she needed to at least talk to him about what had happened, both from his side and hers.

There was too much here she didn't understand.

That was the part that bugged her most. She didn't understand. Grant was involved in something—illegal or legal. But either way, he didn't trust her enough to talk to her about it or confide in her. An unexpected byproduct of the letter was a feeling of knowing him. It was typical Grant—building someone else up and giving them the confidence to do something hard, just like he always did with her. But in the letter he had given some woman named Hope all his faith. Why wouldn't he give Mari that same gift? Why didn't he have enough faith in her to tell her what was going on? Even if he was dealing with a confidentiality issue, he could have told her at least that much—that he had a confidentiality issue and couldn't talk.

At the moment, it only felt like he *wouldn't* talk.

She considered a moment before deciding to open Grant's bag back up. She switched the order of the shirts. She wanted him to know she'd been in there. She wanted to be honest about that part without actually having to come right out and confess. She closed his bag up and turned her attention to the secondary suitcase.

Mari shook her head and finished carefully folding the suitcase's contents so they were exactly as she found them. If there was a woman named Hope sharing this room, Mari wanted to be nothing more than the maid who cleaned it.

No.

She didn't even want to be that.

If there was another woman involved in this picture, Mari wanted to be as far away as possible.

Maybe Mari didn't believe in the "innocent until proven guilty" concept as much as she'd thought she did.

Twelve

Grant hadn't slept in thirty-two hours. Hope had disappeared. They had several marshals watching Dominic's most loyal associates, his house, even his groundskeepers. Hope hadn't been near the estate or anyone in connection to the estate. She had vanished just as Joanne had said.

The only thing he could think to do was go back to the apartment where she'd been staying and pick her room apart piece by piece. *Think like Mari,* he told himself. Mari would see the details. She would know what changed.

He glanced down at the local magazines scattered over the side of Hope's bed and glanced away. He started to walk out of the room, but something familiar tugged him back toward Hope's bed. He bent down and looked closer at the top magazine. It was a picture of The Mariposa well at his hotel, the one in the secret garden where he'd finally had his first real conversation with Mari.

"Joanne, tell me again what she said. Think of her exact words."

Joanne recited everything Hope had said about being afraid because Grant was so far away and how he'd abandoned her and how no one would protect her.

He looked back down at the magazine. Had he said he was staying at the hotel? No. Not exactly. But he had talked about the well with the mosaic of butterflies and how the wishes were carried to the Great Spirit in the sky. He'd thought she'd like that story about wishes being carried on the wings of butterflies. Hope was a whimsical sort of girl, and she had smiled when he'd told her.

"She didn't leave to go back to him," Grant said feeling tired and yet encouraged. "She left to find me." He flicked the magazine where the featured well told Hope exactly where to go to locate him.

His only wish now was that she hadn't managed to lead anyone else to her.

"Carry *that* wish up, little butterflies," he muttered. "Make it happen."

Thirteen

When Mari stepped out of room 913, she felt like a criminal. She kept her head bowed and hoped James and Jeff, the guys who ran security, were watching TV instead of the security screens.

She felt uncertainty that she just couldn't seem to shake. She checked her phone. It was time for her to clock in. She couldn't allow herself to worry about who had been in Grant's room with her, or what the enigmatic bag filled with expensive women's clothes and notes from Grant meant. She had to focus on her job.

Taryn wasn't in the locker room, which made Mari feel even worse. If ever she needed a pep talk and a hug from a friend, it was now. She swiftly changed into her maid uniform, stocked her cart. and headed to the service elevator.

And since cleaning was mindless work, she had all the time in the world to think about everything that had happened and what it all meant. She wanted to check Grant's room, to see if the interloper had returned, to see if that interloper was pretty or not. She hated that she cared what the owner of that designer suitcase looked like.

But she kept her routine in check. She would not clean Grant's room until the end of the day.

During her lunch break, she escaped to the secret garden to try to shore up feelings of tranquility before she faced Grant's room. She leaned over the lip of the well and looked down at all the copper and silver wishes distorted by the rippling water.

"I wish I knew what I was doing," she said aloud. Then she pulled out a penny from her tunic pocket and closed her eyes to make a real wish. "I wish I knew what was going on with Grant."

Mari threw the penny and then popped open her eyes so she could watch the copper coin flutter down to the bottom of the well. She waited a second and then shook her head in disgust.

No new knowledge had immediately downloaded itself into her brain.

Had she really thought that it would?

She must have been totally sleep-deprived to allow her logic to evade her for even a moment. She rolled her eyes at the well and ducked into the foliage so she could sit in her corner and maybe, just maybe, slow her brain enough to get a nap in before her lunch break was over.

After she'd settled into her spot, she set the alarm on her phone so she didn't accidentally oversleep, and she closed her eyes.

That was when she heard the woman's voice and grumbled to herself over the fact that someone had come to ruin her nap.

"Of course I came here. You're so distracted lately. I was worried. We only have a week, and then it's game over."

"It is not game over."

Mari straightened. *That* was Grant's voice.

"You say that, but you can't promise it. I'm not safe anywhere, not with Joanne—did you know she can't hit a bull's eye with a dart? How is she supposed to hit a target with a gun if she can't do it with a dart?"

The woman must have been Hope—the owner of the sundress that cost more than all of Mari's clothes together. Mari leaned forward to see the two talking.

"Darts and guns aren't the same discipline." Grant rubbed his eyes as if he was very tired.

"Like you know about discipline," Hope said. She leaned way over the lip of the well, making Mari have to turn her head away so she didn't see up Hope's embarrassingly short skirt. "You can't even keep your own hotel room secure. Do you have any idea how easy it was for me to be Mrs. Grant Venturi surprising her husband while he's away on a business trip? I could have waited in your room and put a bullet between your eyes before you even got your door all the way open. How is that supposed to make me feel? Dominic would never have been so sloppy in his hotel room security."

Mari waited for Grant to answer, to explain something. She felt desperate to know what it all meant. *Mrs. Grant Venturi?* Was wanting to rip out the hair of a strange woman a bad thing? Because Mari wanted to do just that.

The little vixen who wore a size-four bikini had threatened to put a bullet in Grant's forehead and declared herself his wife in the same breath.

"You're safe as long as you do what I tell you to do. And I told you to stay put."

"I was bored, and Joanne didn't feel safe anymore. And when you come to visit us, you don't stay as long as you used to. If I didn't know better, I'd think you were seeing someone."

Mari craned her neck as far as she could to better see both of them.

Grant stiffened at Hope's words. "What's that supposed to mean? *If you didn't know better?*"

"You're not the sort of guy who goes in for meaningful relationships, are you? You're so married to your job, you don't have room for anything else. You can say what you want about Dominic, but he at least sent flowers when he was away. And if he had a bad night and was a little scary, a pretty blue Tiffany's box was usually on my pillow the next morning."

Grant seemed agitated by the girl's assessment. "Relationships are more than being bought off. You've seen the wishing well, Hope. Let's get you back to my room."

"And what will the hotel staff say about that? Two girls in a room in one day. They're going to wonder how I didn't catch you with your mistress."

"What?"

"You are such a scandal, Mr. Protective Custody."

Grant inhaled a sharp breath and held it before releasing it slowly, as if he was trying to keep his patience. "Hope, I don't know what you're talking about."

Hope laughed. "The woman in your shower. She was singing."

Grant's entire body went rock solid. "What woman was in my shower?"

Hope laughed again. "It's not like I went and checked her out!"

"Mari..."

The way he said her name in that soft whisper sent a ping through Mari's soul. He really did care for her. And he was a cop, not a criminal. Hope had said something about protective custody.

Mari trembled with relief. At least he wasn't going to jail anytime soon.

"Let's go back to my room," Grant said. "You've been out for too long as it is."

"It's a secret garden," she countered.

"Your point being?" he asked.

"Duh, Grant. It means it's a secret, just like me."

"The way you've been going the last forty-eight hours, you seem like the worst-kept secret in this hotel."

Hope laughed again. "No, the worst-kept secret is a secret garden in a hotel with arrows marking the way to it. Give me some money. I want to make a wish."

Grant grumbled something Mari didn't catch, but he fished a penny out of his pocket and handed the coin off to Hope's waiting hand. Hope made a big show of turning around, closing her eyes, and tossing the coin over her shoulder. As soon as Mari heard the splash, Grant was already leading the girl out.

"Don't you want to know what I wished for?" Hope asked.

"Not really," Grant said.

Mari felt gratitude to know what Grant was actually doing, well . . . sort of. Hope had been a lot of help in that area. But Hope had said something else that bothered Mari. She'd commented on Grant being distracted, about his relationship getting in his way of doing his job. Was Mari a distraction?

She emerged from the foliage, feeling almost worse than she had when she'd gone in. Grant obviously worked to protect people. Mari wasn't sure if he was CIA, FBI, or what and felt stupid for not knowing what government entity worked with such things. She now understood his need for secrecy and only wished she'd been more sympathetic. Real lives were at stake. But could she be with someone who had to keep secrets from her? He could have just explained that he worked a top-secret government job and that he couldn't tell her things.

And that was the real problem; he hadn't told her that single small detail that would have helped her be understanding about everything else. The guy was so buttoned up, Mari had to wonder if he ever opened himself for anyone.

The end of her work shift loomed closer and with it the chance to enter Grant's room and talk to him. She knew he would be there, because he was hiding some sort of fugitive in his room. As she approached door 913, Deanne's voice shattered her apprehension.

"Mari? Mari, I need to speak with you." Deanne had an unopened bottle of diet root beer in her hand. She must have just come from where she made the vender stock the obscure beverage choice.

Mari glanced at the brushed silver doorplate of 913.

Deanne gave Mari a look so cold, Mari shivered. "Don't worry about that. I will have it looked after."

Mari frowned, not sure what that meant.

But she followed Deanne to the elevators and down to the basement where Deanne's office was positioned near the laundry room. When Deanne closed the door and invited Mari to sit, Mari knew something was terribly wrong.

Fourteen

"She fired you?" Taryn's indignant voice on the phone was a calming balm to the panic Mari felt over the events inside Deanne's office. Mari stood at the corner bus stop with all her belongings loaded into a garbage sack like some sort of homeless woman. She had to wait another eleven minutes for the bus to come and needed something to keep her from crying in the street.

"Why?" Taryn demanded to know. "What reason could Deanne have to fire the only person who doesn't snitch lotion to take home?"

How did Mari explain that she'd been caught entering a guest's room late in the evening and not exiting again until the next morning? The basic reason sounded so much more sordid than it actually was. But Deanne didn't want to hear what really happened, and Mari couldn't explain if she'd wanted to. The rules had been broken. Maids didn't spend nights in guests' rooms. "What kind of establishment do you think we're running here?" Deanne had said. "This is a five-star hotel, not a brothel."

And she'd fired Mari without any hesitation or regret.

Mari almost explained everything to Taryn but stopped herself for the same reason she had stopped herself in Deanne's office. There was still a woman in room 913 who was supposed to be some sort of secret. Mari couldn't explain without compromising Grant's situation.

So she circumvented the question by asking, "What should I do now?"

Taryn was a planner. That one question sent Taryn off into directions Mari should have seen coming. "You use the money your Bad Decision sends you every month and focus on your schooling so you can get done faster. Then you pass the California bar and sue Deanne for wrongful termination."

But Mari didn't want to sue anyone. She *had* gone into a guest's room and spent the night. She'd broken a rule. Did it matter that her intentions were to help him? She saw the justice in her situation—even if she didn't like it.

"I'll call you later. My bus is coming soon."

Taryn clucked her tongue. "Oh, honey, you're taking the bus? Let me come get you."

"It's your day off. I'm fine. I don't mind. I gotta go, though. I'll call you later."

Mari disconnected the call, realizing that discussing her pathetic situation out in the street made her want to cry even more. Tourists ambled toward the boardwalk and the beach with folding chairs and piles of towels tucked under their arms. They smelled of coconut sunscreen. Seagulls shrieked in the distance. Just last night, Mari had felt lost on Tangerine Street. Today, she felt something else . . . broken?

No. That wasn't it. She felt a little more than simply lost. Grant had kissed her and said he loved her, and nothing of that eavesdropped conversation refuted his claim, but the conversation and the luggage she'd broken into had changed things for her.

It was Taryn's suggestion of Mari using the money her ex-husband sent to her that brought Mari to her heartbreaking realization.

She could not live a life with a ghost. She wanted to be in a relationship with someone who opened up to her and let her see the real him. That didn't mean she wanted details about his work; she understood those sorts of secrets. But it meant she wanted someone who was more than a generic suitcase. She wanted to see the ticket stubs on the counter that showed what kind of movies he liked. She wanted to see snack remnants.

What was she going to do?

She didn't know. But what she actually ended up doing was crying on the street while clutching a bag full of her belongings.

A tourist in a loud surfer shirt dropped a quarter in the empty Starbucks cup someone had left near the bus stop bench by Mari's feet. And she wondered if the tourist wasn't right. Even though Mari had an apartment to go home to, she certainly felt like a homeless person.

Fifteen

Mari didn't come to clean Grant's room. Someone else's voice called out "Housekeeping!" when the knock came at the door. Grant had been prepared to talk to Mari, to tell her his room needed to be checked off for cleaning but that no one could come in for a while. He wasn't prepared to deal with anyone else.

He gave Hope a look and nodded his head in the direction of the bathroom. Hope went as directed and shut herself up inside. Grant called out through the door, "Who is it?"

"Housekeeping," the woman called back.

Grant's blood raced in his veins. Had Dominic found them? "Where is my regular maid?"

"She doesn't work here anymore."

He didn't believe that for a second. He pulled out his weapon and clicked off the safety. "Why?"

"You think they'd tell me? It's an HR violation to discuss the employment status of a coworker. Would you like me to come back later to clean your room?"

"No. My room's clean. I won't need anything today."

"Okay," the voice said through the door. She sounded happy about the arrangement, elated enough to be genuine. Grant clicked on the safety again and slid his weapon back into its holster.

Mari didn't work at the hotel anymore? He glanced at the bathroom door and decided to leave Hope in there a moment while he made a phone call so he had some degree of privacy. He touched Mari's name on his screen.

It rang several times and went to voicemail. He ended the call and dialed again. Did Dominic know about her? Did he get to her somehow? Grant couldn't think of how anyone could have connected him to Hope before she showed up at his hotel room. He'd been careful. And his dating Mari in the evenings helped make him appear to be just a regular guy taking in the sights of Seashell Beach.

She didn't answer that time either.

He placed the call a third time.

"Hello?" Mari answered.

Grant had never felt so relieved to hear any voice in his life. "Mari, where are you?"

"Home."

She sounded . . . wrong. "Are you alone?"

She made a sound that seemed like she'd meant it to be a laugh. "There's a question."

"Mari, I'm serious. I need to know if you're alone."

"Yes. I am."

The words sounded so final, so miserable. "Why aren't you at work? You're scheduled today."

"I . . . don't work there anymore."

"What? Why?"

"Maids aren't supposed to be in guests' rooms."

"Then how are they supposed to clean them?" He knew

it was a lame attempt at a joke even before he finished it.

"Overnight. Overnight visits are not allowed."

He'd known she'd gone to his room, because Hope had said she was in the bathroom. But he figured she was in there cleaning—spraying down the shower or whatever. "You stayed in my room . . . all night?"

"I was worried about you and was only waiting for you to come back so I could make sure you were okay. You just never came back." She rushed to say the words, to absolve herself from the crime her employer had placed on her.

"Look," Grant said. "I know all this looks strange, but—well, I can't explain. But I'll fix things for your job as soon as I can. It just might take a few weeks."

"You don't have to fix anything. You didn't ask me to go to your room. I went on my own, and I pay the consequences for my own choices."

Grant scrubbed his fingers over his head as he tried to decipher what he heard in her voice. He'd never heard her sound so guarded before. "Look, Mari, I don't know where things were going with us, but I think it might have been a good place. I just can't allow it to go any further right now, because there's a lot going on that needs my attention."

"I know. I get it, and I agree you should focus on what's important."

"I'm not saying you're not—"

She cut him off. "I have things to focus on, too, so maybe let's just end things here and know that we had fun and we can still be friends."

Grant wasn't sure what was going on, but he felt like he'd just latched onto a railway that ended at a brick wall. "Mari, I'm not trying to hurt you. I just need time to sort things out." Once he used the word *hurt*, he knew he'd accurately described her guarded tone.

"Don't worry, Grant. I'm fine. You're fine too. We'll both be fine."

"I was just thinking we needed some time, but you make it sound like this is goodbye." He paced the room, needing to move, needing to feel like he was doing something.

"I think that might be for the best. Don't you? There's just too much about you I don't know. It's like you're all locked up—like my ex-husband."

Grant spun around as if to fend off that attack. "Whoa. Did you just compare me to your ex? The guy who you said used you up and threw you away? You think I'm that kind of person?"

"No! That's not what I meant. What I mean is that I don't know anything about you. You're closed up—like your suitcase in your closet and your toiletry kit in the vanity. I'm not the kind of person who will allow herself to be locked out of someone's life ever again. I need keys."

"Keys? Mari . . . I don't understand . . ."

"Keys, Grant. Keys that give access to the other person's life. I don't want to be locked out. I don't want to sit on the doorstep of your soul and wonder what's going on inside. I want to unlock that door and walk in and be a part of whatever *is* going on inside. If I can't do that, then there isn't a reason for us to be continuing this conversation. So, can you do that? Can you let me in?"

"Of course I can. I am."

"Really? So when were you ever going to tell me you've got a woman in your hotel room?"

He ground his teeth together hard and slumped down onto his bed. She knew there was a woman in his room. He wanted to tell her, to explain everything. Wanted to let her into his life the way she wanted to be in his life. But the case was too huge. He couldn't allow Mari to get caught in the crossfire of his responsibilities and mistakes. So instead of telling her the truth or giving her any kind of explanation, he said, "I need you to never mention what you've seen in my room again—not to anyone, not to the other maids or anyone at school. Not to your mom, not even to your supervisor. Can you promise me that?"

"You want a promise with no explanation?"

He didn't answer.

"You don't have to ask for a promise, you know. I wouldn't—didn't—tell anyone. Not even to save my job."

"Mari..."

"I still don't even know what you do for a living. Something-like-a-cop isn't much to go on. If you can't even tell me what you do for a living, then you don't really trust me with your keys after all. But hey, I've gotta go. Finals coming up, you know? Goodbye Grant."

She hung up before he could respond.

Hope leaned against the wall to the bathroom. "You really suck at communication, don't you?"

"For the sake of protection, this is probably better." He clutched his phone in his hand.

"Protection? For you or for her?"

Grant didn't answer, because he didn't have an answer.

"Does she even know you're a U.S. Marshal?"

He gave his head a slight shake.

Hope pushed off the wall and grinned. "I'm embarrassed for you. Even Dominic told me what he did for a living and trusted me to stick with him anyway."

Grant *almost* said, "And look where that got him, since you're testifying against him," but since Grant needed her to testify, he decided it was best not to tick her off. Besides, she had a point. He hadn't even told Mari what he did for a living.

And she'd been fired.

Because of him.

Grant felt terrible but couldn't even place a call to the hotel to explain the situation and get her job reinstated, not until after the trial. He would make it up to her then. He would make everything better then. That was the chant that ran through his head as Hope talked him into playing cards with her, as she flipped through channels without ever stopping on any of them, as she peeked out the window with a look of anticipation and fear on her face as she thought about the boyfriend who would kill her if he could.

When he opened his suitcase to pull out his lounge pants to sleep in, he immediately noticed the change in shirt order. Mari had been there and left her mark.

Mari had left her mark in him as well.

Sixteen

Mari applied for graduation and walked with her class. Her mom and dad were in the crowd waiting to see her get her degree—finally. Taryn sat with them. Even Christina and Raegan had shown up for the graduation ceremony.

The day after graduation, Mari moved away from Seashell Beach to attend law school.

She was sorry to move but glad to start a new chapter in her life. The Mariposa Hotel called her and offered her an apology for her termination and said they were proud of her for helping a government official in an investigation. That was the story Grant had given them: that she'd helped an investigation. They offered to give her old job back.

She didn't take it.

Not just because she was moving and it would be one miserable commute, but because Taryn had been right all along. Mari had the financial means to finish school without working, and it was time she put it to use. Swallowing her pride wasn't an easy thing to do and, come to find out, pride tasted pretty awful, but she had goals and needed to keep them in mind. Taryn had even been right about Mari needing more human relationships in her life. Mari had started spending more time with Taryn, more time with her parents, even more time with some of her classmates, though so many of them were younger.

What she didn't start doing was spending more time with men. Not really. Grant had started writing her. Just text messages at first, a quick *hello* and *how are you doing*. He included a triumphant declaration that the trial had been won and he appreciated her discretion.

She had wanted to ignore him but found herself not up to that task. The responses were curt at first, nothing more than a quick *I'm glad for you. Congratulations.* But he refused to leave things alone. He asked questions that required answers. The more he wrote, the more she felt obligated to respond, the more she found herself wanting to respond, the more she found herself smiling when his name appeared in her phone's screen.

Then he wrote an email. It began with:

Allow me to introduce myself. My name is Grant Venturi. I work as a U.S. Marshal and occasionally have to do things that require me to vanish from off the face of the earth. I recently met someone named Mari Niles, who makes me nervous because I want so much to impress her. My training has taught me how to be almost invisible. I pack light and leave no identifying traces (aside from the DNA on my comb and toothbrush). I do so in case I have to leave things behind.

As part of my training, I do not leave people behind, so I hope you don't mind me intruding on your life even though you consistently tell me you're busy and focusing on your education.

So you know, Hope was my charge, nothing more. I gather you already know that by your comments in our phone conversation several months ago when I behaved badly and you hung up on me, but I wanted to be totally clear on that point.

I miss you.

Grant

Mari hated how much her entire body curled around her laptop as if she was cocooning the email in a protective embrace. She'd even glanced around her empty apartment to make sure no one noticed how the email had affected her.

She had forced herself to wait a few hours before allowing herself to write back.

Grant did not wait a few hours. His response to her response had been instantaneous.

And that was the beginning of her new life with Grant for the several months while she packed, while she moved, while she unpacked and settled in her new place. While she started law school, while she had law questions she thought he could answer, while she wrote papers and analyzed previous trial cases that might give a precedent to her arguments.

He stayed with her every step of the way, revealing himself one word on her glowing screens at a time.

The ghost started to materialize.

When Mari mentioned that she had a few days off for fall break, everything changed again.

It changed with a simple question popping up in her email.

"*If you get to sleep in, what time do you like to get up by?*"

"*9:30,*" she emailed back.

"*That's a ridiculously early time for sleeping in.*"

She smiled at her computer screen, her toes curling a little inside her slippers. "*I'm a morning person,*" she typed.

"*I'm willing to overlook that flaw. Meet me at the Mariposa well on Thursday at 6 p.m.*" He must have calculated how long it would take her to drive to Seashell Beach after getting ready.

Mari's smile faded. What would meeting him face to face again mean to her? She wanted to focus on school like he needed to focus on work. Wasn't being digital pen pals enough?

"*Okay,*" she wrote back before her mind had given her fingers permission to make dates for her. Traitorous, traitorous fingers.

She had a date with a man she hadn't seen in nearly five months. What would it be like? Would it be the same?

She thought of the single kiss, the one filled with life and promise and the simple parting declaration: "Love you."

He'd never repeated the phrase, and she had never broached the subject. Some things were better left alone. But now she had a date. At a hotel where she'd been fired. With a guy she had, sort-of, dumped. Or had he dumped her? The lines on that one were hazy.

Either way. She was going back to The Mariposa Hotel.

Seventeen

"I can't do this," Mari said to her reflection in her rearview mirror. Grant hadn't said what to wear, so she'd put on a skirt—something that could be casual or dressy, depending on where the person wearing it was located. Skirts were so wonderfully universal that way. She thought of the expensive sundresses Hope had packed in her suitcase and frowned at herself.

Was Grant around those kinds of girls very often? Mari didn't know. She wasn't sure she even wanted to know. Did Grant still think of her in a way that would entice him to kiss her? Maybe. He *was* asking to meet her.

She'd imagined this meeting in her mind a million times. What would he want? What would he say? What would she say? She missed him all the way to her bones, but could she say that when she was in law school and he was some traveling FBI agent? Okay, she knew he was a U.S. Marshal, but it was still hard to get the other acronyms out of her head. She hoped she didn't slip up and actually say one of them. She hoped she didn't slip up at all.

"Go inside," she commanded herself. But her butt stayed in the driver's seat of her car. She was halfway tempted to text Taryn to come down to The Mariposa parking garage and see for herself that Mari finally had her own ride.

"Drive home," she commanded herself.

But she didn't do that either.

She'd been sitting in her car for a full eighteen minutes giving commands her body didn't listen to.

Finally, without any command at all, her fingers were tugging on the door latch and her feet swinging out of the car. Her legs straightened and held her upright. "This is a bad idea, Mari Niles."

But her feet started moving toward the parking garage elevators. They didn't stop until she'd wound her way through the halls to the secret garden. Mari put her hand over her eyes and said a quick prayer of gratitude that no one she knew had seen her. The familiar mix of plumerias and hibiscus instantly made her feel like she was home. She scanned the area.

Grant wasn't there.

Mari frowned. Had she taken too long to decide to go inside? She dropped her head in her hands and gave a little groan of frustration. And that was when she saw a small silver key in the middle of the path, just a foot inside the entrance to the garden.

She glanced around quickly, then bent to pick it up. In fine-point Sharpie, a word on the key read SHED. A thin, barely visible fishing wire was tied to it. She gave the string a little tug and followed to where it seemed weighted down. It wrapped around the thin trunk of a white plumeria, where a second key hung from one of the flowers. This key was gold. The word on it read CAR. The wire twisted off in another direction.

THE MARIPOSA HOTEL

"Grant?" Mari said, looking around, but she didn't see him anywhere. She followed the line to another silver key with a fat black top. The word along the key blade read MOTORCYCLE.

Grant had a motorcycle? Huh. She learned something new every day.

She wound around the garden, freeing the tree branches and flowers from the thin wire while collecting keys. There was one for a lockbox, one that had a picture of a thumbprint to indicate that Grant used a thumbprint to open his gun case. There was one for a filing cabinet, one for an enigmatic office, one for his childhood home, which included a little note not to tell his mom he was handing out keys to her house, a numbered passcode for his garage, and lastly a large tarnished silver key hanging from the well.

The word written on it was HEART.

That was where the trail ended.

She felt her lip quiver before she could do anything to stop it. "Grant?" she said.

"I hear this well has butterflies that take wishes to the Great Spirit," a voice said from behind her.

She didn't turn, not sure she trusted herself to face him just yet. No one had ever done anything like this for her before. No one had heard her words and then really listened and acted on them. But Grant had.

She'd told him she wanted keys, and he'd given them to her. All of them.

His voice was suddenly a warm whisper right at her ear. "Do you want to know what I wished for?"

She did turn then, pulled by his warmth and energy. He was so close behind her that as she turned she felt the smooth skin of his freshly shaved jawline. She didn't answer but instead kissed him. He responded instantly. His hand went to the back of her head, his fingers twining in her hair until she was lost in this moment with him, the flowers, and the stone butterflies.

He smiled against her lips before pulling away until only their noses touched. "Yes. That was exactly what I wished for."

"Me too." To prove it, she kissed him again, then smiled against his mouth.

"What?"

"I had no idea a ghost would be so much fun to kiss." A ghost who turned out to be exactly what she wished for.

Part Two

Butterfly Kisses

One

Ridley Lansing shifted his Jeep into fourth gear and appreciated that the classic Mustang convertible in front of him was going the speed limit. That was the perfect way to drive the Pacific Coast Highway. Too fast and it meant the gorgeous expanse of the Pacific flew by; too slow and it was totally inconsiderate of the long line of cars behind you on the narrow highway.

Even more than the Mustang's speed, he appreciated its mint condition. Candy apple red, of course. A '65 should never be any other color, although if someone offered Ridley a black one, he wouldn't say no. But almost as much as he liked the paint job, he liked the contrast of the dark gold hair streaming out in a wild ponytail behind the driver's head. He framed a shot in his mind, the title forming as clearly as the picture: "Classic Summer." He couldn't see much beyond the graceful line of her neck and the relaxed set of her lightly tanned shoulders, but he'd caught her profile once when she'd glanced toward the waves, and she seemed to be his age.

Part of him wished he was ten years younger, when his more reckless college self might have stepped on the accelerator and sped up to catch her eye, then maybe her phone number. He contented himself with enjoying the sight of a carefree woman exploring PCH the right way. No, almost the right way. She'd need a surfboard jutting out of her convertible for the picture to be perfect.

The sign for his exit came up, and he moved to the far right lane, amused when the driver ahead of him did too. Good. He'd get to enjoy the enhanced view for a few more minutes. When she took the same exit, he smiled. The gods of summer had his back today. At the bottom of the on ramp, he strained for a glimpse of her in her rearview mirror but only caught the graceful sweep of her eyebrows over her sunglasses. Aviators. Hot. He was a sucker for women in aviators.

Her hand darted toward her radio and cranked up the volume knob, and just like that, she was holding a private dance party in the driver's seat, her ponytail now bobbing wildly as she bounced along to the song. He turned down his own radio and heard the Rolling Stones pouring out of her car. Of course. Of course a hot woman in aviators and a classic Mustang would love the Stones.

He watched her, a slow grin overtaking him as she rocked out, flinging her arms into the air as Mick Jagger howled a high note. A passing car honked its horn and she jumped, settling her hands back on her steering wheel. She glanced into her rearview mirror, her eyes seeming to lock with his before she shrugged and went back to her car dancing, obviously deciding not to care what anyone else thought.

She was having fun, and he realized he was too. Too bad his perfect woman would disappear when the light changed.

She paused and held up her phone for a second, flicking a quick glance at the map on the screen. She had a California license plate, but the fact that she was using GPS meant she wasn't from Seashell Beach. Good, because he'd hate to think he'd been blind to a woman like this in his own backyard.

The light changed and they pulled out, a smooth tandem heading west, but when she flipped her signal for a left turn onto Tangerine, a hum of awareness ran along his nerve endings. It was the same sensation he got when a wave swelled way out, but he knew before it formed that it was going to give him his best photo of the day.

Sure enough, the next time her signal blinked, it was to turn into The Mariposa Hotel guest driveway.

Oh man. She was in *his* territory now, and he was going to take full advantage of it.

He passed her and swung into the far side of the self-park lot to get a good view of the waves and watched for several minutes. Still soft. Good. That meant the organizers wouldn't be running any heats he had to shoot. He had time to run into the hotel and grab a bite at the Sandpiper.

The spacious lobby was more full than he'd thought it could get, and he had to dodge a bellhop pushing a cart of designer luggage toward the elevator. Ridley checked his watch. Almost three, so that meant people were checking in. Brent wouldn't have time for a chat. He weaved his way to the other side of the lobby, dodging more guys and several women looking more impatient than two dozen people in resort clothes should look.

"Ridley!"

He turned at the sound of Brent's voice and backtracked to where his friend stood in his navy blazer with his name and general manager title pinned to its breast pocket.

"Rough day?" Ridley asked as Brent jerked his head at another bellhop while keeping a calm smile on his face.

"You could say that," Brent gritted through his teeth. "Our turnover time is not on point today, and we've got a big plastic surgery conference checking in. I've also got a concierge out with a flu or a daughter with a flu, or he flew somewhere. I don't know. I couldn't hear him over the panic in my head when he said he wasn't coming in today." He eyed the restless vacationers shifting from foot to foot while they stood in the check-in lines and cast bored glances around the hotel. "This group is going to want entertaining, and Marco's my best for handling them." He pinched the bridge of his nose and straightened his smile.

"I'll do it," Ridley said.

Brent shook his head. "You don't have to. I know you were heading into the Sandpiper for some grub. Go."

"It's not a big deal. It'll be like the good old days." Twelve years ago they'd been students at UC Santa Barbara, working nights at one of the city's most exclusive hotels. Brent worked at the registration desk as experience for his major in hotel management. Ridley had worked at the concierge desk because telling people where to find interesting stuff to do in the city was more his thing. He'd always had a knack for finding cool stuff.

Brent groaned as a bellhop sent half the luggage on the cart sliding off. Ridley snorted. "Go. I'll play concierge."

Brent nodded. "Uniform is in the employee locker room. Just check the racks with the clothes in dry cleaning bags. You know which one you need?"

"Hawaiian shirt, dark blue with white palm leaves?"

"Yeah. Thanks." Brent glanced over the line backing up at the registration desk. "Major thanks, actually. Your room this week is on me."

"Not necessary, dude." Ridley's place was only a few miles from the hotel.

A raised voice from the guest at the front of the check-in line sent both of Brent's eyebrows up. "Yeah, it is. You're covering the Pro/Am surf contest, right? Save yourself the hassle of finding beach parking every morning and stay here. Now get to work."

Ridley grinned and saluted while Brent headed toward the registration desk. Ridley went the opposite direction, down the north corridor to the door discreetly marked "Service." He hadn't been past it before, but he easily identified the employee changing room and rifled through the rack of dry-cleaned backup uniforms, pulling down a crisp Hawaiian shirt his size. It looked ridiculous with his worn-out cargo shorts, perfectly broken in to fit his lenses and filters. Brent was right. If Ridley was going to have to put on the starched khaki shorts that went with the aloha shirt for a whole evening, he definitely deserved to have his room comped for the week.

Ten minutes later he was behind the concierge desk, watching Brent coach his registration clerks in a low voice and casting enough apologetic glances to the waiting guests that Ridley could see the tension leaving their shoulders.

For the next hour, Ridley didn't have to do more than call in a reservation for a doctor and his wife at Ridley's favorite seafood restaurant and book another guest a spa package for the next morning. By then the bustle in the lobby had quieted to a thrum, a steady but manageable stream of check-ins of plastic surgeons coming in for the conference. It was hard to tell whether the middle-aged men had facelifted wives who'd availed themselves of their husband's skills or girlfriends who hadn't started fighting gravity yet.

He personally liked character in a face, imperfections

that told stories, tiny lines that suggested living. He winced as a woman passed his desk on the way to her room, her hand tucked into her husband's arm, her skin stretched drum-like over her cheekbones. She gave him LA flashbacks. He hated having to go down there to shoot, but it was almost unavoidable when two of the top-rated U.S. surfers came out of Venice and Malibu. Malibu was bad; half the women over fifty looked like their faces had been frozen at age thirty in a Madame Tussaud kind of way.

He people-watched for another hour, answering a few questions and booking another reservation, but it didn't take long for the rush to die down. He was about to text Brent, who had disappeared to handle something urgent elsewhere, that he was going to leave, when a flash of dark gold caught his eye, and he looked up to see the Mustang girl crossing the lobby.

Now he could see her fitted jeans and worn flip-flops as she strode to the registration desk with a confidence he liked. No coy strutting, just a brisk business-like walk. She leaned over to talk to the clerk and ran her fingers through her hair. It was messy, he noticed, with streaks the color of corn silk. He wondered if she owed those to the sun or a salon.

The sun, he decided the second she turned around and he could see her face fully. She didn't have a stitch of makeup on, and she was gorgeous. Big dark eyes in a heart-shaped face gave her a sexy girl-next-door vibe. Now that he could see her better, he'd put her age at a little younger than his, maybe thirty, tops.

When she headed toward the elevators, an impulse he couldn't explain made him open his mouth and call halfway across the lobby, "Welcome to The Mariposa."

It startled her; he could see it in her confused expression when she glanced his way. "Thank you," she said, her tone polite. She didn't stop, and he wanted her to. He couldn't peg her. Maybe she was here to meet someone. A boyfriend? Or friends for a girls' weekend. She wasn't with the convention and didn't look like she was a sidepiece for any of the doctors. She wasn't glossed, plucked, and augmented enough.

"I'm Ridley," he said when she kept going. She paused. "I'm the concierge on duty tonight. Can I help you with anything?"

He wished he could come up with a better leading question to figure out why she was staying at the hotel, but at least he'd gotten her to stop for a minute.

"Thanks, Ridley. I'm fine though." A smile peeked through, like she was enjoying a joke she didn't want to share with anyone. "What I need, I don't think you can give me. But I appreciate the offer."

"Try me," Ridley heard himself say.

"I'm in the market for a miracle," she said, her smile fading a tiny bit. "Got any of those lying around?"

"Fresh out," he said, hating that he couldn't tell her yes. He scooped up the binder of brochures Marco kept to help the guests. "I do have horseback riding, wine tasting, chocolate-making, and parasailing." He tapped an empty plastic sleeve and gave her a sad look. "Someone already took the miracle we had in stock."

She laughed, and it lit up her face. "Then I guess all I need right now is a nap. Which binder are those in?"

Ridley slumped and rested his chin in his hand. "I feel like a failure. Please think of something I can do for you so I don't get fired."

She shook her head. "All right. I could use some intelligent company this evening."

Ridley straightened. He was intelligent.

"If Tom Hiddleston turns up," she continued, "point him my direction. Otherwise, you're off the hook. If anyone asks, I'll tell them you tried really hard. You should definitely keep your job."

"Tom Hiddleston?"

"Yeah. He's an actor. Maybe you saw him in *Avengers*. He's Loki."

Ridley quirked an eyebrow at her. "I'd have known him as F. Scott Fitzgerald too."

That sent both of *her* eyebrows up. "*Midnight in Paris* reference? Nice. I love that movie. That was before Tom Hiddleston was even a thing."

"I didn't know he was a thing. I just thought he was a good actor."

"He's both. He's the thinking woman's Brad Pitt." She gave him a tired smile this time. "I need to get to my room now. Don't worry, so far the customer service has been fantastic. I'll tell any official-looking people so." She walked away, heading toward the elevator, and Ridley watched her go.

One lesson he'd learned about living in a resort town was that the relationships were never permanent, and the more drawn he was to someone, the worse it was when they left. He wasn't the kind of guy to get overly attached too soon, but every now and then he struck a different connection with a woman, a distinct spark that was rare. Those two or three had never turned into anything despite the best intentions on both sides.

It was much smarter to stay away from the girls who flitted through the hotel like the butterfly it was named for. They weren't designed to stay long, and he was fine with that. It was plenty fun to play if an especially pretty one drifted through his orbit in the Sandpiper, the restaurant on the hotel's beach side, and lighted next to him for a drink and some company. There wasn't much to say after the small talk, but that didn't bother him.

Still . . .

He walked over to the registration counter, stopping in front of the clerk who had checked the woman in. "Hey, Celeste," he said, reading her name tag. "What's that guest's name? The one you just helped?"

Celeste tapped a few keys. "Brooke Dresden. She came in two hours late from LA."

That surprised him. Maybe she was one of those granola yoga-y types that popped up in LA every now and then.

"Do you need her room number?"

"Yes. I need to send something up for her."

Celeste read it off to him, and he returned to his post, pulling out his cell phone to call Brent.

"Everything okay?" Brent asked. "You ready to be off the hook? It's probably slow enough that I can have the front desk keep an eye on the concierge stand."

"Everything's fine," Ridley said. "But I need to do something for one of the guests before I go, and I need to log on to the computer here to do it."

Brent gave him the staff log in and password and tried to send him home again. "Dude, you saved me. Go pack a bag and tell Celeste we're comping you a room on the top floor. It's yours all week. Don't say no."

Ridley hesitated but then thought about the surf report for the next three days. "I'll take it," he said. "There are a lot of early starts this week. I wouldn't mind being able to walk out of the back door and start shooting."

"Sweet. I'm glad. And now I'm going to go back to figuring out the concierge thing for the week. Turns out it was Marco's daughter, and she's got the flu. I guess he can't leave her at daycare. I can't blame him, but I do have to cover for him. Wish me luck."

"Luck," Ridley said. "Also, I make this aloha shirt look good, so if I've got time I'll jump in again."

"I'm comping your room service too," Brent said before hanging up on Ridley's laugh.

Ridley logged onto the computer and executed a quick Google search before finding what he needed and printing it off. What the lady wants, the lady gets. After all, The Mariposa was all about customer service. His was about to be five-star worthy.

Two

Brooke lifted her suitcase to the pristine white bed cover, but instead of opening it and digging out the dress she should be sliding into, she collapsed onto her back and let her eyes drift shut. She'd learned the art of the power nap at work, and she needed one now. It was stupid that a drive up the coast highway could wear her out more than a full day on the job, but it had. What should have taken three hours ended up five with all the traffic.

She'd teased the cute concierge downstairs, but honestly, the only thing that had made the drive bearable was the audiobook she'd been listening to most of the way. It was a James Bond novel, actually. And Brooke liked James Bond fine—beyond fine if it was Daniel Craig—but she'd mainly picked the book because it was Tom Hiddleston reading it to her. If only she really could conjure her favorite actor out of thin air to be her dinner date. They could go to a third-rate dive, and it would be a massive improvement over the company she'd be dealing with tonight, even with fancy hotel catering.

She dozed for thirty minutes before her annoyingly precise internal clock forced her to get up and dig out the dress she needed. Her hand hovered over her favorite cotton tank dress. If it was up to her, she'd slip into it and curl up by the pool with a burger and a book.

Remember the goal. She reached past it and fished out her cocktail dress, a designer sheath in a bold geometric print any fashion connoisseurs would recognize on sight. It was important to appear affluent to these people, to look as if she belonged in their circles. They would be quick to close ranks on any perceived outsiders.

That could be the theme of her entire twenties, really. "You Don't Belong to This Class."

She checked her reflection in the mirror, glad she'd matched the straps of her tank top to the straps of her dress while she'd driven with the top down. The hours up the coast had given her skin enough color to make the dress pop, and she had no visible tan lines. She'd been afraid she'd sprayed on the sunblock too early, but she'd struck the right balance. A spray tan would have been better, of course, but she never had time for that.

She reached up to tousle her hair. That was an unavoidable casualty of driving a convertible, but there was no way she was giving it up, so she sighed and dug out her curling iron instead. Fifteen minutes later she had her hair tamed, her makeup perfectly applied, and a pair of strappy nude stilettos to step into.

She squared her shoulders and faced her reflection, lifting her chin to practice the relaxed, amused smile she would need to fake for the next hour and a half. She could only begin the process of separating a whole terrace full of plastic surgeons from their money if they believed that smile. It didn't look quite right, so she took a deep breath, thought about the beach in San Juan del Sur, and her smile relaxed all on its own.

She was ready. These guys had no idea what was about to hit them.

"Brooke!"

Ridley's head shot up at the sound of the name in time to see her emerging from the elevator bank. The mussed hair and subtly sexy tank top and jeans had been replaced by long loose curls and a dress so fitted she had to have been sewn into it. Part of him was disappointed to watch her walk toward the man who had called her name and slide her arm into his, an inviting smile on her glossy coral lips, and part of him wanted to thank her for the view of her spectacular legs.

Mostly he was bummed. The dude had twenty years on her, easy. She was one of them, a girlfriend it looked like, based on her lack of a wedding ring, and he was disappointed in himself too. His radar was off. He should have recognized her type right away. He probably would have if he was in LA.

At least he could flirt with her now. There was no danger of a real connection. It would be fun to see how much he could interfere with whatever she had going on with the doctor who had whisked her away. Tomorrow, maybe. If he had the energy after shooting, he'd see how much havoc he could wreak between her and her date. But for right now, he'd issue his parting shot for the night and go home to pull a travel bag together and drive back so he could crawl into bed and get a good night's sleep in before his early alarm.

"Colby," he called, gesturing one of the bellboys over. "Can you take this up to room 529 and leave it for the guest?" He handed Colby the framed paper, and Colby looked down at it, confused. "Yes, this. Put it on the nightstand. Trust me. It's what the guest requested."

Colby shrugged. "I've dropped off stranger things." He took off for the elevators, and Ridley allowed himself a grin before placing the plastic "Please See the Front Desk for Help" sign on his counter and heading for the locker room. He changed and slid the uniform into an unclaimed locker in case he needed to fill in for Marco again, and then he headed out, his thoughts drifting from women who weren't at all what they seemed to his morning photo shoot and how to capture the surf exactly as it was.

Brooke uncurled her fingers from her sweating glass and flexed them a few times. She needed to relax, she reminded herself. Intensity would only be her enemy here, but when she spotted Gavin Dillard making his way toward her, she had a hard time squashing her intense dislike of him. He started with his standard opening, and she almost mouthed it with him, wondering if it would startle him to realize she could rehearse his words.

"Hey, Dr. Beautiful. Looking good."

"How are you, Dr. Dillard?"

She kept her smile relaxed even though she hated the nickname.

"Great. Be even better when I hit the links tomorrow."

"Are you going early or late?"

"Mid-morning. Sleep in, brunch, golf. Perfect vacation."

"Sounds like a good morning, but . . ."

Dr. Dillard groaned. "Don't even say it. I know that look in your eye. You want something from me."

"Wrong," she said, now offering her mischievous smile. "I want to do something for you."

"And what's that?" Dr. Dillard asked.

"I want to offer you the kind of quality of life that money can't buy."

He glanced around the hotel terrace, the tables overflowing with lush fruit and high-end cheeses, the flames of tiki lamps flickering in the sea breeze. He held up his whiskey glass in a mock salute. "I don't know. Money has bought me a pretty good quality of life so far."

Brooke wouldn't let that deter her. "Imagine then what I can offer you if it's something you can't even put a price tag on."

Vanessa Dillard joined them in time to hear that, and she frowned. "Are you trying to pull Paul away from his work again, Dr. Dresden?"

Vanessa was exactly like the kind of patient that drove Brooke craziest—the ones who came in just as their faces were reaching the point that character could make them interesting and then asking for a scalpel to take it all away. But these kinds of clients kept Brooke's practice going and ultimately funded her trips with Smiles from the Heart to the remote native villages to do the work that actually mattered, so Brooke smiled and schmoozed her. "It's more like I'm trying to offer him a different kind of work with a totally different reward."

Vanessa flashed her a tight smile. But really, with a face lift that fresh, any smile would have been tight. Her tone left no doubt that she was annoyed though. "Brooke, we've got three kids in private school, one about to graduate and attend an even more expensive college, and you know how California taxes are. We can't give up three weeks of paying clients for Gavin to go camping and play superhero."

Brooke's smile didn't falter. She knew Vanessa didn't mean to be as demeaning as she sounded. If anything, she was sure it was guilt pricking at Vanessa that caused her to be so sharp. The Dillards were privileged but had forgotten or maybe never realized it. If only Gavin would come down to Nicaragua this winter, it would forever change him. And that's probably exactly what Vanessa feared. It would add a whole new dimension to their already hectic lives. But if Brooke could just get Vanessa to see that it was the kind of dimension that would make them rich in . . . well, in their souls.

But highly competitive LA plastic surgeons didn't talk in terms of souls. Rumor was they didn't have them.

Brooke being the exception, she hoped. She had so much soul that it ached for the kids she couldn't get to. The thought put her back on track. "I know you have a tee time tomorrow, but that's when I'm presenting on new maxiofacial surgical techniques. You should come and check out for yourself the difference it makes. You'll want to make a difference too after seeing it." If he had a heart he would, anyway. Only a zombie could be immune to the smiling post-op faces she stacked in her PowerPoint.

Gavin opened his mouth to answer, but Vanessa beat him to the punch. "Since you're not a parent you may not understand this, but making sure Gavin gets in his round of golf matters. His work schedule is punishing. He needs to recalibrate and reset emotionally so he can be a fully present father to our kids when he gets back. I know what you're doing is important, but our value of trying to find the work/life balance is a good value too."

Brooke's smile slipped, and Vanessa detected it, her own frown reappearing. Great. That meant Brooke's "judgey face," as her sister liked to call it, had shone through her social mask. Vanessa's eyes narrowed. "Gavin can't be a walking billboard for his business the way you can," she said, her voice pleasant despite the irritation in her eyes. "He has to work much harder to build a client base than you do. He can't give up weeks at a time to go do charity work when he already has a family to provide for."

There were so many things wrong with Vanessa's words that Brooke didn't know where to start. She decided to take them in order. With the most even tone she could manage, she waded in. "I'm not a billboard for my business."

"Then who did your work? I hope you're giving him credit. Is it Dr. Markmarian?" Vanessa asked, tossing out the partner name that graced the glass doors of the fancy medical suite where Brooke worked.

Dr. Dillard interrupted before Brooke could answer. "She hasn't had any work done," he said, eyeing her, but he did it with the same analytical study she used on her own patients.

"You have something against it?" Vanessa asked with a lift of her reshaped chin.

"I can't win with you, can I?" Brooke asked, letting all of her irritation go. The Dillards were a lost cause, and she had no energy to waste on that. "If I'm getting work done, I have an unfair advantage because I'm a walking brochure, and if I don't, it's because I think I'm too good for it? Is that it, Vanessa?"

Vanessa only lifted one tan shoulder and let it drop again. Brooke had no problem retreating so she could regroup and wage her campaign in less combative territory. "I'm sorry, you guys. I definitely don't want to upset you, especially when you should be enjoying the resort and your free time. Ignore me. I'm going to get myself something to eat. Maybe that will civilize me."

Vanessa gave her a cool nod, and Dr. Dillard wouldn't meet her eyes, so with a murmured goodbye she turned toward the fruit buffet. She'd picked up a few pieces of grilled pineapple when she turned at a light touch on her elbow to find Gavin Dillard standing there.

"I'm sorry I can't do more right now, but with the kids, and my surgery schedule . . ." He trailed off and extended a check to her.

"I can always find people to write checks, Dr. Dillard. I need people who can go down there and do the work. I need your skills."

He shrugged. "I can't. I'm sorry."

He pushed the check toward her, and she took it, finally glancing at the amount. Five thousand dollars. She could put all of them to good use. But she could have put him to even better use. Still, she took the peace offering and smiled, a real one. "Thank you. I'll make sure every penny counts."

He nodded and headed back to his wife. Brooke scooped a few strawberries onto her plate and turned to survey the crowd, nibbling at the pineapple as she considered who she could go after next. She'd come to the conference determined to bag a surgeon, and she'd do it by hook or crook. But she really hoped the hook worked, because she didn't have the faintest idea of how to be a crook.

Two hours later, she dragged back to her room. She'd scared up a few more donations to Smiles from the Heart. But the thing she needed most, skilled surgeons, eluded her. She leaned her forehead against her hotel room door for a full minute, breathing in and out until the tension in her chest eased. When she straightened and walked in, ready to map out her game plan for recruiting surgeons tomorrow, she took one look at her bed and burst out laughing.

A framed picture of Tom Hiddleston's face in full Loki

getup scowled at her from her pillow. She snatched it up to read the note scrawled with Sharpie in the corner. "It's a pleasure to be of service to you. Let me know if there's anything else I can do."

The sheer cheekiness of the concierge in sending it up collapsed her into giggles. Oh man, she must be overtired. Her cheeks began to hurt. *Oh well. If I laugh my face off, I know how to fix it.* And that only made her laugh harder, all the way until the tears came and she wasn't sure which ones were from hilarity and which were from frustration.

Three

Friday morning Ridley glanced at the text that had just come in and called out to Brent. "Gotta go! Sorry, man!"

"No worries," Brent said. "I appreciate you doing it."

But Ridley was halfway across the lobby heading toward the beachfront exit, so he waved over his shoulder, not checking to see if Brent had seen the acknowledgment. Pierce Van Wagenen was about to surf a heat and the magazine wanted a whole photo essay on him, one showing the progression of his form through the stages of the competition. The man was lethal whether he was loose and easy like he tended to surf during the qualifying heats or laser focused during the elimination rounds. Either way, he dominated. No other pro had such inconsistent form while posting consistent wins.

"Ridley!" Brent called when he'd almost reached the sand. His friend jogged to catch up with him. "I know you're in a rush, but talk to me about this when you get a chance, okay? I don't know what it means." He handed Ridley a sheet of paper. "It came in off of our guest request app last night, but no one's sure what's up, so let me know if you do." He flipped Ridley a fake salute and hurried back toward the front desk.

Ridley glanced down at it and grinned as he hustled past the bleachers set up for the spectators.

Mariposa Guest Request from B. Dresden, Room 529:
Text: *I appreciate you sending Tom up. I do enjoy some Loki. But not every lady is looking for a man to reform. Sometimes she needs a Captain Nicholls. Your efforts are noted though.*

His grin faded at the "but . . ." It figured she'd be one of those high-maintenance women who needed more even when someone had gone the extra mile. Whatever. Not his problem. He reached the sand and almost had to muscle his way to a prime spot. Several of the other photographers did a double take when they saw him in the hotel's Hawaiian shirt. "Whoa, dude," said Laddie Burroughs, Ridley's biggest competition for freelance work and a complete tool. "You do not look like you."

"I'm shooting this incognito for kicks."

"You're not famous enough to need a disguise," Laddie said, confused.

"You're dumb but cute, Laddie."

"I don't even understand our conversation."

"Just smile and look pretty," Ridley said, clapping him on the shoulder before turning his lens on the waves again. Laddie didn't understand because there was nothing to understand. It was a nonsensical conversation, but Ridley liked to throw him for a loop sometimes, see if it gave him an edge in the shooting.

Ridley disappeared into the rhythm of the waves, watching the surfers cut across the surface, framing his shots. Pierce won his heat and made it look like he hadn't even tried, but he'd executed some epic cutbacks. The guy was a beast. Ridley stayed after Pierce was done, shooting a new kid coming up through the women's ranks, a girl out of San Clemente who had impressed him in the last two junior competitions. She was one to watch now that she'd hit the adult circuit. It wouldn't be too long before sponsors were knocking down her door, and he could hurry that along if he had some great shots to send in to his editor.

Eventually the waves turned mushy again, so he put his camera away and hiked back through the sand to The Mariposa. He really wanted to get out of the hotel uniform and into his own threads. He checked his watch. He might even have time to finally get his sandwich at the Sandpiper before he had to jump into his photo edits.

"Thanks for Tom."

The slightly husky voice snapped him out of planning his exciting to-do list. He glanced up to find Brooke smiling at him from her table for one at the sand's edge. A half-eaten salad sat in front of her, and she'd slid her sandals off and stretched her legs out in front of her. Her long, lovely, peach-turning-gold legs. She was a Ralph Lauren ad in her loose white linen sundress, wholesome and gorgeous, but he'd dated enough women to know that her effortless appearance had taken a lot of time and enough money to feed a Bangladeshi family for a year.

"What the customer wants, the customer gets. Or almost gets," he amended, remembering her close-but-no-cigar response through the app.

"I got a laugh. A big one. It was almost as good as Tom himself in that moment."

"Glad you enjoyed it," he said, crossing so he was at the edge of her table. "I make it a point to please. Care if I join you?"

The skin around her eyes contracted the tiniest bit, so quickly that he doubted most people would have noticed it, but there was no mistaking it: a touch of disgust.

"Are you allowed to do that?" she asked.

"Am I—" he almost repeated the question until he glanced down at his concierge duds and realized what she was asking. And that his uniform turned her off. She was obviously here hunting bigger prey, not a lowly lobby monkey. *Snob.* He smothered a grin. He was definitely going to mess with her now. He pulled out the seat opposite her and made himself comfortable. "I'm off duty for the day," he said. "My time is my own. For the rest of the night."

She flinched at his innuendo. "Time doesn't really belong to anyone, does it? It just *is*."

"Deep," he said and watched a light blush color her cheeks at his mocking tone. He didn't apologize. She'd been a jerk first.

"Blame the view." She waved toward the Pacific. "It makes me wax philosophical. How was work today?"

He smiled at her new tone. It was polite to the point of painfulness. *Keep your distance* underlined every word she spoke. "It was perfect. I couldn't love what I do more."

Her eyebrows drew together. "That's good." Now she sounded concerned. "You definitely went above and beyond what you needed to for me. And is that why you were on the beach with the camera? Were you taking pictures for a guest?"

He glanced down at his camera bag. "Something like that."

"I can relate to taking pride in your work. But do you ever feel... restless? Like you want something more?"

She meant professionally. And it bothered him that she would sit in judgment of his job, even though she wasn't judging his real job. But she didn't know that, so he stretched out even more in his chair, making sure his legs grazed hers before coming to a rest so close to them that he could feel her heat. She didn't move. He didn't know how to read that. Was it because she was open to flirting?

Her chin rose the tiniest bit. He grinned. Her stillness was because she wasn't going to back down from a challenge. "How's your stay at The Mariposa so far?"

"Not super productive," she said, her forehead wrinkling.

"How productive do you need to be when you're staying in a beach resort?"

She lifted her glass to him in acknowledgement and took a sip. "Fair point."

"Can I ask what you're trying to produce?"

"I told you."

That stumped him until he remembered. "Miracles?"

"Miracles."

He wondered what miracle she needed. She looked stressed now that he could study her, but not a life-or-death kind of stressed. Maybe it was financial stress?

He'd ask Brent to check whether or not she was paying for her own room. If she was handling the bill, what did that mean? That she was hoping to pick up a wealthy connection here to make it worth her while?

"What kind of miracle?" he asked, but the noise of chairs scraping at a nearby table cut him off halfway through.

Brooke frowned, glancing at the slim watch on her

wrist. "I've got class. Enjoy your lunch," she said as she dug in her purse to pay her bill.

"Class in the middle of a gorgeous afternoon? Stay. Enjoy it." He shifted and brushed against her leg again. It was an accident this time, but it sent a fiery ripple all the way up his body.

"Can't. See you around."

The only classes going on were the plastic surgery ones. He wanted her to be the carefree girl in the car, the one who did her own thing, not this calculating woman who stalked her prey by sitting in on their classes. "That's the definition of a lame vacation. Do you know one of the teachers or something?"

He became a bug in her salad beneath her cold stare.

"I *am* one of the teachers." She turned around and walked off before she could even see his jaw fall open.

Oh, this was bad. This was so very bad. He'd made every sexist assumption he could possibly make because he'd misinterpreted the facts in front of his face. He was a pig. He'd written off every female in the doctors' vicinity as their arm candy.

He knew better. He groaned and shoved his hands through his hair. If it wasn't for the fact that most of the conference guests were coming up from LA, his mind never would have run down that track. Stupid LA.

But it wasn't LA's fault. It was his stupid fault.

What an idiot. What a total, ridiculous waste of a progressive liberal arts education. His mother would be ashamed. His sisters would kill him.

He owed Dr. Brooke Dresden the hugest conceivable apology for not seeing *her*, not looking past the surface, for being too lazy to recognize his own biases.

He sucked.

So much.

And yeah, he'd made some sweeping generalizations about the male surgeons attending the conference too, but it was so much more insulting that it had never crossed his mind that she was one of them.

He was also a hypocrite, he realized. It wasn't cool that she was stuck up about his job, but he'd judged her so much more harshly with way less evidence. It didn't get stupider than that.

There was no way he could make up for it.

But any woman, most especially the one who he had just completely marginalized, deserved the best apology he could make.

He dropped his head to the table.

Oh, he *sucked*.

Four

Brooke wasn't a crier. It bothered her mom, who thought she was bottling her emotion in an unhealthy way. But the reality was that not being a crier was a huge asset and had been time and time again in her career. She'd seen fellow male residents break down in tears from exhaustion and stress before she had.

As her whopping audience of three rustled at the end of her presentation, shifting in chairs and eyeing their watches, she was glad for the no-crying thing. Because if she were a crier, this is exactly the kind of thing that would have set her off.

Two of the doctors left without a word. The third, a doctor she didn't recognize but who didn't look much older than her, nodded without meeting her eye before hurrying out.

She slid her iPad into her tote and headed back toward her hotel room. She knew her presentation on advances in cleft palate repairs wasn't going to be the biggest draw at the conference. That would be Inagen Corporation's launch of its new sclerotherapy procedure. And she'd known being scheduled at the same time as that demo was going to kill attendance in her class. But she'd figured anyone who showed up was already going to be sold on the idea of Smiles from the Heart, and all she'd have to do was give them specifics and start syncing calendars for the winter trip to Nicaragua.

She couldn't even convert the three doctors who'd wandered in to her cause. Maybe her neediness had shown through, and they'd worried about getting tangled up with someone who would be a drain on their professional resources. She wanted to chase them down and shake them, hollering, "It's not *my* neediness! It's the kids! Did you see the slides?"

Yeah. Because that would put those fears to rest.

Pressure in her head indicated a pending tension headache, which was the bonus she needed to make her day extra awesome. But only enlisting more surgeons would make it go away, and she'd blown her best chance.

The rest of the symposium schedule flashed through her head. There was another cocktail party tonight where she could try mingling again, but it would be more of the same. By now, word had probably spread that she was looking for doctors to do international pro bono work, and she'd spend the entire cocktail party as a pariah.

This was miserable. There had to be a better way.

Well, screw getting all dressed up and trying to fit in. These weren't her people. She wasn't going to torture herself by sucking in her stomach in a little black dress for two hours and pretending to be interested in her colleagues' golf scores or spa experiences.

She'd duck into two of the classes tomorrow that she'd promised Dr. Markmarian she would check into. Stuff like that was a cash cow for the practice, and it funded her Smiles from the Heart work. But she wasn't playing the schmooze game anymore. Once she cleared those classes, she was going to use the remaining two days to recuperate, reset, and regroup. She'd need to go back to Beverly Hills on Monday refreshed, ready to face clients and figure out how to convince them that if they could give up $6,000 for a tummy tuck, they could cough up another $1,000 for her charity.

She slipped into the elevator, glad that Ridley guy wasn't at the concierge desk. He'd gone from hot to not with his chauvinism. It's not like she wasn't used to the constant surprise when people found out what she did for a living. It wasn't even the assumption itself that bothered her, because she'd gotten so used to that kind of ignorance. It was the subtle condescension she'd detected from the guy. He was funny and flirtatious yesterday, and then today, patronizing.

That wasn't even an unusual experience for her either. Some men were idiots. But it was somehow worse coming from a guy who clearly was old enough to have set himself on a meaningful career path but who chose instead to work a cakewalk job as an employee of a luxury hotel catering to the whims of rich people. There was nothing wrong with wealth, and nothing wrong with working for the wealthy, but . . .

She sighed. Maybe she was guilty of her own prejudices, but she'd seen his type all over LA: pretty guys who chose jobs that put them in the path of the socialites drifting in and out of hotels, country clubs, and restaurants looking for handsome distractions. And these guys were ready to reap all the benefits of being the boy toy of a bored millionaire's wife.

Maybe it was different here, a few hours north. But even if it was, how did he, as someone who really hadn't made stellar choices in his life to end up as a concierge at the age of at least thirty, get to sit in judgment of her?

He had intelligent eyes. She was used to studying faces, and she could read a lot about a person in the way the lines of their faces fell. His were faint, only beginning, but they told her that he spent a lot of time thinking and even more time smiling. She hoped it wasn't his slightly sardonic smile or his blatantly flirtatious smile she'd seen. Those lines were best when they were carved out by real smiles.

He'd flashed her a couple of real smiles, like when his leg had touched hers and sent heat up from her calf all the way to her stomach. Had he smiled because he'd felt that too?

Whatever. She sighed and twisted her hair up with a hotel pen as she stepped out of the elevator. She was displacing her frustration over the day onto this Ridley guy, and he didn't deserve her emotional energy. She needed to be channeling all of that in figuring out how to staff the Chinandega clinic. She'd clear her head, get a good night of sleep, and attack the problem with a better attitude in the morning.

She hurried to her room, anxious to shed her work clothes for something comfortable, digging into her suitcase for a pair of running shorts and a sports bra. She'd barely slipped into them when a knock followed by "Housekeeping!" sounded at her door, and she padded over to let whoever it was know that she didn't need maid service today. But instead of pushing a cart, a woman her age wearing a name tag that read "Mari" stood at the door holding an iPad. "Dr. Dresden? This was sent up for you." She swiped something on the screen and handed it to her. "You're all set."

She took it, too confused to argue for a second, but when the maid turned to leave, Brooke called out for her to stop. "What am I supposed to do with the iPad when I'm done?"

"You can leave it here. We'll get it back to the right place. Have a good evening."

Brooke watched until she disappeared around the corner, then felt like a jerk for not tipping her. She grabbed a five from her purse and chased after her, calling to her again as she stepped into the elevator. "Wait, Mari? I forgot to tip you!"

Mari smiled. "That was taken care of too." And with a whisper, the doors shut, and she disappeared with the answers Brooke was barely formulating questions for.

She returned to her room and picked up the iPad, waking up the screen. It was a note.

> *Dear Brooke,*
>
> *You didn't look like you had a great day today. You looked beautiful, like you have from the second you walked through The Mariposa's doors, but you looked like you had troubles hanging around you that even the ocean breezes weren't blowing away. And then I added to them by making a completely sexist assumption. I'm sorry. I'd tell you myself, but you don't deserve even more of me and my idiocy. You need a man of refinement and culture. You need . . . Tom Hiddleston. Please enjoy.*
>
> *~Ridley, your concierge and Hiddleston dealer*

He'd pasted a link below the note.

He was overstepping. It was totally inappropriate for him to make such personal remarks, but it was hard to get too mad at someone who was beating himself up as much as she'd wanted to earlier, and even harder to get mad at a guy who was trying to buy her forgiveness with Tom Hiddleston pictures.

She clicked on the link and within seconds burst out laughing. It was Tom Hiddleston, all right, but a video, not a picture, and he was reading poetry. It was glorious, as Hiddleston tended to be. His smooth voice wrapped around the lovely words of W.H. Auden and curled up in her stomach, a soothing antidote to the stress roiling it. Laughter tickled her chest at the idea of maybe-not-so-awful Ridley scouring the Internet trying to find this for her and pushed away the last bits of bad feeling.

Maybe an undemanding job wasn't the best application of his intelligence. But maybe he had good reasons for choosing the job, and she needed to let go of the judginess she'd been holding onto toward him since he was obviously repenting of his.

She watched the entire clip, smiling bigger as it went on. Tom Hiddleston was perfect. Tom Hiddleston reading poetry was more perfect. And Ridley the Concierge was perfectly ridiculous for sending this to her. She picked up a piece of the hotel stationery and slid the pen from her hair.

>Dear Ridley,
>I watched the video. I'm worried about you. I think you've peaked. This is untoppable and I'm still here for two more days. We're even. You're forgiven. I probably have wrong ideas about you too.
>Thanks for the laugh,
>~Brooke

She secured her hair in a ponytail and snatched a beach towel out of the bathroom, slid into flip-flops, and swept up the iPad on the way down to the lobby, leaving it with the concierge on duty. "Can you make sure Ridley gets this note?"

"I'm sorry, who, ma'am?"

"Ridley? The guy working this desk last night? And this morning?"

The girl furrowed her forehead. "Yes ma'am. May I get your room number in case there's any follow up?"

"He'll know who it's from," Brooke said, walking away with a wave.

She made her way out to the beach, passing the tiki torches edging the back terrace, already lit even though the sky still showed more lavender than indigo. She turned away from the early arrivals to the conference mixer and headed for the water. She wanted to clear her mind so it would be wide open for solutions, not navigate a terrace of tan, well-dressed obstacles.

The beach had emptied in the last couple of hours, and that already made her breathe easier. She spread her towel out on a stretch of sand far from the hotel and opened with a sun salutation. She'd sworn to her father never to lose her Nebraska farm roots when she'd accepted her job in California. "You're going to start eating avocados on everything and doing yoga all the time," he'd complained when she told him where she was moving. She'd laughed and promised not to convert to "California-ism," as he'd called it, but she had to admit she loved having avocado *and* citrus trees growing in her condo complex's courtyard, free for the plucking, and she'd definitely come to love yoga.

She moved through several more poses, opening up her breathing and letting the weight of the day fall from her body before ending in lotus. She listened to the waves, her eyes closed, her mind finally quiet. She wasn't sure how long she was there, but she could sense that the light had faded pretty completely before she even opened her eyes. And when she did, she looked out over the water with clearer vision and a renewed sense of hope that she could leave this conference with everything she needed to help Smiles from the Heart.

Five

Ridley studied Brooke from a distance. He didn't want to come any closer and disturb her even though he knew she wouldn't hear him over the waves. He wasn't sure he wanted to approach her even when she opened her eyes. People, usually women, came down to the beach to meditate or do yoga all the time during the off peak hours. Sometimes it seemed like some of the women did it for show, wearing super skimpy outfits and holding themselves with an awareness that suggested they knew they were being watched, because that was the point.

But then there were the women like Brooke, who showed up looking comfortable, and who was deep down inside of wherever her meditation was taking her, her face serene.

It made him like her more, and it kept him rooted to the sand, thinking. He'd been hoping his Hiddleston apology would win her over a little, give them a chance to relax with each other and see if the electricity he felt near her was only on his side. But she already had more depth than he'd guessed, and that was a little dangerous.

Then again, she was a plastic surgeon. It was hard to imagine getting too caught up in someone whose whole career depended on the vanity of others.

He took a few steps closer to her. He'd liked their sparring. He could go for more of it. But he didn't know if she would, and the uncertainty intrigued him. He shook his head. He was being that guy, the one who liked a challenge. He didn't care. Brooke was clearly intelligent enough to figure that out and decide if she wanted to play.

He relaxed, slinging his camera across his body and settling back on his heels to take in the newly fallen evening sky. He'd think through his shots for the morning semi-final round and wait for Brooke to finish. It was another ten minutes before she stirred, and he straightened and walked over as soon as she unfolded her long, gorgeous legs to stretch them out in front of her.

"Hey," he called out, just loud enough to be heard over the surf. She whipped her head toward him. "Sorry. Didn't mean to surprise you."

She stared at him in confusion for a second then focused. "Hi. What are you doing out here?"

He dropped down beside her. "The question is what are *you* doing out here? It's getting chilly. Don't you want to be up on the terrace or maybe in the dance club with the rest of your compadres?"

She leaned back on her hands and shook her head, peering into the horizon instead of at him. Interesting. "This is more comfortable than in there," she said, nodding back at the hotel. "Those bars and cocktail parties are always the same. But this?" She inhaled as if she were trying to breathe in every molecule of the breeze that toyed with her hair. "This never gets old, is never the same. Watch." She closed her eyes for a few seconds and smiled out at the ocean again. "See? It's already different."

"I get it." It was why he'd shot surf contests for the last eight years without getting bored. It wasn't different from beach to beach and contest to contest; it was an entirely different ocean with each wave that rolled in. His pang of understanding twined around a touch of unease. She was definitely more his type than he'd thought.

He tested her to see. "So the fancy stuff over there isn't for you, huh?"

"No."

She didn't elaborate, but he pushed for more anyway.

"Do you not like the people or the setting?"

"Yes."

He laughed. "Give me something to work with here. Which do you dislike more?"

She finally glanced over at him but instead of answering him her eyebrows rose. "You must like both if you're here even when you're out of your uniform."

"I'm working."

"I wouldn't think their dress code would be so laid back," she said, shooting a glance at his board shorts and TK Froghouse shirt.

"Oh, I wasn't on concierge duty."

She glanced at his camera. "More photography for the guests? I guess it really is an all-inclusive hotel."

He laughed at her tone. "Don't say that like it's a bad thing. It's why you're getting your daily dose of Hiddleston."

She turned her first real grin on him, and he immediately plotted to win another one from her. "The video was genius, by the way. Thank you. You're relieved of your Hiddleston duties. I couldn't stand putting the pressure on you to top that."

That only made him laugh again. "Sometimes the universe really, really wants you to get things right. And the universe really wanted you to have that video, so it helped me out."

"Do the rooms have comment cards? Because I'm going to fill one out: 'Ridley is the best concierge ever in the history of hotels. His skills are unmatched.'"

"Awesome. The manager will love it."

She smiled at him before returning her gaze to the water.

"Is that it? A good concierge and beach proximity are all The Mariposa has going for it?"

She groaned. "I sound like a brat."

"You sound like the opposite, which means you don't sound at all like The Mariposa usual."

She glanced behind them at the hotel bathed in perfectly positioned landscape lights. "It's beautiful. I think I'm uncomfortable with the . . ."

He wondered what word she was struggling to find. "Furniture? Ambiance? Price?"

"Excess. I'm uncomfortable with the excess."

Right then and there, he fell a tiny bit in love with her. That was bad. And he didn't care. "This isn't how you roll at home?"

She laughed. "That's an understatement. I'm the queen of Ikea."

"The Mariposa is the pride of Seashell Beach. You know that, right? Before the city won the contract for it, we were a lot more like the other sleepy beach towns you passed to get here. Ramshackle, dilapidated."

"Charming?"

He tilted his head toward her. "You don't think The Mariposa is charming?"

"Impressive, maybe. But not charming. And it's really... new? Everything is so shiny and kind of antiseptic."

"Have you explored the grounds at all?"

"I haven't. Been in classes all day."

"Teaching all of them?" he teased her, getting another laugh. He was getting addicted to that sound.

"Now you're going too far the other way. I'm not *that* good. I've been checking out some new techniques."

"I think maybe you need a tour," he said. "I'm not really into defending major developers who come into towns like ours and make them comfortable for the rich and unlivable for everyone else. But The Mariposa has been good for Seashell Beach. They work hard to contract with locals, and they pay well."

"For as much as they charge people to stay here, they should."

"It's a decent wage. And a lot of the businesses around here have seen business boom. Morgan at the floral shop can barely keep up, and it's the best problem she ever had. The kitchen uses the local bakery for their breakfast pastries, which is an extra $200 a day for Delilah's shop. That makes a difference when you're an independent business. She had to hire another one of the high school kids to help her out for the summer season. Job creation, right there. And it's happening all over town." He leaned back on his hands, matching her relaxed pose. "You came up from LA, right?"

She nodded, but he caught a small twist to her mouth and wondered what it meant.

"I'm surprised that a plastic surgeon from the cosmetic surgery capital of the world would even count the cost of staying somewhere like this. Seems like you guys, and by guys I mean women too," he said, grinning at her, "would be doing well enough not to even think about the bill."

"I'm not most guys. I'm not even most women," she said, quirking an eyebrow at him. "This is very different from where I'm from, and different from where I like to spend my time."

"And where is that?"

"From? Nebraska."

"And where do you like to spend your time?"

She didn't answer at first. Finally she glanced at him. "I'm more of a mountain girl."

"A mountain girl from Nebraska?"

She only smiled.

"So you're saying it's hard for you to relax in those surroundings." He indicated the hotel behind him with a jerk of his head. "Because you don't like rich people or conspicuous wealth."

"Right. Like I said, I sound like a brat."

"No. But it makes you a contradiction."

"Is that a nice way of calling me a hypocrite because I'm staying here at all?" She turned to study him, her face expressing curiosity rather than defensiveness.

"No. A hypocrite would complain about the conspicuous consumption while lounging by the pool in expensive clothes and summoning cabana boys for drinks. You're sitting on a sandy towel in your comfy clothes. You're hypocrisy-free." He straightened, brushing the sand from his hands. "Here's the thing. All this would be a little much for me as a lifestyle too. But I'm seriously offended on behalf of The Mariposa that you find it lacking in charm. Can you really tell me this isn't the best conference you've ever been to? The event manager, Raegan, puts together some great stuff, I hear. She's starting to attract a lot of celebrity business. KC Wood is even doing a big charity thing next month."

"I see a lot of celebrities as it is in my work."

"I guess you would. So I'll try something else. I noticed on one of the event lists that my friend Abbie is teaching a class. She's writes this cool kids' book series, which might not seem like it has much to do with surgery. But she always finds a way to tie stuff into the conference, and people love her. A lot of conferences book here just so they can get her to present. You should drop in her session."

"I saw that one, but it's geared toward managing partners in a surgery practice, so it doesn't really apply to me."

"Fine. None of that impresses you. You're a tough case. This is my last resort: let me take you on the tour and show you the coolest thing at The Mariposa."

She laughed and glanced down on her clothes. "I promise I'm not high maintenance. I mean, look at me. It's more that I've just checked out on the day already. And that means not dressed for walking around The Mariposa."

"You're the guest so you're the boss. If you decide to roll into the lobby in your footie pajamas, as far as the staff is concerned, then that's the way it should be done."

"What about the other guests? I have a bunch of colleagues up there who are going to think I've lost it if they see me wandering around in my workout clothes looking like I don't have a clue about protocol."

He stood and extended a hand to pull her up. She accepted it. Hers was cool from the sand, but the friction of her palm sliding against his sent heat racing up his arm anyway. He froze for a split second, and when he pulled her to her feet, he was slow to let her go, meeting her eye and offering his everything-will-be-fine smile. "We'll avoid your plastic pals. And as far as what they think, do you care?"

She returned his smile with a slow one of her own

before tucking a stray hair behind her ear. "You've got thirty minutes to make your case."

He leaned down to scoop up her towel. "Anything to please," he said, shaking it out and folding it before tucking it under one arm and holding the other arm out to her. "Charmed yet?"

She threw her head back and laughed. Maybe she wasn't yet, but he was falling under a spell he didn't understand. "The Mariposa will get its chance," she said. "Tell me where to meet you. I need to put this towel away."

"You really don't have this luxury thing down yet. You've got to make yourself way less thoughtful and way more entitled. Watch." A waiter walked by as they skirted the far edge of the terrace. "Hey, Brady," Ridley said, squinting at the waiter's name tag. "This guest is done with this towel. Can you take care of it for her?"

"You don't have to d—" Brooke started to say, but the waiter took the beach towel with a smile and a cheerful, "Sure thing."

She narrowed her eyes at Ridley. "That wasn't his job."

"Rule number one at a luxury resort: everything is everyone's job the second a guest makes a request. I promise that's not even the most annoying thing he's even been asked to do today."

She tilted her head at him. "You think the guests here are annoying?"

"Yep."

"Then why work here?"

He stalled by crooking his head toward a path branching off of the main one leading to the hotel and guiding them toward it. He should admit to not being an actual Mariposa employee. But some stubborn part of him wanted to win her over on sheer personality, not because she might find his job glamorous. He had no problem with using someone's career to figure things out about them, but she already knew he loved photography. He'd too often been a notch for women, something to check off their list: globetrotting photographer, check. He was probably the next best thing to pirate or explorer, as far as fitting the "adventurous type" category went.

Brooke's expression had grown more intent as he took his time with an answer. He realized he was the one verging on hypocrisy here. He'd fully intended to draw her into fun and games during her stay, and suddenly here he was, not wanting to just be a guy she could tell her girlfriends about when she reported back after the weekend then forget.

"It's kind of a side gig with decent perks." *Like a free room.* "Watch your step," he said to distract her. "My grandmother used to always tell me the best things were bends, as in 'around the bend.' Because every bend in the road meant a surprise, and you never knew what you might find. A spectacular view? A dip? A hill? Anyway, prepare yourself, because around this next bend in the path is where the awesomeness happens."

"I'm excited. Is it a pony?" she asked, cracking him up.

"Yes. Because The Mariposa understands that not even its richest guests ever outgrow their childhood desire for a pony."

The path straightened out again, but a smaller one forked off to the left, away from the hotel, and about thirty yards down it, a soft glow from more outdoor lights diffused over the top of a hedge of hibiscus bushes.

"What's that?" Brooke asked. "A gazebo?" She sounded game but not overwhelmed by his surprise.

"No. Something way better," he said, sliding his hand down to hers to tug her toward it. It felt . . . right. "You're about to discover how The Mariposa got its name. Do you speak Spanish?"

"Menu Spanish, mainly. But I know 'mariposa' means 'butterfly.'"

"Have you wondered why they didn't name this place The Breakers or White Sands or something beachier?"

"Yeah, actually. Mariposa almost seems . . . quaint."

They stepped through the opening in the floral hedge, and she gasped. Ridley squeezed her hand. "Not a gazebo. A wishing well."

Brooke slid her hand from his and hurried over to it, making him regret bringing her somewhere that would make her let go of him.

Brooke leaned over the well and yelled down. "Andy, you Goonie!"

"*Goonies*? Nice." She kept zigging when he thought she would zag.

"I like that you like that," she said, glancing at him over her shoulder.

"So my Tom Hiddleston skills, my cutting-edge camera, my official Mariposa aloha shirt all do nothing to impress you, but liking *The Goonies* is what does it for you?"

"Yeah," she grinned. "But the poetry video? It even edged out knowing the Goonies."

"I'm feeling so much pressure now," he said, leaning against the well with his arms folded across his chest.

"Yeah, you look super stressed," she said, rolling her eyes. "You must have something good up your sleeve."

Ridley shrugged. "Depends on how you feel about nerdy wishing-well trivia."

She pressed her hand over her chest. "*Who told you? Who told you I love it?*"

"Smart aleck." He couldn't have quit grinning if he

tried. Good thing he didn't feel even the least bit like trying. "So yes, The Mariposa has only been around for a year. But that doesn't mean it doesn't have character. This well is older than the city of Seashell Beach."

"Really?" She ran her finger across the mosaic-encrusted beams edging the canopy. "I thought maybe this was a faked patina to give it some credibility."

"Nah. This thing is stone-cold legit," he said, tapping the stones forming the well itself.

"Boo," she said. "You owe me the well trivia for making me listen to your bad jokes."

"Let's start with this: it's three hundred years old. The landscape architect hunted it down in this tiny Mexican village and had it brought here."

"Oh. That's . . . that doesn't seem right." She stepped back from the well and rubbed her palms on her shorts like she was trying to wipe away some guilt. "Just because a corporation can buy something doesn't mean it should."

"You can enjoy it guilt-free," he said. "The village was a ghost town, and the state government had no interest in keeping it. The Mariposa's owner made a hefty donation to the state of Yucatan's historical preservation society along with a promise to let them buy it back if they ever decided they wanted it. Unless that happens, it's here, with all of its stones and mythology intact."

"It *is* pretty perfect with this butterfly design." She stooped to trace one of the monarch butterflies in the tile work near the base of the well. She straightened again, leaning over to peer down into it, as if she could make out anything in the inky blackness of its shaft. "Did you say mythology? Like the usual toss in a coin and make a wish?"

It fascinated him how quickly she could transition from relaxation to stress over the well's origins back to relaxation again. He cleared his throat. "The owner of The Mariposa is Native American. Or half, anyway. His tribe has a tradition that butterflies carry wishes up to the Great Spirit who grants them, which is a cool-enough story. But on top of that, the legend in this little village the well came from is that if you dropped a coin into the well, you would get your heart's desire. So you can tell it your wish, but it gives you what your heart really wants."

"If I promise I'm not a gold digger, will you loan me a quarter?"

He suppressed a wince at the gold digger reference, regretting his earlier assumptions again. He dug into his pocket and produced a quarter, presenting it to her with an obnoxious flourish. "It's a gift, not a loan."

"Moneybags."

Was that a tiny shiver he saw when her fingertips brushed his hand?

She closed the coin in her fist and grinned. "Thanks. Now I'm going to throw my precious in the well."

"What if it comes flying back up, Goonies-style?"

"Then it will officially be the coolest thing that's ever happened."

"Oh man, I got your hopes up. You're not going to see that coin again. Sorry. How can I make it up to you?"

"Give me another quarter to wish with?"

He fished two more from his pocket. "I'm wishing too. I'll tell you mine if you tell me yours."

She plucked a quarter from his hand. "I know what yours is."

His eyebrows flew up. "Prove it."

She ignored him and closed her eyes for a moment, her expression intent before she tossed her first coin in and listened for the splash.

"That was a serious wish," he said.

"Miracles usually are. And now wish number two." She slipped his wishing quarter from his fingers. "I'll toss mine in with yours to make sure it comes true," she said, dropping them into the well.

"You're that sure you know what I want?"

She glanced around the garden enclosure and smiled. "A tropical garden with the ocean in the background, a rising moon, a wishing well, a guy and a girl? I think we might have wished for the same thing." She reached out and tugged on his shirt with the barest pull, but it was enough to draw him to her. "Can I get away with saying this is how magic happens?"

"Only if I can make fun of you for it later."

"Done," she said, and he smiled as she slid her hand behind his head to draw him down.

But he was done too, done waiting, and he dipped down and kissed her. She smiled against his mouth and he lifted his head slightly to smile back. "You have not one time in two days been anything I expect."

"That makes two of us, because I haven't done a single thing in the last hour that I've expected. So we're even, yeah? And I'm going to keep the streak alive."

She leaned into him for another kiss, her fingers now drifting up from his neck to brush through his hair, tickling him, but that's not what sent a shiver racing down his back.

"Cold?" she asked, leaning back.

"Opposite," he said, kissing her again, deepening the kiss until a small moan escaped her.

"Hot," she agreed, dropping her head against his chest.

He held her there, amazed that it was enough for him to simply feel her there, no thought about what came next or how the night might end. She withdrew her arms from his neck, and he mumbled a protest, but she only moved them to his waist, sliding them around him and resting her cheek against his chest. The wind kicked up a strand of her hair, and he brushed it back behind her ear. "Are you checking me out, doctor? Listening to my heartbeat?"

"I'm just *being*. I don't do that a lot when I'm here."

"At the hotel?"

"I mean LA, I guess."

"You're three hours away from LA. You can leave it behind you. I'll let you just *be*."

She nestled into his chest even further. He smiled out at the ocean, moonlight painting the calm water with tiny brush strokes of silver. "Brooke?"

"Mmm?"

"Sorry. I lied. I can't let you just be," he said, tilting her chin up and kissing her. She sighed against his lips and returned the kiss, long and slow. He sat on the edge of the wishing well and drew her to stand between his legs. She rested her hands against his chest and smiled at him, their faces level now.

"I believe in the wishing well," she whispered.

He stole another kiss. "Repeat after me: The Mariposa has charm."

She reached up to ruffle his hair. "It has charm, all right." But instead of dropping her hand, she kept brushing her fingers through his hair. "Soft."

He turned his head to trace her palm with his lips. "Soft," he agreed.

She met his eyes, still smiling, but after a couple of seconds her smile wavered, and she blinked. He knew before she even stepped back that the spell was broken. "You're thinking again."

She shrugged.

"About what?"

"Tomorrow. And about the day after that. I go home Monday. Back to reality."

"Reality? I thought you said you live in LA."

"Nice one," she said, with a fleeting grin. Her body hinted at a turn toward the garden exit.

"That's it?" he asked. "You're going to toy with the handsome concierge by the wishing well and walk away without looking back?"

A sound of regret puffed out of her on a tiny sigh. "Let's agree that no one got played here and that, yes, it's time for me to go back."

He caught her hand and drew her in again. "Tomorrow is the last day of the conference, right? But you don't leave until Monday. So what are you planning to do all day Sunday?"

"I don't know. I'm staying because I promised my mother I would take a day to spoil myself. I don't really know how to do that, so I'm open to suggestions."

"Oh, we're getting into my specialty now, Dr. Brooke. Will you give me your number and let me be in charge of your Sunday? I promise not to even make myself part of it if you don't want to, but every time I've seen you until I found you meditating, you've done a version of this." He furrowed his brow and frowned slightly. "No one should look that stressed unless the world is caving in on them. Is it caving in on you?"

She shook her head and dropped her gaze to their hands. He still held hers, feathering light strokes against her palm. "I'm glad," he said. "Listen to your mother. Take one day to appreciate all of this." He swept his free hand toward the hotel. "And if you still can't get behind the idea of the luxury, at least spend the day appreciating that." This time his hand encompassed the ocean.

She nodded, and he liked the measured movements of her head, like each tilt and drop of her chin was a promise, one she was making seriously. "All right. I'll listen to my mother. Give me your phone." He unlocked it and slipped it into her hand, waiting for her to program her number in. "Ridley?"

"Yeah?"

"I want you to be part of my Sunday."

"You know how to say all the right things."

She laughed and took a step back, tugging on his hand to pull him to his feet. "Race you to the hotel. Scared?"

"Not even a little," he said and took off running.

"Cheater!" she called, but he could hear her behind him already, and he wondered if his sandals versus her bare feet would mean she could catch him. She was gaining on him, and as she pulled even with him, she stuck out a foot and tripped him, sending him sprawling onto the manicured lawn. She stopped beyond his reach. "Surgeons are cutthroat, didn't you know that? We'll do anything to even the score."

He pushed himself up and grinned. "I deserved it."

"Are you all right?"

He held out his arms and did a quick turn. "No injuries, Doc."

She cocked her head and narrowed her eyes. "You totally deserved that. But just so we're clear, I would have beaten you without cheating. I went to college on a track scholarship."

"Um, that's sexy."

She sketched a mocking curtsy, gave him a small wave and ambled back toward the hotel, all relaxed lines and soft edges. He watched her progress up the steps and shook his head, still smiling. What had he gotten himself into?

Six

Brooke fell onto her bed far too wired even to think about sleep. It was the kind of wired where everything in her body was electric, from the feel of her own eyelashes against her eyelids each time she blinked to the way the thoughts zipped through her head, bright and neon and perfect.

Not thoughts. Feelings. A carnival of them. When had she last felt that?

She hadn't played that way since last summer, when she'd gone home to Nebraska for the Fourth of July weekend and spent it on Lake McConaughy with her high school friends, laughing like she'd never left. It was an effervescence that only happened with summer, but somehow Ridley had made that happen again. Ridley was summer personified—messy dark blond hair, warm skin, lazy smiles.

She climbed off the bed and headed for the mirror, fingers still on her mouth, wondering how long before the feeling of his lips would fade, and if the giddiness would fade with it. She grimaced then laughed at the reflected Brooke laughing back at her, a tousled-hair mess of a woman who had most definitely been kissed. Maybe she should hire Ridley to hang around her office and kiss all the women who came in wanting fillers. She was sporting the look they all paid her to give them.

Except she'd rather keep Ridley's kisses to herself. Which was stupid. And a pointless way to feel. A few mornings from now she'd be driving away from the hotel and not looking back.

Wait. Wasn't that the perfect reason to kiss him? To spend a few sun-soaked days being carefree? Getting her "head right," as her mom would put it? It was the whole "filling her bucket" thing, replenishing her emotional energy so she had more to give the little ones who needed her in Nicaragua. Being down there, doing the surgeries, always rejuvenated her in a way no amount of meditation and yoga could. It was the lead-up to that, the scrounging money and supplies, recruiting doctors, organizing details, that wore her down. She'd need more emotional fuel than what she had in her reserves right now.

Dr. Markmarian wasn't expecting her back in the office until Wednesday. She'd planned to spend Tuesday after she got back from Seashell Beach working from home on Smiles from the Heart stuff, which meant she had a space in her schedule. So yeah, spending all of Monday here, soaking up a couple more days of Seashell Beach and Ridley, instead of driving home, were exactly what the doctor would order for herself.

"Dr. Dresden? Dr. Dresden! Brooke!"

It was hearing her first name that finally broke through her mental fog. "Dr. Benson?" she asked, hoping she'd come up with the right name for the guy hurrying across the hotel lobby to reach her. He'd been in her class the day before and refused to make eye contact with her directly, but she'd caught him staring at her out of the corner of her eye several times. What did he want? Was he going to try to make a move now? Boo.

"Yeah, Leland Benson," he said, reaching her. "I took your surgery technique class."

"I saw you there. What can I do for you?"

He scrubbed his hand through his hair, and it didn't move. Super gel. Nice. Up close she could see the glint of a wedding ring on his hand and guessed his age to be mid-forties, but with a little work around the eyes and probably a jaw reshaping.

"I've been thinking about what you said. I have a practice down in Orange County. It's a nice place, nice people, but my wife and I have been talking about how we miss the diversity from my surgical residency in New York. The other day, my youngest, who's eleven, said . . . Never mind." He slid his hands into his pockets. "Suffice it to say we've recently come to the conclusion that our kids need more exposure to real life than what they're getting in our gated community."

Brooke gave him a nod that was an invitation and a plea. *Tell me more. Please let it be the words I want to hear.*

"I was trying to figure out how to help with your Nicaraguan project, but I kept getting hung up on the whole idea that there's no way to include my family, and we really want to create some family experiences around humanitourism. Have you heard that expression? Where you go on vacations and do good for others? My kids' friends do these mission trips, I guess they call them, but we're not really religious."

"I get what you're saying," Brooke said, beginning to smile.

"Yes, well." He cleared his throat. "I called my wife and told her about it and how I wished that there was something we could all do but where I could still use my surgical skills. She looked into Chinandega village, and she called me back this morning." A smile, half rueful, half proud, spread across his face. "Tracy is a force of nature. She's spent the last day and a half doing research, and she's figured out how she and our kids can go work at a nearby orphanage for the week while I work at the clinic. She's excited. Which will probably be overwhelming to the orphanage, but I'm excited now too. And our kids will be once they get down there. But I'm wondering if you still have room for another surgeon?"

Brooke's mouth fell open.

"So that's a yes?" Leland Benson asked, grinning.

She grabbed him and hugged him. "Give that to your wife for me. Yes! We need you! And her! And all other Bensons!"

"Brooke?"

She whirled to find Ridley standing a few feet away, once again not in uniform. "Hey." She turned and hugged her newest recruit. "I'll find you later and get your information. This is going to be awesome!"

Dr. Benson strolled away, still grinning.

She walked toward Ridley, not caring that her smile was huge and he might think it was for him. Maybe it was. It was for sexy Ridley coming to meet her with his wind-tousled hair, for Dr. Benson and his force-of-nature wife, for The Mariposa, the conference, the world.

"Do you have plans already?" Ridley asked, his voice even. Too even. Like he was working awfully hard to keep it so nonchalant.

"Not really."

"It looked like you and . . ." He jerked his head after the retreating Dr. Benson.

Brooke's insides felt like they were smiling too, stretching and expanding in happy ways. "*That* was my miracle, not a date. The well worked. The Mariposa is one-hundred-percent charming!" She slid an arm through his and peered up at him. "How cute that you're already jealous. Or maybe I should be disturbed? Should I be disturbed?"

Ridley pulled her against his side and laughed. "You should probably be thrown over my shoulder and carried to the pool so I can drop you in for that."

"You wouldn't dare."

"If I was sixteen, sure. But as a grown man, I'll just use my words. I like you. I have no claim on you. And I'm not jealous. But I will definitely do a better job of entertaining you than Dr. Dork."

She burst out laughing. "He's happily married. Not that it's your business."

"It isn't," he admitted. "But I like hearing it anyway. So what's the miracle?"

She turned so she could slide her arms around his waist. "The miracle is that I finally got a commitment I really needed for work, and that means that for the first time in months, I don't have to think about that project for a little while." It always felt like she was bragging about herself as the Super Humanitarian to say more than that in casual conversation, so she changed the subject. "What are you doing here? Are you coming to take over my Saturday too?"

"Maybe. Are you busy?"

"Possibly not, but first I'm going to need another comment card. 'Plus side: Concierge has excellent interpersonal skills. Negative side: He forgets stuff.'"

"What stuff?"

"My day has been annoyingly Hiddleston-free so far."

He winced. "I had *one* job, and I messed it up."

"Yeah. If you don't want me to report you to corporate, you're going to have to make it up to me."

"Absolutely. Whatever you want. What can I do for you? Send a towel-warming rack to your room? Fetch all your shoes for a complimentary polish? Come and read you the newspaper every morning?"

Brooke jerked her head back. "Please say you made that last one up because you have an overactive imagination."

"No, ma'am," Ridley said, leading her toward the back terrace. "I once had a guest with macular degeneration who came and stayed for a month. And he liked to get the news from the papers because he said TV news wasn't trustworthy. So I sat and read him the news section every morning."

Brooke had a niggling suspicion that the guest hadn't asked for Ridley to do that so much as Ridley had volunteered. "You're an interesting guy," she said. She wondered how long he'd been at this "side gig" and how long he planned to stay at it. But really, when it came right down to it, she catered to a wealthy clientele as the means to an end. Maybe that's what Ridley was doing too: using his upscale hotel job to fund a different dream, like photography. "You still haven't convinced me not to report you to corporate." She let a teasing smile play on her lips, and he flicked them an appreciative glance.

"Name your price."

She shook her head. "Not how this works. You failed in your Hiddleston obligations. You have to surpass my expectations, and I don't know what I expect. Good luck figuring it out."

He slid his hand down to tangle their fingers together

"Not really."

"It looked like you and . . ." He jerked his head after the retreating Dr. Benson.

Brooke's insides felt like they were smiling too, stretching and expanding in happy ways. "*That* was my miracle, not a date. The well worked. The Mariposa is one-hundred-percent charming!" She slid an arm through his and peered up at him. "How cute that you're already jealous. Or maybe I should be disturbed? Should I be disturbed?"

Ridley pulled her against his side and laughed. "You should probably be thrown over my shoulder and carried to the pool so I can drop you in for that."

"You wouldn't dare."

"If I was sixteen, sure. But as a grown man, I'll just use my words. I like you. I have no claim on you. And I'm not jealous. But I will definitely do a better job of entertaining you than Dr. Dork."

She burst out laughing. "He's happily married. Not that it's your business."

"It isn't," he admitted. "But I like hearing it anyway. So what's the miracle?"

She turned so she could slide her arms around his waist. "The miracle is that I finally got a commitment I really needed for work, and that means that for the first time in months, I don't have to think about that project for a little while." It always felt like she was bragging about herself as the Super Humanitarian to say more than that in casual conversation, so she changed the subject. "What are you doing here? Are you coming to take over my Saturday too?"

"Maybe. Are you busy?"

"Possibly not, but first I'm going to need another comment card. 'Plus side: Concierge has excellent interpersonal skills. Negative side: He forgets stuff.'"

"What stuff?"

"My day has been annoyingly Hiddleston-free so far."

He winced. "I had *one* job, and I messed it up."

"Yeah. If you don't want me to report you to corporate, you're going to have to make it up to me."

"Absolutely. Whatever you want. What can I do for you? Send a towel-warming rack to your room? Fetch all your shoes for a complimentary polish? Come and read you the newspaper every morning?"

Brooke jerked her head back. "Please say you made that last one up because you have an overactive imagination."

"No, ma'am," Ridley said, leading her toward the back terrace. "I once had a guest with macular degeneration who came and stayed for a month. And he liked to get the news from the papers because he said TV news wasn't trustworthy. So I sat and read him the news section every morning."

Brooke had a niggling suspicion that the guest hadn't asked for Ridley to do that so much as Ridley had volunteered. "You're an interesting guy," she said. She wondered how long he'd been at this "side gig" and how long he planned to stay at it. But really, when it came right down to it, she catered to a wealthy clientele as the means to an end. Maybe that's what Ridley was doing too: using his upscale hotel job to fund a different dream, like photography. "You still haven't convinced me not to report you to corporate." She let a teasing smile play on her lips, and he flicked them an appreciative glance.

"Name your price."

She shook her head. "Not how this works. You failed in your Hiddleston obligations. You have to surpass my expectations, and I don't know what I expect. Good luck figuring it out."

He slid his hand down to tangle their fingers together

and lead her toward the restaurant entrance instead of the terrace. "I'm going to need fuel for that, so we're going to eat the best ceviche you've ever had, and I'll have it solved by the time we're done."

The hostess smiled as they approached. "Outside for two?"

"Definitely," Ridley said.

They followed her to a table at the furthest edge of the restaurant's patio, giving them the closest view of the ocean, which was at high tide. "Ceviche," Ridley said to the waiter, who nodded and left. Ridley pulled out his phone. "I promise I'm not being rude," he said, tapping and scrolling. "This looks like I'm ignoring you, but in reality, this is me being all about you."

"I'll take your word for it," Brooke said. And she did. Despite his eyes being on the screen, a heightened awareness prickled between them. She could still pick up the scent of his laundry detergent over the ocean breeze, and when she crossed her legs and sent the fabric of her dress floating against his leg for a whisper of a second, a muscle twitched in his cheek.

"How adventurous are you?" he asked, still not glancing up.

"Ceviche isn't adventurous for me."

"No kidding? Raw seafood stew is no big deal for a landlocked Nebraska native?"

"Nope."

"Good. But I'm not talking food. How about life?"

She thought of the simple buildings she'd slept in skirting the wild Nicaraguan forests, and the rough-and-tumble Jeep rides up mountainsides not meant for wheels that had miraculously delivered her to remote villages to follow up with patients. "Very adventurous."

"Then I know how to make up the Hiddleston thing to you."

"Do I get a hint?" she asked. A delicious restlessness shivered down her spine at the promise of mischief in his eyes.

"Sure. After we're done here, can you be dressed in shoes that are okay for slippery rocks?"

"Is it weird that proposing slippery rocks is even sexier to me than someone suggesting I slip into something more comfortable?"

Ridley laughed. "That goes onto my list of reasons you might be awesome."

She leaned forward, her expression serious, and laid a hand on his arm. "Not might. Am."

He leaned forward too, and stole a kiss that made her head swim. "No argument."

The ceviche arrived. It was fresh with notes of aji peppers, and she savored it as Ridley asked her more about her previous day in classes and she gave him a snarky version of the ins and outs of nose jobs.

"I have to admit that you're not at all how I thought a plastic surgeon would be," he said.

"Female?" And even though she'd only been teasing him, she regretted the question when he looked embarrassed.

"I'm really sorry about that."

"I'm sorry. I shouldn't have teased you. I know you meant your apology."

"I meant that I expected a plastic surgeon would be more . . . plastic. Um, not physically or whatever. More fake inside. Or maybe totally real and upfront but with zero depth."

She nodded. "A lot of them are. Some of us enter this field purely for the money. Some of us do it because the hours are much better than a regular surgeon's. And some of us do it because the stakes don't seem as high."

"Which one is your reason?"

She shook her head. "None of them."

"Then what is?"

She almost told him—about her little sister born with a cleft palate and how surgery made it possible for Hailey to live a completely normal life without any hint of a birth defect. She almost told him about how a fifth-grade social studies report had led her to stumble across the harsh reality that in other places a cleft palate meant a life on the margins. She would have told him, if it mattered for him to know, that she had found her life's passion at the age of eleven. But it didn't. So she kept her answer simple. "There's an opportuneity for real good in plastic surgery. But to do it, I have to fund it."

A look of understanding crossed his face. "And to fund it, you need a lucrative practice in LA."

"It makes it easier," she said.

"So the miracle you were looking for . . . it's related to the good you think plastics can do?"

"Yeah." She changed the subject. "This was the perfect thing to eat right this second." She loved her work, and it fired her up, but it wasn't exactly light conversation. With Dr. Benson's commitment, she could afford not to think of it for a while. She could be present, here, now, and now was about Ridley, and soft hair dancing in the sea wind, and his crooked looking-for-trouble smiles. "Weren't you about to promise me an adventure? Slippery rocks, et cetera?"

"Definitely some et cetera," he said, leaning forward for another kiss. She loved that he did that. It was a casual intimacy that she never found until deep into a relationship, but it felt right, like he wasn't thinking too hard, just feeling and doing. "Meet me by the sand in thirty minutes?"

"I'm lower maintenance than I look. See you in fifteen. Just have them bill this to my room, okay?"

He smiled. "I've got it."

Right. He had connections around here. "Great. Thanks. It was delicious. See you by the sand."

Fifteen minutes later he smiled at her again as she walked up wearing her yoga clothes from the night before, only she'd laced up her favorite sneakers too. "I'm ready."

"We're going about a mile. Do you want to do it the easy way or the beach way?"

"Is that a real question?" she asked with a laugh as she walked past him toward the water.

"We're heading north," he said, catching up to her. "Do you know this area?"

"Not really," she said.

"Want me to tell you a little about it?"

She appreciated that he asked instead of diving in like a showoff. "I'd like that."

"Besides your usual cranks, the only people who really hate The Mariposa coming in are the surfers." He waved behind them to where the temporary bleachers were receding into the distance. "This beach has always been famous among California surfers, but the town never had the infrastructure to capitalize on it. So surfers have been coming here since the 50s, but with the hotel here now, the city has attracted a couple of major surf competitions because there's room to host everyone. The secret is out, and everyone's coming to Seashell Beach to try the ride. Great for the businesses, but it ticks off the local surfers."

"Doesn't seem to bother you. You don't surf?"

"I do. But it's good for business so I don't mind."

"I don't know how to say this without sounding incredibly condescending, but it surprises me how invested you are in The Mariposa doing well. You talk about it like you helped build it, not like you're a payroll employee."

"The concierge thing. Right." He slid his hands into his pockets. "I wasn't really talking about that. I'm just filling in this weekend. I do other work."

It didn't feel right to ask what that "other work" was if he wasn't volunteering the information, but she wished he would. She wanted to fill in the missing details so she could understand him better. Was he a teacher and this was his summer job? She hoped not. That would make him too sexy. Or maybe he was a struggling novelist trying to make ends meet with a job on the side.

Stop. For right now, this handsome man, late summer sun, and ocean waves were all she needed. The rest didn't matter.

He reached for her hand and told her more about Seashell Beach as they walked, how it had changed since he was a kid, what he loved and what he missed. The tide receded as they walked, and soon they had unbroken expanses of wave-packed sand to walk on. "Are we going there?" she asked, pointing to an outcropping of rocks in the distance. "And if we're not, can we?"

"That's exactly where we're going," he said. "That's why I checked my phone earlier. If you get to them right after the tide goes out, the tide pools are amazing. We're going to catch them just right, but they'll be full, and it's going to get pretty wet."

Brooke knew she had a little kid grin on her face, but she couldn't help it. "I love tide pools. Can you run in those?" she asked, glancing down at his sport sandals.

He rolled his eyes and dropped to the ground in a mock runner's crouch. "Ready, set, go!" and he took off toward the rocks. Brooke had no problem keeping pace with him, but she could tell he wasn't trying to take it easy on her, and it was another mark in his favor. "It's a half mile," he called over the crash of a wave.

She grinned. "A sprint. What do I get if I win?"

"Same thing I do."

"Et cetera?"

"Et cetera." He poured on some speed, and she laughed out loud, matching his pace and liking that she had to work for it.

She pulled away in the last twenty-five yards, and when he joined her a few seconds later, they exchanged smiles but not words as they caught their breath, him bent over with his hands on his knees, her walking in a small, slow circle while she waited for her lungs to cooperate.

Finally he straightened and caught her as her cool-down loop brought her into his orbit, pulling her to him and kissing her, sliding his hand around her neck so his fingers threaded through her hair and his thumb rested against her pulse. His kiss sped it right back up, and he smiled against her lips as he felt it accelerate. "Et cetera," he said, brushing his lips against hers. "Et cetera." Now he trailed a kiss along her jawline. "Et cetera." The last kiss replaced his thumb against her pulse.

She took a step back from him, suddenly aware that the sand and sea and a beautiful sky had all shrunk to become just him, only him, during those kisses. She hadn't felt this light-headed around a boy since Channing Singer in eleventh grade. It confused her. She knew many of the doctors were open to one-night stands when they traveled to these conferences, but her Midwestern values ran a little too deep for that.

But what else was this supposed to be? She'd agreed to let Ridley take over her Sunday because only a crazy woman turned down exploring a new town with a guy as charming as he was. And yet barely an hour with him had her heart pounding and her head spinning. And she didn't care. *She didn't care.* She should be running straight back to her hotel room.

There was no way she was walking away from him. At least not toward the hotel. She turned and shielded her eyes to study the rock jetty. "This is taller than I thought it would be." The top was six feet over her head.

"Yeah, it takes a little work to get up there, but it's pretty awesome. We might even see starfish."

She wrinkled her nose.

"You don't like starfish?"

"I do. But we don't have to, um."

"Um?"

"Touch them? I kind of have a thing about that."

"Wait a second. Haven't you had to peel people's faces off and stuff like that in your job?"

She cleared her throat. "Yes. This is different."

"I will protect you from the starfish, Brooke." His voice was serious.

She planted her hands on her hips and glared at him. "I'm not scared of them. I just think they're going to feel funky."

"Okay. So we'll only look. Feel better?"

"No. I feel like an idiot."

"Aww." He pulled her into a hug, her head tucked beneath his chin. "Sorry I teased you."

She tickled him to get away. "No, you're not. Let's go find starfish. I'm not a pansy."

"Follow me."

He led her to a section further from the shore with several natural handholds, and she followed him up. When he reached down and pulled her up to stand on top, she gasped. "I love this!"

Shallow pools dappled the whole top of the jetty. The nearest one was only a foot away, and the feathery tentacles of the anemones inside waved at them. She knelt and peered into the water.

"Careful of the starfish," Ridley whispered next to her.

She poked him in the side without even looking, gasping instead when a shore crab the size of a half dollar scuttled out of the other side of the pool. "I want it."

"Too little to eat."

"No, for a pet. It can come live with me."

"Good idea. You can keep it on a leash and buy it one of those carriers that looks like a purse, then take it out for walks on Rodeo Drive between patients, and you'll start a whole new trend. First it was purse dogs, then babies as accessories, and now Brooke will give us crabs." His eyes widened when he heard how it sounded. "Wait. That is the dumbest thing I've ever said out loud."

But Brooke was laughing too hard to tell him not to worry about it.

He groaned. "I promise to forget you're scared of starfish if you'll forget I said that."

Instead of an answer, she braced herself on one hand so she could stretch the other one out to the opposite bank of the tide pool, resting it in the crab's path. A moment later it scuttled up onto her palm, and she straightened and held the crab out to Ridley, who stretched out his own palm for the crab to explore.

"Shelly and I forgive you," she said.

"Shelly? Seriously?"

"Is there a better name for a crab?"

"I guess that depends on how you feel about calling a dog Spots or a cat Fluffy."

"Those sound like pets named by people with a real instinct for calling it like it is."

"You know it's totally crazy that you'll pick up a pinching crab like it's nothing but you're afraid of starfish?"

"Is this where I get to remind you that you implied I have a sexually transmitted disease?"

He cleared his throat. "I meant to say that anyone who thinks your starfish phobia is funny should see you handle these cra—er, crustaceans like a boss."

"Thought that's what you meant."

They spent two more hours exploring the pools, joking and playing. He was quick. Very quick. She loved how fast his mind worked, jumping from hilarious one-liners to a thoughtful discussion about ocean ecology to the best seafood each of them had ever eaten. When they finally climbed down from the rocks and walked back to the hotel, she slipped her hand into his without even thinking about it. She couldn't wait to see what he'd planned for them the next day.

He walked her toward the elevators but veered right instead of stopping in front of them, drawing her through a door labeled "Employees Only Please."

"How do you feel about slumming with the help?" he asked, stepping toward her and forcing her to back up against the wall. He braced his hands behind her on either side of her shoulders, making it hard for her to escape. Except she didn't want to.

"I feel awesome about that." She tilted her head up at him, and he leaned down and kissed her, a slower, hungrier kiss than he'd given her yet.

A whole lifetime ticked past before he drew back to touch his forehead to hers. "I wish I had more time right now. I'd take you out for real dinner and show you more Seashell Beach secrets."

She wished that too. So hard. "Why can't we do that?"

He pushed himself away from the wall with a sigh. "I have to work. I'm not sure how long. But part of you enjoying this whole experience is having time for yourself, so being in charge of your day means that I'm assigning you to have some alone time. The only condition is that you can't go to anything related to your conference. I think you should take a nap. In fact, I strongly, strongly urge it."

She smiled like she wasn't disappointed. "You're only supposed to be in charge of my day tomorrow. You don't get any more say over today."

"What about tonight? Can I have any say over that?"

Her eyes widened and he grinned at her, dropping a kiss on her forehead. "Get your mind out of the gutter."

She delivered a mock-angry slap on his arm then got distracted by how much she liked the lean feel of it. He tensed beneath her hand, and she glanced up at him through her eyelashes. A muscle twitched is his jaw, and his expression suggested she was about to end up against the wall again. "So you're saying I'll see you later?"

He pulled her to him for a hard kiss. "Yeah. You're killing me. We need to get out of here before I forget what I'm supposed to be doing right now." He pulled her back through the service door and walked her to the elevator bank. It dinged right away and sent a sad pang through her stomach.

"See you, Doc."

"Later, Ridley," she said as the door closed between them.

In her room she closed the door behind her and leaned against it. She should open her computer and review her notes. She should pull up her spreadsheets and figure out where she wanted Dr. Benson on the surgery schedule for the fall.

But she wanted to lean here and pretend Ridley was still hovering over her, ready to claim more kisses. It had been a good thing she'd had him for support after the last one because her knees wouldn't have survived it on their own.

She straightened and walked to the desk, cracking open her laptop and opening her Smiles from the Heart file to start a new document for Dr. Benson.

She had to shove Ridley to the outer corners of her brain a few times, but she'd managed to synthesize most of the overview information Benson would need by the time someone knocked on her door. Ridley. She hurried to open it and frowned when a smiling room service runner stood there with a covered dish.

"For you," the runner said, lifting the fancy silver dome to reveal a Loki picture. Brooke laughed and took the picture, waving off the grinning runner with a thank you when he refused a tip. Ridley had scrawled a note in the corner. "I don't get it. Why would all the ladies want me like this when they could have me like this?" An arrow pointed for her to turn the paper over, and she gasped and then flat out giggled when a smoldering Tom Hiddleston in a Louis Vuitton ad confronted her. The note on this side read, "Sorry I can't come round, love. Ridley told me no. Ring me up if you're ever in London."

She needed to pay Ridley back, but she didn't know how. What would be his dream type? A blonde surf girl? A model? A wholesome Nebraska girl with gifted surgeon's hands?

She wanted to zip down to the lobby and peek at him working, like she was twelve and spying on her sixth-grade crush. Instead, she'd work on the preliminary surgery schedule for Nicaragua based on the most recent report from the clinic director there.

Another hour passed, and an alert from her cell phone startled her out of a case file. She picked up the phone and smiled when she saw it was a text from Ridley.

If I knock on your door, am I going to freak you out?

Depends. Are you going to do something weird, criminal, or otherwise offensive when I open it?

Define offensive. KIDDING. No. I'm going to surprise you.

A knock sounded, and she texted back before she answered. *I'm already surprised. And I like it.*

She opened the door and found him leaning against the doorway, smiling at her, a large tote bag with The Mariposa logo emblazoned on the side resting at his feet. "I'm about to see if you have bona fide adventure credentials," he said.

"Bring it."

He grinned. "This actually requires me to bring *you* somewhere. But not too far. We won't even leave the hotel. You down?"

"I'm down. What do I need?"

"A sweatshirt and flip flops."

"Hang on." A minute later she had her Nebraska sweatshirt on and was sliding her feet into her favorite two-dollar flip flops. "Ready."

He held out a hand for her, led her to the elevator, and pressed the button for the top floor.

"Let me guess. We're going to sneak into the penthouse and pretend to live like kings for a few hours."

"No. That wouldn't require a sweatshirt, would it? I mean, if it does, I think I have the wrong idea about how rich people in penthouses live."

When they exited the elevator, he led her down the hall, winding around two turns until they reached the end of the hall and a door marked "Stairs" with a discreet sign next to the jamb. He let go of her hand to pull a key from his pocket, and her eyebrows shot up. At the top of the stairs he unlocked another door spray-painted with a stern red "No admittance" in block letters.

"Things are getting real," she said, teasing him.

He paused to smile back at her. "Yeah."

Something about the way he said it made her pulse go thready.

He held the door open for her, and she stepped past him to discover that they were on the roof. "Wow," she breathed, taking in the view. The pool was a bright aquamarine below them, strung like a jewel inside the gentle curve of the hotel stretched around it. The ocean rippled beyond it, inky except where it captured moonlight and tossed it back up.

On the roof itself, two of the pool's lounge chairs waited for them, complete with cushions and beach blankets. A cabana table sat beside one, and he'd placed a rose in a vase and a couple of candles next to it.

"So pretty," she said. "It makes me want to climb onto

one of the chairs, burrow under a blanket, and let my mind drift out with the waves."

His expression relaxed, and it was only then that she realized he'd been holding on to a little anxiety about how she would take it.

She squeezed his hand. "I love it."

"Good. I kind of had to cobble it together with stuff I boosted out of the restaurants from servers who like me. Full disclosure, I think the candles are going to have to be for show. I'm pretty sure the wind is going to work against me."

It was windier on top of the hotel than down by the waves, but Brooke loved the feel of it riffling through her hair. "I give you full credit for the thoughts. And I love everything you've already done, but is there any chance you smuggled food up here too?" She gave him her little sister's best buy-me-a-puppy-daddy expression, and he laughed.

"Follow me, madam." He set the bag down on the cabana table, and Brooke curled up on a deck chair and burrowed as he pulled item after item from the bag. "It's the Mary Poppins bag," she said as he set out a binocular case, a small picnic hamper, a bottle of wine and two goblets.

He tinkered with his phone, and music filtered from a portable speaker. "Music is the trickiest part," he confessed. "Too smooth and it looks like I'm trying to put the moves on you. Too random and it looks like I put no thought into it at all."

She crossed her fingers and closed her eyes, muttering, "Put the moves on, put the moves on, put the moves on."

"Oh, I will," he said, and the wicked grin he flashed her made her stomach flip. "But I want it to look effortless."

"Got it. I'm going to pretend I don't notice." She listened to the music for a minute and smiled. "Avett Brothers. Good choice."

"I was worrying I oversold this all when I called it an adventure."

"Any time a guy I barely know knocks on my hotel room door and invites me through restricted entrances and hidden stairwells, that's definitely an adventure."

"A guy you barely know," he repeated. "It's true, but it's strange that it's true. Does that make any sense?"

"Complete sense." It was the ease between them. She would have given some thought to why it was so easy, but it would have made things complicated again. So she didn't think about it. She nodded at the wine bottle, her eyebrows rising to ask a question, and he smiled and uncorked it, pouring it into the goblets.

She held her glass up to him and smiled. "To summer nights."

"To summer nights."

For a couple of minutes the only sound was the mellow music and the distant crash of the waves.

"I'm glad you wandered through the lobby on Thursday." Ridley's voice wove through the spell that had fallen over them rather than breaking it. "The truth is, I saw you before you got to the hotel. I was behind you on PCH when you were driving in. I thought you looked like the classic California girl, sun soaked and having fun. You have mad car-dancing skills."

She gasped and shot up. "That was you behind me? You're the hot guy in the Jeep."

"I'm the guy in the Jeep, anyway." He looked pleased that she'd noticed him too. "It was funny when you walked through the lobby the second time that night looking like a totally different person. The fact that you were with the conference crowd led me to think that you were . . ."

"As shallow as the patients I work on?"

He shrugged. "I can tell you're not."

She was quiet for a long moment. "I know a Beverly Hills cosmetic surgery practice is an easy target. And some of my patients probably deserve to be made fun of. They really are shallow. But I've been surprised. For every injection I do because someone wants Kardashian, there are two more patients with much more complicated stories. Breast augmentations for women whose lives have been ravaged by breast cancer, or cleft palate repairs or work on burn victims. But even with the purely cosmetic stuff . . . I don't know. I'm learning there are stories underneath."

"Maybe you see stories because you're a cool person and you assume the best about people, like maybe lip injections aren't about better duck face selfies. But maybe that's all there is to it."

She turned to study him. "I didn't take you for a cynic. Is it because you have to work with rich people too much?"

"Maybe." He took a long swallow of his wine. "Probably. I think I've been itchy for something more, something better."

"Like in your job? In your life?"

"Yeah."

"Well, that's specific."

He only smiled. "Yeah."

She left him to his thoughts, staring out at the ocean and feeling a peace that, despite its frustrations, her career let her make a difference in the world. A breeze blew her hair into her face, and the strands tickled as she pushed them behind her ear. She shivered, and Ridley immediately scooted onto her chair and lifted up the blanket so he could squeeze in with her, sliding an arm around her and pulling her close to his side.

She leaned against him and sighed, content. Distracting

thoughts bubbled up—how often did he do this? Was this a routine when he met a pretty hotel guest he liked? Did this feel as natural to him as it did to her?—and she pushed them away. She didn't care. She didn't want to analyze everything about the space and time and mood they were sharing.

She'd drifted away, almost, when Ridley spoke again. "Is this okay?" he asked. "I like just sitting here being quiet with you, but I can bust out my sparkling conversation skills."

"This is pretty perfect." She turned her head to meet his eyes and smile. He took it as an invitation to dip down and kiss her, and she discovered that despite the easy way they were already draped together, she could, in fact, melt into him further.

Seven

This woman was killing him in the best possible way.

He growled as she deepened the kiss before drawing back to drop her head against the lounge chair. He took it as an invitation to press kisses along the curve of her neck. When she spoke he could hear the smile in her voice as he worked his way toward the hollow where her collarbones met. "That wasn't a hint," she said, laughter lacing her voice.

He didn't look up, brushing a kiss against the hollow. What was this bit called? Dr. Brooke would know. But he wouldn't ask her because he didn't want to interrupt the kisses to form words. She sighed and ran her fingers through his hair, tugging his head up.

"You want me to stop?"

"Definitely not," she said, pulling him up so their mouths met again for more kisses.

When they finally came up for air, she turned herself so she was tucked against him, her head beneath his chin, burrowing into his chest. It was the kind of thing a girlfriend did.

He glanced out over the water, feeling the soft rise and fall of Brooke's breathing. He'd told himself she would be a good distraction until she cruised back to LA. He'd told himself he would play the part of the handsome hotel employee and be a little bit of wish fulfillment for her for a few days until she went home. It was one of the biggest perks of living in a beach town. He could be an item on someone's vacation bucket list whenever he wanted.

He'd told himself this is what he wanted.

But Brooke had flipped the script, and now he realized that everything he'd told himself about her was a lie. She wasn't a distraction or a fling. The glimpse he'd gotten past the surface of who she was wasn't enough.

Was it possible to fall for someone in a couple of days? He'd never done it before, but it felt like that's what he was doing now.

What was he supposed to do with that? With her? About her? Bring her to his room and end this weekend like it was a clichéd vacation hook up?

No.

Tomorrow he would take her hiking in the Channel Islands and tell her about the rest of him, not the vacation fantasy he had presented himself as by feeding her misunderstandings about his job. He hoped she'd be cool with it, because he wanted to see her well past her checkout date. He stroked her hair and quit thinking, listening instead to her breaths grow deep and rhythmic. Her head rested more heavily against his chest as the waves lulled her to sleep.

At some point he drifted off too, waking only when she gave his shoulder a soft shake and he opened his eyes to see her smiling up at him, sleep creases from lying on his chest the whole night lining her face. She was adorable.

"Good morning," she said, her voice scratchy. "I'm sorry I fell asleep on you, and please, I'm begging you, don't tell me if I drooled."

"I'm not sorry," he said, sitting up and groaning at the way the damp sea air had crept into his joints. "And you didn't drool."

"Smart boy."

"Truthful boy." Well, almost. He'd be all the way truthful in a couple of hours. "We're doing a real adventure today. Hiking, exploring, dependent on a ferry to return us to civilization. What do you say?"

"Yes. And also, I decided to check out on Tuesday instead of tomorrow."

"Oh yeah?" he said, his voice soft. "Why's that?"

She shrugged, but her smile was a confession. "Reasons."

"I'm on board with your reasons." He brushed a kiss against her lips. "I have to do a few things for work this morning; then I should be off for the rest of the day. Want to meet me in the Sandpiper for brunch in two hours?"

"Will there be hashbrowns?"

"Yes."

"Then yes."

He gave her a wounded look. "There will also be Ridley."

This time it was her turn to kiss him. "Bonus."

He walked her down to her door and headed home to work on his more powerful Mac, determined to fly through his photo edits and submit to his editor in record time. This woman had him wanting to bend and twist time so he could steal more of it with her. He jogged out to his Jeep and slammed it into gear, racing home so he could race back.

Oh man, this woman.

Brooke couldn't find her phone. It was up on the roof, she realized. Dang. She probably couldn't even get back up there without Ridley's keys. Maybe he was at the concierge desk? She called down.

"Guest services, Leslie speaking."

"Hi, Leslie," Brooke said to the perky voice on the other end of the line. "Is Ridley working this morning?"

"I'll check for you. Is he at the front desk? Porter services?"

"No," she said, feeling confused. "He's a concierge."

"Really?" Short pause. "Well, no. No Ridley here."

"Thanks." Brooke hung up the phone, wondering how many concierges it took to staff a hotel the size of The Mariposa. She could at least try the roof door herself, and if that didn't work, she'd see if someone from management could get her in, but she wanted to save that for a last resort. She had no idea if Ridley would get in trouble if the bosses knew he'd let guests up there, or even gone up there himself, but she really needed her phone.

She took the elevator up to the top floor and followed the corridor around until she recognized the door to the stairs. It opened beneath her hand, and she did a fist pump. One down, one to go.

Her luck ran out at the second door. With a curse under her breath, she leaned against it and considered her next move.

She could probably do without the phone for another

hour or so, but if the office tried to reach her, it would be a problem. She'd have to call in from her room and let them know to reach her there if something came up. She pushed away from the door, relieved she had an option besides ratting out Ridley.

When she rounded the corner to head back toward the elevator, she stopped short at the sight of Ridley walking out of one of the guest rooms. She almost called out to him but changed her mind. Something wasn't right.

He wasn't in uniform, instead wearing a pair of beat-up cargo shorts and flip flops, a big camera bag over his shoulder. He walked toward the elevator without glancing back.

He was acting a lot more like a guest than an employee. Maybe there was a simple explanation, but other things buzzed around the edges of her memory. Like how he never seemed to be "on duty." And how no one at the concierge desk ever recognized his name.

But why on earth would he have been behind the concierge desk when she checked in if he was a guest here? And if he was a guest, why didn't he want her to know that?

That bothered her more than anything. If he was hiding that, no reason would be a good reason. She didn't believe in hiding *anything*, because too often it was a pattern. When people got selective about the facts they shared, she could only wonder what else wasn't coming out.

But her medical training led her to seek evidence before drawing conclusions. It didn't take her long to jet back in her room and do a quick Google search, hoping that an uncommon name like Ridley would get her the information she wanted as she typed "Ridley + Seashell Beach" into the search bar. The entire first page of results was him, all links to photo essays he had done about surfing. His face, along with some of his work, popped up in thumbnails across the top of the page, and when she clicked a few of them open, they took her breath away. He was incredibly talented.

So why was he moonlighting as a concierge? Did he have to fill the gaps between photography jobs with something more stable?

But... that had been Ridley the guest walking out of the room several floors above her, not Ridley an employee. She walked to her window and stared at the beach, looking southward to where a work crew was disassembling the temporary bleachers from the surf competition. He had to have been shooting that.

She went back to her computer and dug into some of the links. His LinkedIn profile identified him as Ridley Lansing, a photographer based in Seashell Beach. It weirded her out to be in possession of his last name when he hadn't given it to her, but it also seemed fair given how much more he knew about her than she did about him.

Other links were for industry blogs interviewing him about his technique, and his answers struck her as having the same level of expertise about photography as did the articles she read in her medical journals about plastic surgery. He took his profession seriously.

One link led her to a Santa Monica art gallery selling limited-edition framed prints of his work, and she gasped at the price tags. If he was selling these even semi-regularly, he definitely didn't need a fallback job like concierge.

She sat back down in front of the laptop and scrolled through more of his work. He shot from fearless angles and captured the ocean in light that brought it alive. The more links she clicked on, the more it became obvious that he wasn't just a skilled professional; he was world renowned. She sat back and stared at the evidence on the screen.

A world-renowned photographer who had misled her so she would have no clue.

A slow anger kindled in her stomach, a sense of hurt that made her madder for feeling it after knowing Ridley for only three days. But they had spent real time together, more real than the polite time she'd spent with any of her dates over the last two years. She'd gone out with a couple of guys for a few months and connected with them less than she had with Ridley just by racing him across The Mariposa's lawn, or watching the ocean from the rooftop. And by kissing. And being herself without trying to fit into some neat box.

Somehow knowing he would have to stay within the five calendar boxes she was spending at the hotel had made it easier for her to simply be herself. She didn't have to think about whether he would misinterpret anything she was saying to mean she wanted a relationship, or worry about impressing him. And so she'd relaxed, been herself, laughed and been spontaneous and made jokes and let him in, because it was easy to do that knowing she'd check out and leave him behind.

So why did she care so much about what he'd chosen to reveal or conceal about himself? It would have all ended Tuesday anyway. Today and tomorrow were supposed to be the last adventures before returning to real life. She should go on it anyway, see where the day took her.

But the idea had lost its appeal. She stepped out onto her balcony and breathed in the ocean air, trying to figure out why everything suddenly felt different, why she suddenly felt hurt.

He'd lied to her, and it was a strange lie—to underplay who he was instead of exaggerating it. Obviously he'd been keeping her at a distance too. But it was the kind of lie that reminded her of a movie where a prince or a millionaire hides his roots so he can be loved for himself. For all of Ridley's hotness, she didn't think his job, however good he was at it, was enough for him to have to disguise his identity to discourage groupies.

She'd put limits on their flirtation by giving it the deadline of her checkout date. It looked like he'd imposed limits by deciding to be someone he wasn't for a few days.

It shouldn't hurt. She shouldn't be bothered that he wasn't interested in giving up every piece of his life to a stranger. Before last night, she wouldn't have cared. Much. But to spend hours talking about their childhoods and goals and what they loved and didn't, to feel so connected to someone and find that he hadn't told much of the truth about himself at all . . .

She dropped her head to her forearms resting on the railing and closed her eyes, trying to quiet her thoughts, but one bubbled up over and over again. At some point the night before, she'd mentally erased the last box on her vacation calendar, leaving it open-ended to the possibility of more. And she felt stupid.

She was so good at boxes. Time to remember that. She put her feelings in a box so she could handle high-maintenance clients. She put her feelings in a box so she could work on her cleft palate patients and not die a little inside over the ones she couldn't get to. She put her feelings in a box whenever a new guy entered the picture because it was messy to have feelings on the loose.

She tucked her feelings back into a box now. Her mom would be upset with her checking out early, but she needed to be at work more than she needed to take an extra vacation day. Even if she spent a day being frivolous in LA to make her mom happy, she had a feeling thoughts of Ridley would intrude and she would end up fluctuating between hurt and anger all over again. But she'd just proven to herself that both were stupid reactions. Ridley's omissions had ultimately been harmless. It was her own stupid fault for caring that he hadn't felt attracted enough to her to be fully himself, and her own stupid fault that she'd read more into an evening of talking under the stars.

And kissing.

The kissing...

In her defense, she didn't know how someone wouldn't read something into those kisses. Their first few kisses by the wishing well had been both curious and hungry, but last night they'd gone from hungry to tender, from a flash fire to a deep burn.

Or she'd thought so, anyway.

She wandered back into her room and set her suitcase on her bed. She didn't need to fall any farther down this rabbit hole. She could still check out without getting charged if she was gone within the hour. She would only need half that.

Eight

Ridley pulled back into The Mariposa parking lot and grinned as he swung himself out of the Jeep, his hiking boots hitting the asphalt with a thud. It was stupid how much he wanted to see Brooke, but he didn't care. And when they finished their hike, he'd figure out how to convince her that the end of the day couldn't be the end of their connection, whatever it was. He would take more assignments in LA. He needed more of her.

He was knocking on her door in record time. When she didn't answer, he pulled out his phone and texted her on his way down to the lobby. She didn't answer, but there was a chance she was sleeping in to make up for a late night, or in the shower so she couldn't hear the knock or text.

He stopped by the concierge desk and grinned at Marco. "Can you send something up to room 529 for me?"

Marco shook his head. "You the one sending up actor pictures?"

"Yeah."

"You going to explain what this is about?"

"No."

Marco laughed. "Yeah, sure. I'll send one of the boys up. Brent lets you get away with murder around here. And I heard you covered for me. I owe you. Where do you want it this time? Taped to the TV? Stuck on a mirror?"

"Nah. Maybe slip it under the door this time so it doesn't disturb her. I'll find one and email it to you to print right now."

"Sounds good," Marco said, pulling out an envelope and writing her name on the outside. "Ms. Brooke..."

"Dresden," Ridley said.

"Is that Brooke with an E?"

"I'm not sure," Ridley admitted.

"I'll look it up." He clacked on the keyboard and frowned. "We maybe have a problem, buddy." He turned the screen so Ridley could see it. "She checked out this morning."

Ridley leaned over and read it without processing it. "She said her reservation was through tomorrow."

Marco shrugged. "It was. She checked out a day early. Talk to Lainey at the reservation desk. She might know what's going on."

Lainey nodded when she pulled up Brooke's information. "Yes, I checked her out about a half hour ago. She said she forgot about an important meeting at home and needed to take off. Your name is Ridley, right? Room 1427?"

"Yeah."

"She left a letter for you for when you checked out, but I might as well give it to you now since you're here." She pushed an envelope toward him exactly like the one Marco had been ready to send up to Brooke's room. "We had to send up maintenance to unlock the roof access. Somehow her phone got up there."

"Interesting," Ridley said, keeping his expression neutral.

"Someone brought two lounge chairs up there too."

She was fishing for information, and Ridley didn't blame her. An abandoned phone at a midnight picnic scene, a guy looking for a woman who didn't seem to want to be found, an unexpected letter that was clearly going to blow him off.

"Thanks for the letter," he said. "I appreciate it." He slid the envelope into his pocket and walked out of the lobby and away from Marco and Lainey's curious eyes. Hotel staff could sniff out drama better than a surfer could spot a poser on the waves. He didn't blame them for being curious, but he didn't really want to give them any more to discuss. He might as well check out too, and limit the number of times he had to walk through the lobby and avoid their knowing looks.

In his room he sat on the bed and stared at the envelope for a second. Her absence already gnawed at him, an emptiness in his day that he had expected to fill with her. And now it stretched in front of him as one long blank.

A few days ago an open day would have represented freedom and possibility. He glanced through his balcony doors at the gray pall of the marine layer pushing down on the ocean. That seemed about right.

He slid her letter from his envelope. Her handwriting on the hotel stationery looked like her, strong and elegant, no curly flourishes.

Hi, Ridley.

I decided to leave this morning instead of tomorrow because you're Ridley Lansing and you didn't tell me. I'm not really sure why you let me think you were a hotel concierge when I told you all about myself. I Googled you, and you don't have any deep, dark secrets that the Internet has discovered, so I'm not sure why you didn't want me to know who you really are.

Honestly, I shouldn't care. I know that. But while I had every intention of letting this weekend be the beginning and end of our time together, somehow by this morning I'd let the edges blur. Blame it on moonlight and wine, but it muddled me into thinking it was real beyond this weekend. I don't want to be all dramatic, but I connected to you like I haven't to anyone in a long time. And the fact that I didn't have good enough instincts to sense that it was a false connection makes me feel stupid.

I'm leaving you this note because I'd want to know why someone walked off. I don't have any bad feelings toward you or anything. And I should be preserving my dignity and not saying anything at all, just taking off without a word so you'd never know I got turned around on this. But that's not really my style. For better or worse, I'm about no-holds-barred honesty, and frankly? I guess I have enough ego that I wanted you to know I uncovered your secret identity. Let's ignore that it took me much longer to demonstrate critical thinking than it should have.

~Brooke

Ridley cursed, frustrated at himself. The hours they'd spent talking and laughing last night had taken him right back to high school. Two days before his senior prom, his date, a girl he'd been going out with for less than a month, had given him a kid's book about this wedge that was going around looking for its missing piece until it eventually realizes it's part of a wheel and they're better when they're together or something like that. His date had written an intense explanation across the two pages of the flyleaf about how he was her missing piece, which had led to a disastrous prom-night meltdown when he'd had to explain that he thought she was fun but didn't necessarily see himself as somehow becoming whole because of her.

But that's exactly what being with Brooke had felt like. The hollow feeling somewhere between his chest and his stomach felt like a piece of him had been carved out and misplaced, like Brooke had performed surgery on him and removed something vital: herself.

The worst part was that it was his fault. He could have told her at any point that he didn't work at the hotel, about what he really did. But he hadn't because . . . because why?

Because that wasn't part of the game plan. To say out loud to her that he wanted her to know who he really was meant making a confession—that he liked her, that he was introducing reality into what should have been a diversion. And he'd thought he didn't want that. That was his buffer: to be only part of himself with her, to withhold so that there was no way the game could turn serious.

He'd given up his illusion of distance too late. He'd been so sure his plan to tell her when they went hiking today would magically make everything work out.

Man, he was an idiot.

How was he supposed to fix this? He reached for his phone to call her but stopped before he dialed her number. No. If she even answered, she'd probably feel like talk was cheap coming from him, and she had every reason to feel that way.

He reached for the hotel phone and made a different call entirely.

Nine

Brooke hung up the last dress from her suitcase and stripped down to shower off the residue of a top-down road trip. She couldn't foresee ever giving up her convertible, but there was no question that cruising in it for three hours left a thin film of highway on her. Finished and feeling much cleaner, she climbed into a tank top and knit pajama shorts even though it was early afternoon. She was tired enough for bed.

She couldn't even blame a lazy drive in the sun for the droopiness. After the marine layer had burned off to reveal blue skies, the day had stayed gray to her. She'd gotten Ridley's first text and braced for another one when he figured out she'd left, but no follow-up text ever came.

No surprise, really. They were always meant to be done when she was gone. But the grayness inside her had become something more like television static, frenetic and restless. She hadn't left her condo on Thursday thinking she lacked a relationship, but as she glanced around her place, she wondered how she'd missed that everything about it screamed the truth: she was lonely. She was busy filling up her hours and being useful, yes. Useful to the point of thinking she had no room in her life for more. But her coffeemaker made single-serve cups. And she only had a loveseat because she didn't need a full sofa just for herself. Her tiny cafe table would only fit two people if all either of them had was a drink, but only one person could comfortably eat there.

She'd thought she was so independent when she'd moved in, proud of herself for being able to afford a Beverly Hills adjacent property all on her own without needing to decorate around a roommate or boyfriend's whims.

Ha.

Except it wasn't funny. Now she looked around, and it felt sad. How could a place Ridley had never been be so full of Ridley's absence?

She'd have to figure out what to do about that, but she had no answers right now. All she had was an overwhelming desire to climb under her blankets and wake up in a day where this weekend was a dream that hadn't happened.

Rather than risk a long nap that would screw up her sleep later, she hauled out her laptop and opened her email, smiling when she saw an email from the Nicaragua clinic about Rosa, her all-time favorite patient. She clicked it open and wished she could hug her little friend grinning from the picture the director had attached. Rosa was happy, and before long, Brooke would get to perform the same miracle for dozens of other kids. She couldn't justify spending emotional energy on Ridley when she had this to take care of and worry over.

Two hours later, she'd written up a fairly good overview of what Dr. Benson could expect. She'd spend some time plugging in details throughout the week, but the eight patient profiles she'd chosen for him were a good start. It washed some of the gray out of the day. She glanced at the time and sighed. Still too soon to go to bed. Instead, she poured herself a bowl of shredded wheat and turned her TV on. A *Friday Night Lights* re-watch and Tim Riggins were the perfect antidote for her Ridley hangover.

She groaned when he crossed her mind again. At least that time she'd pushed him out for a full two minutes. A text went off on her phone, and she picked it up, squeaking when she saw Ridley's name. She'd been expecting her sister, or even her sassy grandma who had become a texting fool once they'd gotten her the giant iPhone to accommodate her arthritic fingers. She opened the text.

If I knock on your door, am I going to freak you out?

Her heart stuttered and rebounded with an extra-hard thump. Was her phone glitching and re-sending his previous texts? It did that sometimes when she moved in and out of her coverage areas. It just sucked that it had to resend the one text she liked best out of the half dozen she'd gotten from Ridley. She deleted it and moved on to delete the texts before that. She was on her fourth, finding it satisfying to do them one by one instead of as a batch, when a knock on her door startled a yelp out of her.

"Brooke? You okay?" Ridley's voice drifted in through the window she'd left open for the evening breeze.

She scrambled out of her seat and opened the door to stare at him on her doorstep.

"Hi," he said, his smile wobbling. It melted her a tiny bit; it had been so sure every other time she'd seen it.

"Hi."

He jingled his car keys, and realizing it, he winced and slid them into his pocket. "I hope showing up like this looks wildly romantic and not borderline psychotic. I'll leave the second you tell me to go. Do you want me to go?"

Her heart stuttered again. The man was practically giving her an arrhythmia. "No," she said, dragging it out the tiniest bit. A flash of worry crossed his face, and he took a step back.

"I mean it," she said. "It's okay that you're here. I'm not freaked out. More like totally confused."

"Me too. Or I was. But now I'm not. Which is why I promised Brent I would tell the police I hacked into the hotel's customer database to get your address and not that he gave it to me in case you were mad."

"Brent?"

"The manager at The Mariposa. We go way back."

She nodded, still dazed. "It's fine that he gave it to you. Why did you want it? I mean, why are you here?"

"A few reasons. The most important is that I wanted to apologize. I'm sorry I didn't give you the whole picture of me. I know it's easy to say now that I don't have to prove it, but I was going to tell you today when we were out hiking."

"The fact that you drove all the way down here sort of proves your point. I believe you. Look," she said, glancing behind her. "Do you want to come in?"

"Yeah," he said, his smile back at full heartbreaker wattage. "I'd like that."

She led him to the love seat and cursed herself for not getting a full sofa. She didn't feel like squeezing in so close to him while they had this conversation, whatever it might be. She led him to the table instead, and he took a seat.

"I like your place," he said, glancing around.

"Thank you. I don't have much to offer you. I'm kind of a take-out girl. Do you want some water? Or tea? Or coffee?" She rummaged through a cabinet for tea, wondering if she even had any. Why had she offered him tea? She didn't even drink tea.

"I'm fine."

Too bad. Now she had no excuse not to sit down. But instead of taking her seat, she leaned against the counter and crossed her feet in front of her.

He cleared his throat. "This is so awkward, I'm sorry. But I read your note this morning—"

She colored, remembering how frank she'd been, not expecting to see him again.

"—And I felt like I owed you more than an apology text."

"You don't owe me anything. It was just a weekend."

"No, it was *supposed* to be just a weekend. That's why—" He broke off, his forehead crinkling, and he looked like he was about to confess to hitting her parked car. "That's why I didn't say what I do for a living. There's a resort culture that happens at hotels like The Mariposa. I worked in it for a long time. I'm still around it pretty often because of all my traveling. And single women who come to resorts tend to fall into a few categories."

She frowned, not liking the generalizations she could sense looming.

"There are categories for all of the male guests, the married women, the families, for everyone," he said, catching her expression. "I'm explaining the pattern you'll see if you hang out somewhere like The Mariposa a lot."

"Is that what you do? Hang out there a lot?" She hated to think of him as someone who sat around trolling the registered guests for women to pick up. She'd like to think she had better judgment than that.

"No. I mean, not really. I shoot along that stretch of beach all the time because it draws so many surfers. And I stop into the hotel pretty often to chat with Brent. I knew him because in college I really did used to be a concierge at the same hotel where he was a valet, and I was pinch-hitting for him the other day when his regular guy had a family emergency. So for that day, I wasn't faking."

"But the rest of it?"

"So the categories I mentioned." He cleared his throat and squirmed some more. "A lot of times single women who are coming to the resort at the same time a conference is happening are looking for a fling."

"You mean a sugar daddy," she interrupted, giving him credit for at least having the decency to turn a deep red. "I'm going to hate everything you're about to say, aren't I?"

"If I were you, I would."

She sighed. "All right. Let's agree that sometimes women think doctors are an easy meal ticket. Let's agree that some of them are predatory. Let's agree that this is a very, very small minority of women."

"Completely agreed. But it's a pretty high proportion of the single women who come to the resort."

"Stipulated," she muttered.

"I know it's not *all* the single women. But usually the ones who want solitude don't come to The Mariposa. They go to spa properties, like in Ojai or Sonora."

She waved for him to get on with it.

"I've made it a strict rule not to get involved with women I meet while traveling or who come to The Mariposa. There's no potential there, because even if the connection is amazing, the distance would always be an issue. But sometimes, it's fun to flirt. Does that make me sound like a pig?"

"Not if the other person is playing too, I guess."

He looked relieved. "You caught my eye on the highway. I thought you were local, and I saw at the stoplight that you didn't have a wedding ring on, so I was sitting there wishing I would bump into you around town. And then when we both pulled into The Mariposa, I couldn't believe I'd lucked out. But right away it created a conundrum: if you were someone I'd want to date in real life, I needed to stay away from you for the weekend. But if you were superficial, then maybe it would be a fun weekend, done and forgotten by Monday. I know that sounds so calculating, but honestly, I think I can tell when someone's too invested, and I would never lead someone on to entertain myself for a couple of days."

"Okay, but how were you supposed to figure out if I was a weekend distraction or a true fit?"

The clock over her stove clicked loudly at least a dozen times before he answered. "Before I answer this, I understand that I've been guessing wrong about you from the start. Could I convince you to sign a contract promising you won't hate me for what I say next?"

"You don't need a contract. You'll be fine." It did sound pretty calculating coming out of his mouth this way, but she had an equally analytical mind. If she articulated the way she'd approached most of her dating relationships, it wouldn't sound much better. He'd been practical, and she could understand that. Mainly, though, she believed him when he said he would never take advantage of someone who wasn't interested in the same level of an uncommitted good time.

He took a deep breath. "So the single-woman-at-the-resort profile . . . I figured you were there either to snag one of the doctors, in which case I thought it might be fun to see if I could distract you. And if that's not what you were there for, then experience has shown that a lot of the women like flirting with the help."

"Like *Dirty Dancing?* Baby and Johnny?"

He smiled at her disbelief. "Yeah. Happens all the time."

"Wait, you know the movie?" That surprised her even more.

"I have three sisters. It was on a time or two, or two hundred, in my house growing up."

She nodded. "So you were basically seeing if I took the bait, and I did. Nice. I can't believe I confirmed all your awful stereotypes."

He dropped his head into his hands and groaned. "I kind of hate myself right now. You should kick me out." He scrubbed his hands through his hair and straightened. "But I'm never going to assume anything again. I'll let the stories unfold around people. Seems like a less cynical way to deal with the world anyway. I swear I'm cured."

She smiled. He was so earnest, like her sister's buy-me-a-puppy face. His shoulders relaxed a fraction when he saw her smile.

"I'm not going to kick you out," she said. "I do it too. Spot another doctor at a party and make assumptions. Sum up guys in a single glance. I get it. I probably wouldn't even care except—" She broke off, not wanting to rehash the contents of her note. *Except that I really liked you, and I felt stupid.*

"If I'd been able to see you for who you really are, I would have never even talked to you, and I don't mean that as an insult. I mean that I would have known right away that I would get lost in you." He took a deep breath and grew as still as she felt inside, every part of her having drawn a breath she didn't know how to release as she waited an eternity to hear his next words.

"I did, Brooke. I got lost in you. Having me here probably makes it feel like you tracked some annoying sand all the way home from Seashell Beach, but I have something else to say besides I'm sorry, and I need to get it out or wonder what if."

"What if . . . ?"

"I swear everything I told you about myself except for my job is true. You saw more of me than you think you did. So what if I told you I feel connected to you in a way I can't explain? I understand if you want to say thanks and move on, but I just couldn't let you think that you were the only one who felt something special."

Her insides felt the way the ocean had looked from the hotel roof last night: kinetic and restless and glinting. But these were flashes of hope, anticipation that wouldn't subside even as waves of common sense tried to swamp it. "Thank you for saying that." She kept her voice neutral. She still wasn't sure what he was doing in her kitchen other than being a standup guy. That was a good thing, and she appreciated him for it. But she didn't want that to be the only reason he'd chased her three hours down the coast, just so she wouldn't think he was a jerk.

Her words made his shoulders tense again, and she realized he'd hoped for a different reaction. He pushed back from the table and walked toward the door. Panic squeezed her insides. She didn't want him to go but didn't know how to say she wanted him to stay.

"Thanks for not calling the cops on me for stalking you," he said. "I'm sorry again I wasn't straight with you."

He opened the door.

"Wait," she said. "Do you think if I reported you for stalking it would mean you'd have to stay in town for a day or two?"

He turned toward her with a small smile. "Do you think they'd throw me in the Beverly Hills jail? Maybe it's nicer than other jails."

"We could find out," she said, her heart pounding.

"I don't really want to go to jail, even if it might be a fancy one. But I'd love to hang out with you here. I just . . . I can't read you, Brooke. You don't seem mad, but I can't tell how you feel."

She let out a long breath. "Confused. Part of me wants to throw myself at you, and part of me can't figure out the point when you'll have to turn around soon and go on living two hundred miles away. It scares me how much I want to pretend like that distance isn't a problem."

He dropped his hand from the doorknob and crossed to her in a few long steps, pulling her in for a long kiss, as hot as the first fiery one they'd shared by the well. She moaned and slid her hands around his neck, suddenly desperate to be close to him, wrapped around him, drowning in the taste of him. He slid his hands down her hips, backing her up, lifting her to sit on the countertop so he could step between her knees. He sank deeper into the kiss, and she followed him, loving the feel of the tense muscles in his back and chest, the hard pounding of his heart beneath her palm. She had no idea how long it was before they came up for air and he rested his hands on the tops of her thighs to run his thumb along the hem of her shorts while he let his breathing even out.

He rested his forehead against hers, and she traced his lips lazily, wondering what it was about their shape that made them so good for kissing.

"I Googled you too," he said after a minute. "You're amazing."

"Did you check my Yelp reviews or something?" she said, smiling. "Those reviewers are all hoping I'll see them and give them a complimentary Botox injection."

"I'm talking about Smiles from the Heart. Why didn't you tell me about that?"

She shifted in her seat like it had suddenly developed lumps. "I don't know. Seems like bragging. I talk about it to people who I'm trying get to fund it or work for it, but not really anyone else."

"Hold on," he said, easing away. She whimpered in protest, and he laughed and scooped her up, carrying her like a bride to the love seat, where he set her down with a soft kiss on her lips. "I'm going to grab something from my car. I'll be back in a second, I swear."

She barely had a minute to think about how crazy her evening had turned out to be when he was back with an iPad in his hand. He sat beside her and repositioned her legs so they lay across his lap. "I need to show you some pictures." He swiped through a series of stunning surf photos. "These are in Aschunchillo."

"That's beautiful. This is near the clinic where I operate."

"I know." He said it in a way that meant he was waiting for something.

She wrinkled her forehead and looked back at the pictures then at him. "What are you . . . I don't know what you're telling me."

"I took these pictures. Your website says you're down there next in November. That's an awesome time for surfing. I was thinking I would make that my next trip down too. I haven't shot Nicaragua in three years. What do you think? Do you even have time to breathe when you're there for surgery?"

"No."

His face fell.

She ran her finger across his lips again. "I want you to come anyway. Is that selfish?"

He smiled and drew her fingertip between his teeth to give it a light nip before answering. "Yes. I like it. Mostly because I hope it means I get to be selfish too. I think I'm going to start shooting in LA a lot more, and I want to lock up every minute of your free time that you'll give me." He set the iPad on the ground and leaned forward to kiss her again, and she melted into him, tilting her head so he could explore her mouth as she returned the favor. "How much free time can I have?" he murmured before moving to trail kisses down her neck, each brush of his lips igniting a tiny flame.

"What if I say all of it?"

His kiss gave her the perfect answer.

Part Three

Dreams Come True

One

Raegan Stone stretched her arms over her head until she felt the familiar pull of her shoulder muscles. It had been one of those days. Constant emails, dozens of phone calls, and finally she'd booked The Mariposa Hotel for the charity event of the season.

As the new events coordinator at the resort hotel in Shell Beach, Raegan was still digging out from under the disaster the last event coordinator had left behind. Mrs. Perry had been a cousin to the hotel manager or something, and her management was to collect a paycheck, make a million promises, then disappear on vacation while the hotel staff tried to carry out the convoluted instructions that were often scrawled onto the complimentary hotel pads of paper.

No longer. Raegan prided herself in her spreadsheets, in which she had half a dozen fully automated and linked pages that coordinated each event down to the number of rolls of toilet paper that were needed for the attending guests. If Raegan Stone was good at anything, it was details.

Her stint as a florist in north L.A. had given her experience with frantic customers as well as nourished her secret love for design. But it was impossible to become a designer in L.A. without spending hundreds of thousands of dollars attending the Fashion Design and Merchandising Institute. So Raegan had been relegated to working in one of the top L.A. florist shops, and when she heard about the job opening at The Mariposa up the coast, she'd been one of the first to apply.

"Coming to lunch, Raegan?" Jill asked, cutting into her thoughts. Jill was the director of catering, and their offices sat next to each other.

"I brought a bagel and juice," Raegan said.

Jill shook her head, red curls bouncing. "One of these days, I'm going to force you to eat a burger and fries."

"It's a plan," Raegan said with a smile. "I've got to finish these spreadsheets, so maybe next time."

"I'm holding you to that," Jill said. "Can I bring back anything?"

"No thanks. I'm fine." Raegan watched Jill grab her purse and leave the office. Jill was a carryover from the old system, and they'd butted heads quite a few times. But over the past few weeks, things had started running smoothly.

Raegan placed her hands on the keyboard in front of her and typed in "Booked," then highlighted it in yellow. Nothing was ever final, and her yellow highlighting kept the account active. The Dreams Come True charity organization she'd just booked was a relatively new one, but with the backing of prominent millionaires, it had gained attention by the media. The media always loved a sob story, and Dreams Come True was full of them. Raegan had to admit that her heartstrings had been tugged a time or two as well. Who wouldn't feel for the young girls shuffled from foster home to foster home, never having any real families and never getting opportunities for further education?

Dreams Come True raised money for college scholarships for those girls chosen by the program, and the girls also received a five-day, all-expenses-paid trip to Disneyland once a year. Disney quickly jumped on board, throwing in even more perks, and other theme parks jumped on the bandwagon as well. It seemed that if charity organizations could be a hot trend, Dreams Come True was at the top of the list.

And it didn't hurt that one of Hollywood's biggest producers had started the organization. With KC Wood's connections, actors and actresses had come forward, creating television ads and other campaigns to fundraise.

Raegan clicked over to her next spreadsheet. The *Who's Who* list was amazing. Actors who commanded millions of dollars per film were coming to the hotel for the event. She was sure millions would be raised and foster girls all over the nation would be accepted into the program. It all looked good on paper, Raegan supposed, but was it just another way for the actors and the movie industry to get media attention and thus raise their net value even more?

She guessed there was an underbelly of business tactics associated with every charity organization. A few more clicks on her computer, and Raegan pulled up the profile of KC Wood, founder of the charity. Surprisingly there was no picture of him, but Raegan painted one in her mind regardless. Hair implants, bleached hair, faux tan, Rolex, white veneered teeth. She was about to search out his picture on Google, but instead she got caught up in reading some of the vignettes submitted by girls who'd been selected by the charity.

Yep. The stories were tearjerkers. She was wiping away a

tear while reading one particular story when her phone rang. Even though Raegan was technically on lunch break, she picked up the phone.

"Mariposa events office," Raegan answered.

"Is this the events office?" a young woman asked on the other end of the phone.

Raegan tried not to let out a sigh. "Yes, how may I help you?"

"This is Tiffany, from Dreams Come True. I'm the personal assistant to Mr. Wood, and I'd like to discuss his suite accommodations."

"Let me transfer you to reserva—"

"I've already talked to them, and the man at reservations didn't seem to get what I need," the woman bulldozed over Raegan's offer. "I need to speak directly to the events manager."

Raegan cringed. This was one of *those* clients, and she happened to be KC Wood's personal assistant, which meant Raegan had to play nice. *The customer is always right*, she repeated in her head. "I'm Raegan Stone, and I'm the events manager."

"Finally," the woman said. "I figured the events manager would understand the need for Mr. Wood's complete privacy and the fact that I need to share his suite as well, but my name should not be on any of the receipts or documentation."

Raegan wanted to laugh out loud. So this young, pushy, female assistant was trying to keep her love affair with a prestigious film producer secret from the media and the hotel staff. Raegan had dealt with crazier situations, one involving an actor who insisted on brand-new, ironed sheets on his bed each night, and a high-powered executive who requested three power strips in her room. As a precaution, the reservations manager had brought in an electrician to give them an estimate of how much electricity the sockets would handle without an overload.

"We will be happy to keep your name off all documentation, Ms..."

"For your purposes, Tiffany is just fine. But you must keep that between you and me. Can I trust you, Raegan?"

Raegan had a sudden image flash to her mind of Tiffany walking around a private pool, wearing a white bikini, phone in one hand, glass of chilled wine in the other. Tonight after work, Raegan might laugh, but at this moment, everything inside her clenched with disgust. She loathed people who acted as if they owned the world and treated anyone without the same financial status as they were like an ant on the sidewalk. Tiny, insignificant, and squashable.

At the age of thirty-two, Raegan felt that she might be old enough to deserve respect from those younger than she. And Tiffany sounded like she was perhaps twenty. What was such a young woman doing as the assistant of someone like KC Wood? Not that Raegan had ever met or even seen Mr. Wood, but his name was on the credits of major blockbuster films, so she assumed he was in his late thirties, or forties, or even fifties.

Oh yeah, that's right, Tiffany is KC's hot young thing. Again, Raegan's imagination took over, and she pictured Tiffany walking beside that pool only to be joined by a fifty-something man wearing only board shorts and a Rolex.

"I'll text you the list of what's required in our room, and I expect you to delete it after the requirements are fulfilled," Tiffany continued. "You'll also save my name in your phone as *T assistant*. Did you get all of that?"

"Yes," Raegan said, although she was tempted to ask her to repeat it. But she knew she had to keep it professional. The customer might always be right, but it didn't mean Raegan had to like it.

Moments later, when Raegan had hung up with Tiffany and was picking at her bagel, a text came in from *T Assistant*. Raegan was grateful she wasn't drinking her juice, because she probably would have choked on it.

Tiffany's texted list had twelve items on it. All of them made Raegan's neck burn.

Two

Kevin Wood popped open the trunk of his car, then climbed out of the car to retrieve his bag. He'd driven the two hours from his LA home to Shell Beach, hoping the long drive would clear his head. His sister was suing him. Working in the film industry since he dropped out of college as a freshman, he'd seen plenty of lawsuits. He'd been at both ends of them.

But this was personal.

His sister had been a textbook case of the troubled teen. Although they'd both grown up in the same neighborhood with the same two parents and the same black Labrador, Rita took the hard way with everything. From her drug use to her teen pregnancy, to her parents getting custody of her daughter, Tiffany, to the most recent lawsuit against Kevin, everything was always everyone else's fault.

When he'd opened his mail from Rita's attorney that morning, his mood had plummeted. Despite the stacks of scripts on his home desk and two movies in final production, nothing sent his emotions into a ping-pong battle like Rita could. Since their parents' death two years ago, Kevin had taken over care of Tiffany. She was twenty now, but she looked to Kevin as an older brother-slash-father.

She was the reason he'd started the charity Dreams Come True. It was to involve Tiffany, who needed to stay busy and focused. She loved attention, and she was outgoing and beautiful—all things Rita would rob from her if she had a chance. Kevin had been to enough therapy appointments with his niece to know that her own mother was madly jealous of Tiffany.

Rita's latest judgment against Kevin claimed defamation of character. Rita claimed Kevin had turned Tiffany against her, and it was his fault their relationship was so poor. She claimed his charity Dreams Come True portrayed her as a terrible mother to the world and that Tiffany's "story" was full of lies.

Kevin had hired Tiffany as his assistant, but she also brought in the money from sponsors. When she got up in a crowd of people—as a beautiful, bubbly woman—and told how she spent her childhood moving from town to town while her mother was looking for the next hit, it brought people to tears. If Tiffany hadn't had her grandparents take over guardianship, she would have been thrown into the foster system.

Kevin still remembered the tear-filled phone call from his mother when they had located Rita after she'd gone missing with her daughter for years. "We found her, Kevin. Tiffany is safe with us."

Since the death of his parents, the emotional rollercoaster had taken its toll, and Kevin had stopped most things he loved—things that used to give him a stress outlet. Now he was lucky if he ran a couple of times a week or read a book for fun or watched a movie he hadn't produced himself. But he was grateful Tiffany was in a really good place right now, and though he'd had to dig deep for patience as she worked with him hand-in-hand on the charity, things ran relatively smoothly.

Until this morning. And it would have to come on the day that he was supposed to be checking into The Mariposa for the annual charity gala. In its third year, Dreams Come True had attracted mostly favorable attention, and a half dozen notable actors would be attending the event this weekend. Tiffany was ecstatic. Every time someone confirmed, she called him, squealing about it.

That thought made him smile. If he could only forget Rita and her poor choices and focus on the good that came from them—Tiffany—then he could find something to be happy about.

Carrying his bag into the hotel, he checked his phone. Two texts from Liz. He let out a groan. They'd been on again, off again for several years, and apparently now she wanted to be on again. Liz was model gorgeous, but she was one of those women who used her looks to manipulate those around her.

There was a reason Kevin worked out of his home for the most part; he even had his production meetings in his spacious living room. He avoided the smooze fests that went on in the movie industry. The less he was around the ladder-climbers, the more work he could produce. This weekend was an exception. He'd come on Thursday so he could spend the evening and the following morning preparing for the board meeting that would take place on Friday afternoon.

Walking into the hotel, he was surprised to see the reservation desk empty of employees. He glanced around for the concierge, but that station was empty too. Showing up at 1:00 p.m. on a Thursday could be any hotel's dead hour, and it seemed no one was in sight. He eyed the ringer on the reservation desk and walked toward it.

Just as he was about to ring it, a woman came out of a door to the side of the reservation desk. She didn't have a typical hotel uniform on but was dressed nicely, as if she was a manager or something. Her dark hair was smooth and straight, and she had the deepest blue eyes Kevin had ever seen. For a moment he just stared at her, thinking she could easily be in the film industry with her kind of face.

"Oh, sorry. There's no one here," she said. "Do you need to check in?"

He barely had a chance to say, "I do," when she turned away.

"Let me go find someone." She opened the door she'd come out of, hesitated for a second, then turned back to face him.

Kevin blinked a couple of times, trying to tell himself he hadn't just been checking her out. But the list tallied in his head anyway: about 5'8, average build, skin that looked like she'd babied it . . . and those eyes. What was wrong with him? This woman was beautiful, but he worked around beautiful women all of the time. As she came in again and walked toward him, he tried to figure out why he was so struck by her.

"I think it will be faster if I just send a couple of texts." She smiled at him. "Sorry about this." She looked down at her phone.

Kevin was smiling back, like a twelve-year old boy to his crush, but she wasn't even looking at him.

"It's probably just a miscommunication," she continued. Kevin noticed the light freckles across her nose. "Paulie might've thought she was cleared for her lunch break, but

José had to log in some specific requests for the charity event this weekend."

Kevin wasn't completely listening to what she was saying. Instead, he looked at her ring finger—no wedding band, but that didn't necessarily mean anything in today's world. He guessed her to be about thirty, five years younger than he. Maybe she was divorced with a couple of kids. Maybe she had a boyfriend. Maybe she was very happily married. With those eyes and her low sweet voice, there was no way she was single.

"It's all right," he said when she looked up at him after typing into her phone. "I'm here at an odd time. Although, I was hoping my room would be ready."

"I'd check you in myself, but I'm afraid you might end up in the laundry room."

He laughed. "Are you the hotel manager?"

She returned his laugh. "Hardly. I'm Raegan, the events coordinator."

He stuck out his hand. "Kevin."

"Welcome to The Mariposa, Kevin," she said, shaking his hand slowly, her eyes still filled with laughter. "I hope you'll enjoy your stay . . . as soon as we can get you checked in."

"I'm sure I will," Kevin said, wanting to smack his own head as the cheesy words came out. He released her hand, reluctant to do so for some reason, and wondered if it would be too forward to ask her out to dinner. *I must be sleep deprived.* One meeting with a strange, beautiful employee, and all of a sudden he was daydreaming about asking her out for dinner tonight.

"Oh, I'm so sorry," a woman's voice interrupted. A blonde woman rushed around the corner, smoothing her short hair back. Her name badge read *Paulie, Front Desk*. "I'll get you checked in right away, sir. Are you here for the charity gala?"

"I am," Kevin said, handing over his credit card.

Raegan disappeared through a door behind the reception desk before he had a chance to thank her or say anything more.

Paulie took the card from him, read the name, and her eyes widened. "Oh, Mr. *Wood*, it's wonderful to meet you." She held out her hand above the counter, and Kevin shook it, trying not to groan.

Her face flushed when their hands touched, and her eyes lingered a bit too long on him. It was the money, he thought, and the name, and the illusion of his glass-bubbled world that attracted the women. And this Paulie apparently was no different.

"I hope it's all right that I'm here a little early," he said. "My assistant will be checking in tomorrow."

"Of course, no problem." Paulie's smile was huge.

It made Kevin feel a little queasy. He was thirty-five, unmarried, unattached, and he wasn't interested, even though Paulie was making it more than clear that she was. He took the room key she offered and nodded politely as she told him about the pool hours and the laundry facilities. "Although," she rattled on, "I'm sure your assistant will handle those types of things. But our staff is here to help you with anything, Mr. Wood."

Another smile from Paulie.

Kevin thanked her and stepped away. A quick glace around the hotel lobby confirmed that Raegan hadn't come back out; she was nowhere to be seen. He headed for the elevators. He'd get settled in his room, then scout out the ballroom where the gala would be held. Maybe he could request that Raegan give him an official tour. He usually didn't care so much about these sort of details—he left that to Tiffany—but he wanted to see Raegan again.

Three

"Wow," Raegan muttered as she told herself what had just happened in the lobby with Kevin hadn't *really* happened. She hadn't been struck with lightning-stunning attraction to a random guy who was staying at the hotel. Dark and slightly wavy hair, warm brown eyes, and nice, broad shoulders. He was obviously in good shape, but not one of those marathon-runner types who was too thin and jittery. Kevin was maybe six inches taller than she, the perfect size to hug . . . what was she thinking?

This was why as soon as Paulie appeared, Raegan had left, grabbed her utility bag from her office, then walked the long way through the halls until she reached the elevator. All without hardly taking a breath or allowing herself to fully absorb the attraction zinging through her.

Raegan was far from interested in any relationship—be it a fling or longer. After the past six years of on-again, off-again dating with Brandon—who could never completely commit—she'd walked away from him once and for all.

Raegan needed time to just be Raegan. Not "Brandon's girlfriend" or anyone else.

Raegan pushed the elevator button, and when the doors opened, she slipped inside. She refocused on her current to-do list and what she could make herself busy with until her rational mind took over. Up on the third floor was a neglected floral arrangement. Raegan took pride in the fresh flowers she brought in twice a week and arranged herself. Sure, she could pass the task onto one of her staff members, but flower arranging was something Raegan still loved.

It would be the perfect activity after running into that man—the man who set her heart racing and made her voice sound too high-pitched. The elevator dinged open, and Raegan wiped her hands on her pants. She was sweating—really? Unbelievable.

What was this? A mid-life crisis at the age of thirty-two?

She shook her head as she walked toward the foyer that was on every level of The Mariposa. The lobby on the main floor was exquisite, but one of Raegan's favorite features in this hotel was that each floor also had a lobby of its own. They were more secluded than was the main lobby, and many of their visitors commented on that fact.

Raegan arrived at the foyer and surveyed the drooping flowers. It must have just been a bad batch. She'd arranged the flowers the day before, and they'd been on the cusp of blooming. Today, they should have been in their full, glorious bloom. Instead, the pink and yellow roses were still closed and turning brown on the edges. The daisies were the only flowers that seemed to have any life.

She picked up the vase and tilted it to see how much water remained. Maybe she'd forgotten the water?

"Raegan?"

The voice startled her, and the vase slipped from her hands, crashing to the floor. The vase didn't break, since it landed on the massive area rug, but flowers and water spilled everywhere. In the back of her mind, Raegan was aware that Kevin was the one who'd startled her, and he was now rushing over to help her clean up the mess.

Of all the people, of all the moments...

"Sorry," he said. "Let me help you."

Her heart was hammering so hard she didn't reply for a moment. She wasn't upset by the accident—she was glad the vase hadn't broken, and the flower arrangement might have had to be thrown out anyway—but how was she supposed to get this guy out of her head? Two chance meetings in the same twenty minutes.

"Thanks," she said as she gathered the roses from the rug, careful not to bunch them together and bruise the petals.

Kevin put the vase back on the alcove, then picked up all the greenery and daisies.

When she rose, holding the roses, he was standing there with the dripping mass of daisies in his hands, looking like a sheepish six-year-old just caught throwing a rock at a car.

"I'm so sorry," he started, but Raegan cut him off.

"Really, it's all right. This arrangement was having issues anyway."

He raised a brow and continued to stare at her in a way that made her feel too hot. "Can flowers have *issues*?"

She had to smile, so she did, despite her better judgement. "They very much can have issues. Big issues, you know. I mean, flowers are perhaps the most emotional plants in the world."

"Really," Kevin deadpanned. "Like what kind of issues?"

Raegan crossed to the alcove, not wanting him to see her blush madly. She started putting the roses into the vase, one by one. "Take the rose for instance," she said. "It can bruise easily when mishandled."

Kevin joined her next to the alcove. "And the daisy? What's her issue?"

"She loves the sun, so she pouts when she has to stay inside."

Kevin laughed, which made Raegan feel all melty inside. She tried to snap out of it—this mini-infatuation she had with this guy. She'd finally started feeling like herself again after the deadend relationship with Brandon. She'd found her center, her true self, or whatever the latest trendy word for it was.

Bottom line, she was enjoying just being Raegan. She was happy. Content. And this stranger with a contagious laugh and dreamy eyes had nothing to offer her. Nothing at all. Right?

He was leaning on the shelf, watching her with a crooked smile on his face, as if she was the only person in the room. Well, she was technically the only person around, so correct that to the only person in the hotel, or Shell Beach, or even the world. The thought sent a tingle across her arms.

This was ridiculous. Raegan reached for the daisies, and Kevin handed them over.

"That's looking remarkably decent," he said.

Raegan lifted a brow and slid her gaze over to him. "Do you know much about flower arranging?"

"Nothing at all," Kevin said. "I just know when I see something I like."

But he wasn't looking at the flowers any longer. This guy had no problem with eye contact, and Raegan didn't know exactly what to make of that.

Four

Kevin could literally see the interest in Raegan's blue eyes. He had to admit, it was a boost to his male ego that she was interested in him, but not because she was a beautiful woman. It was because she was real . . . from her smile, to her curvy body, to the green stains on her fingers from floral arranging. She wasn't the made-up, surgically enhanced, botoxed women he met at many of the promotion events he attended.

Kevin was quite surprised that he was so drawn to this woman. It wasn't like he was looking for a relationship—or even had time for one—and despite some of the habits of his colleagues, he wasn't looking for a fling with random women he met in hotels. Not that she was here on vacation or anything; she worked at the hotel.

And he found her charming, especially as she listed the emotional attributes of various flower species. "Are you married? Kids?" he asked, when she paused to turn back to her flower arranging.

The moment he asked the questions, he wanted to take them back. He couldn't have been more obvious, but then again he was thirty-five. Couldn't he ask a beautiful woman a straight-forward question?

"No, and no," she said, lifting her right brow slightly. A tiny dimple appeared above her eyebrow. Kevin found it fascinating.

"And you? Lovely wife, three children at home?" she countered.

He laughed. "No and no."

"Gamer?"

He shook his head, still grinning.

"Creep?"

"No, just busy."

"Ah. One of those." Raegan reached for the greenery he still held.

He gave it up, easily, catching a whiff of her subtle perfume. He knew enough that her scent wasn't from one of those cheap body sprays. His mother had worn the real stuff—and apparently Raegan did too.

"It's all about the career—not enough time for anything else," she continued, her tone light and teasing.

But Kevin knew she was feeling him out as well, trying to figure out what kind of man he was. "The career is part of it," he said. "But the older I get, the more complicated life becomes."

Raegan gave a sage nod, although her eyes were gleaming. "You couldn't be more right."

"I like being told I'm right," Kevin said with a wink.

"Of course you do." Raegan did another adjustment on the flowers. "There. What do you think?"

Kevin looked at the arrangement. It certainly didn't look like it had been spread across the floor just a few moments before. "You're really good at that—it looks like a professional arrangement."

DREAMS COME TRUE

"Well, it is," Raegan said. "I used to work at a florist shop before coming here." She gave him a sideways glance. "What industry are you in?"

"Film, mostly," Kevin said, sliding his hands into his pockets. Was she teasing him again?

"Are you here for the charity gala this weekend?" Raegan said.

"Of course," Kevin said, wanting to laugh at her question; but she didn't seem to be joking. "I heard the hotel is fully booked."

"I think it is." Raegan turned her blue gaze on him. "I'm usually too caught up in the events to know the number of room bookings, but the charity gala is all everyone has talked about for weeks." She brushed her hands together and stepped away from the alcove. "Dreams Come True . . . that's a pretty clever name."

"Thanks," Kevin said. His cell phone rang, and he glanced at the caller. Tiffany. He should have called her as soon as he arrived to tell her about his change of plans.

"Go ahead and get that," Raegan said. "I've got to see if any of the other floral arrangements need my attention."

Kevin sent the call to voicemail. "I'll call back in a minute. I wanted to know if, uh, you're free tonight. Maybe we could meet for dinner at the hotel restaurant, and you could tell me all about Shell Beach?"

Raegan hesitated, but Kevin was glad to see she wasn't put off by his question, merely surprised. He was surprised himself.

"I . . . Maybe. I can't guarantee anything."

She'd said *maybe*. That was a good sign, right? "When do you get off?"

"It just depends on what's going on," Raegan said. "Usually about 5:30."

Kevin decided then and there that he loved her smile. She didn't have large fake, white teeth framed by botox-red lips. "Great to meet you," he said, sticking out his hand. A bit formal, but when she took his hand, he was grateful he'd offered. And when she didn't pull away immediately, he hoped that meant something as well.

Hoped he'd be seeing her at 5:30.

As Kevin walked down the hallway to his room, energy zinged through his body. He felt like he could go for a run and get in another couple of extra miles than normal. It had been a long time since he'd felt this way after asking a woman out. Too long. The next few hours would drag, that was for sure.

His phone started to ring again as he slid the keycard into the hotel room door.

"Hey, Tiff," he said, balancing the phone on his shoulder as he carried his bag inside and set it on the couch in the living area. Tiffany had booked a two-bedroom suite.

"You're there a day early?" she said into the phone. "How come you didn't tell me?"

"I did—I left a message."

"KC, you know what I mean," she said, a pout in her voice. "I had everything arranged. Your favorite treats are supposed to be waiting and—"

"Let me guess," he cut in, "chocolate-covered strawberries and sparkling water?"

She laughed. "And fresh flowers—are there fresh flowers?"

Kevin scanned the room, thinking of Raegan at the mention of flowers. On a side table near the immense window was a gorgeous arrangement. "As a matter of fact, there are fresh flowers."

"Oh good, at least they got that right," Tiffany said.

"You know, I'm not a celebrity," Kevin said. "Some people might get the wrong idea if you keep demanding this kind of stuff."

"Oh, KC, let me take care of you—that's what you're paying me for," she said in a cheerful tone. "Besides, it's no trouble at all when I'm spending your money."

"Yeah," he said with a chuckle. "That's what I figured. When the strawberries show up, I'll save a couple for you."

"You'd better!" Tiffany said.

Kevin laughed. He loved it when his niece was in a good mood. He decided to wait before telling her about her mother's lawsuit. It could wait until he absolutely had to.

Five

The phone was ringing when Raegan walked back into her office. She snatched it up and answered, only to be filled with dread. It was Tiffany calling again. "KC checked in early, did you know that? And the things that I ordered aren't there."

Raegan clicked onto her calendar on her computer. It was Thursday, and the gala was on Saturday. "Which day was he supposed to check in?"

"Tomorrow, but—"

"Everything you ordered is scheduled for tomorrow," Raegan said, trying to keep her voice light and smooth.

"But he's there today," Tiffany protested. "And he's expecting—"

Raegan let out a silent sigh as the young woman on the phone went over everything they'd already gone over. At the end of the tirade, Raegan simply said, "We'll get everything in as soon as possible. If you have any more concerns, you can speak with reservations. Do you want me to transfer you?"

The phone went dead. "Hello? Tiffany?"

Raegan shook her head. How could she go from the pitter-patter elation of flirting with Kevin on the third floor, to utter disgust and despair? She dialed reservations. "Paulie? I have a huge favor to ask of you..."

Five minutes later, Raegan had effectively delegated all of Tiffany's demands and could now focus on double-checking that everything was running smoothly with the gala that weekend. Just as she hung up with Rob, the audio visual director, Jill came into her office.

"Do you ever take a break?" Jill asked, folding her arms and leaning against the doorway.

"As a matter of fact, I went up to the third floor and rescued some flowers," Raegan said. "And got asked out to dinner by a hot guy."

Jill's mouth fell open. "Wait. What?"

Raegan laughed at Jill's astonishment. "Kevin... Forgot to get his last name, but we're going to dinner tonight at the hotel restaurant. Totally original, I know."

"Oh. My. Gosh." Jill clapped her hand over her mouth. "You're serious! You're totally blushing."

Raegan touched her cheeks. "I am. Wow."

"Oh no," Jill said, her mouth pulling into a frown. "I have to leave in an hour to pick up my kids."

"And?" Raegan prompted.

"And I won't be able to see this Kevin guy." She snapped her fingers. "I know, take a selfie with him."

"You're kidding me, right? I'm not thirteen."

Jill blew out a breath of frustration, but her eyes were twinkling. "I'm happy for you anyway," she said, crossing to Raegan and giving her a hug. "And if there's any way to work in a casual photo, text it to me!"

"You're funny," Raegan said. "He's staying at the hotel, so it's not like I'm going to see him again."

"Good point," Jill said, straightening. "But that makes it all the more romantic. Hot date. One night. Anything could happen."

"Please," Raegan said. "Don't make me regret telling you."

After Jill went back to her office, Raegan found that she was checking the clock way too often. Where was an all-consuming crisis when she needed one to pass the time? For some reason that she didn't want to analyze, she found that she was staring out the window a lot and replaying the conversations she'd had with Kevin. She knew she was overanalyzing everything, and she told herself that was the only reason she'd be meeting him at 5:30. To burst her own bubble.

She spent a few minutes in the bathroom, trying to refresh her makeup with only the lip-gloss in her purse and then finger-combing her hair. She narrowed her eyes at her reflection, seeing that she was definitely not in her twenties any more. Well, there was nothing more she could do now. Kevin was going to get her thirty-two-year-old self as a dinner date.

Raegan was sure that by the end of the meal, she'd have a good list of why Kevin was a harmless flirtation and nothing more. Despite her attraction, she was sure that, just like in an episode of *Seinfeld*, she'd discover a deal breaker soon enough. And that was assuming Kevin was completely interested in her, not the idea of a random woman at a vacation resort hotel who happened to be available for dinner.

Striding out of the restroom, Raegan shouldered her purse and headed for the hotel restaurant. It would be a bit

DREAMS COME TRUE

awkward at first since she knew the regular employees and they'd be witnessing the date firsthand.

"Raegan," someone called out behind her.

She turned to see Mari. "Did you just get to work?" Raegan asked. She hadn't seen her all day.

"Yes, working full shifts this weekend," Mari said with a sigh. "I guess there's a big event." Her brown eyes twinkled.

"I might know something about that," Raegan said.

Mari laughed. "I'm actually pretty excited to see some of these hotshots up close." She lowered her voice. "Not so excited to clean up after them."

"Can't wait to hear the stories," Raegan said. "I'm sure there'll be some good ones." She was about to launch into her experience with Tiffany, but the housekeeping manager poked her head out of a nearby room and motioned for Mari to help her.

"Gotta run," Mari said. "You off for the day?"

Raegan nodded. She'd tell Mari about her date later. If there was one friend she could confide in at the hotel, it was Mari. Raegan had enjoyed their friendship over the past few months, swapping horror stories about quirky guests.

Raegan continued down the corridor, then slowed as she approached the lobby. Her heart was thudding like mad. This was perhaps one of the craziest things she'd ever done. At least she wasn't going off-location with him. Kevin was nowhere in the lobby, and Raegan was trying to decide if she should check the restaurant, when he stepped out of the elevator.

Their gazes met, and Kevin smiled.

Raegan found herself smiling, then schooled herself to not seem too excited. She meant to keep this all light-hearted, even though her pulse was drumming.

"You made it," Kevin said, crossing to her.

"I finished everything for today, and since I was feeling kind of hungry, I thought I might see what you're up to."

"Funny," Kevin said, grinning. "I wasn't quite sure if I'd be seeing you again, so this is a nice surprise."

"Do you like surprises?" Raegan asked, falling into his flirtatious trap.

"Good ones," Kevin said, tilting his head. "What about you?"

"We have something in common it seems." She adjusted her purse on her shoulder.

"Let's go see if there are any good surprises on the menu then," Kevin said.

As Raegan walked beside him, she was struck by his easy gait and how natural his height felt to hers. He wasn't too tall, like Brandon sometimes felt. As they walked the short distance to the restaurant, he said, "How long have you worked at this hotel?"

"About six months," she said. "It was a big change at first, coming from a florist shop, but the customer service portion wasn't too different."

"How so?" Kevin asked, looking over at her.

"Oh . . ." Raegan realized she had almost criticized the wealthy and famous and their demands at the posh florist shop she'd worked at. She didn't know how Kevin fit into the scheme of things with his work in the film industry, but surely he was friends with a lot of those wealthy and famous people. "Customer service is always entertaining."

He raised a brow and laughed. "I'm sure you have a lot of stories."

They'd reached the host stand, and Raegan was relieved that the host tonight was a new woman she didn't know. Soon they were seated at a quiet table next to a huge window overlooking the ocean.

"This view is amazing," Kevin said, gazing out over the panorama.

"Yeah, I've been spoiled," Raegan said. "I need to take the time to appreciate it more."

He leaned back in his chair, his gaze sliding over to her. "Living in a tourist town where people come to relax probably isn't the same for you."

"Living the dream at some point becomes work," Raegan agreed.

"True," Kevin said.

Their waitress appeared, and her eyes widened when she looked at Kevin. "Welcome to The Mariposa Restaurant. C-Can I get you something to drink?"

Raegan knew who the waitress was by name—Cathy—but they hadn't really spoken. Cathy's face flushed, and Raegan was suddenly very interested in how Kevin would react. Raegan agreed that he was good looking, but not like one of those drop-dead-gorgeous actors who'd be coming to the gala this weekend.

Raegan ordered water with lemon; then Cathy turned to Kevin, her coloring deepening. While Kevin ordered a drink and an appetizer, Raegan couldn't help but notice Cathy's hands shaking while she wrote down his order.

Really strange, Raegan thought.

"Thank you, sir," Cathy said in a breathless voice. "I'll bring out your drink right away." She turned away, then rotated back. "And did I tell you it's a pleasure to have you as a guest at our hotel this weekend?"

Raegan frowned. Cathy was really going overboard.

"I appreciate that," Kevin said, glancing at her name tag, "Cathy."

The waitress's face couldn't have grown any redder. "I'll be right back, Mr. Wood."

Raegan stared after Cathy. Mr. Wood? *Kevin Wood.* She hadn't asked his last name, and now that she knew it, something cold rushed through her. She looked over at Kevin, who'd opened the menu and was scanning the contents.

"I should have asked her about tonight's special," he said, lifting his gaze to Raegan and giving her a half-smile. A smile that might have melted Raegan's heart . . . but . . .

"Your name is Kevin Wood?" she asked in a faint voice.

His brows lifted. "Yeah. I told you my name, right? You didn't just meet a complete stranger for dinner, did you?"

He was teasing her, but it was as if Raegan had been caught in a cold rain. "Why is that so familiar?"

"The public calls me KC, but my name is Kevin—" He stopped. "Wait, what's wrong?"

Raegan needed a drink of water, but Cathy hadn't returned yet. Kevin—KC—KC Wood. She was having dinner with *KC Wood*, one of Hollywood's most prestigious producers. The phone call from Tiffany echoed through her mind, the demands, the favors, the secrecy. Tiffany would be arriving the next day and sharing his suite. Kevin was in a relationship with a twenty-something blonde bombshell.

Well, to be fair, Raegan didn't know if Tiffany was blonde, but that wasn't the point.

She brought her hand to her mouth and inhaled, hardly believing this was happening to her. She should have known that the connection she felt toward Kevin was too good to true. He was a player, the worst sort of kind. The kind that asked her out within minutes and wasn't afraid to take her to dinner in front of all her co-workers, flaunting his station in life.

"Here you are, Mr. Wood." Cathy was back, drinks and appetizers on a tray. She set down the things on the table, then pulled out a pad of paper from her apron pocket. "I hope I'm not imposing. But could you sign this paper for my nephew? Actually, sign one for me and one for my nephew. He'll be ecstatic."

Raegan watched in disbelief as Kevin obliged, writing a short note, then signing the pad of paper. He spoke with Cathy for a few more minutes, although Raegan had no idea what he said. Her mind was racing, drowning out all comprehension. All she knew was that she had to leave. She had to think, and she couldn't do it in the middle of the restaurant with people watching and with her pretending to enjoy a conversation with Kevin.

Raegan realized that people *were* watching, and she hadn't noticed it before. Glances shot their way from the surrounding tables—glances that admired and appraised, not only Kevin, but Raegan.

"Excuse me," Raegan said, rising to her feet. She picked up her purse and clutched it against her chest.

Kevin and Cathy both looked at her in surprise.

"I suddenly remembered that I . . . uh . . . forgot about something. I need to go, and I—sorry." She stepped back from the table, looking at anything but him.

"Raegan," Kevin said, rising to his feet as well. He flashed Cathy a smile, then looked back to Raegan. "I'll walk you out."

"No, it's all right," Raegan said. "Very sorry." She took another step back, then turned and walked out of the restaurant, her heart pounding so hard that she was sure everyone could hear it.

She thought she heard Kevin call her name again, but she didn't turn around to be sure. She crossed through the lobby. Thankfully there was a line at the check-in counter, and no one paid attention to her.

Only once she was settled in her car, the door shut firmly, keys in the ignition, did she allow the shock to reverberate through her. For the past several hours, she'd been living in a *what-if* dream, and that dream had just turned into a thunderstorm.

Angry tears spilled onto her cheeks. The worst part of it was that she'd allowed herself to hope. She decided that she hated every woman who'd ever been seduced by Kevin Wood, but most of all, she hated herself.

Six

Kevin paced the lobby, although it was only 7:00 am. He'd been up for hours and finally, at 5:30, he'd gone for a long run. The beach had been stunning in the early morning light, and the cool ocean wind had cleared his mind just a little.

What he really needed to do was speak with Raegan. Her abrupt departure the night before wasn't normal, that he knew. But what was going on? He'd told her his name, and after tossing and turning all night trying to come up with a reason, he realized that he hadn't told her his last name. Or had he?

It was all a blur now. But Raegan knew he was there for the gala, and he was almost certain he'd said something about working in film. Still, Kevin had the feeling that she hadn't known who he was. Somehow she'd been blind-sided at the restaurant last night.

And it bothered him to no end that the only woman he'd been interested in for a long time seemed to have an issue with his career. He admitted that living in the

Hollywood spotlight for years might intimidate a woman used to small-town life, but Raegan hadn't seemed particularly intimidated . . . more like disappointed, or even disgusted.

He exhaled with frustration. But then again, could he really blame her? Maybe that was why he'd never been in a solid, long-term relationship. Those types of women stayed away from men like him.

His phone buzzed, and he looked down at the incoming e-mail. Rita's lawyer was up early. Kevin clicked on the email and skimmed through the formal language. It was as he suspected. A lawsuit had been officially filed, and now he'd have to tell Tiffany. He'd wait until after the gala—no use making both of them upset.

Kevin only hoped he could keep it away from the media.

It was Friday, and Kevin decided Raegan probably didn't come into work until 8:00 or 9:00. He went up to his room and showered, wishing he'd gotten her number. And then as soon as he thought it, he berated himself for obsessing about a woman he'd just met and whom he barely knew.

Despite his arguing mind, he found himself back in the lobby after his shower. He sat in one of the chairs facing the hotel entrance and scrolled through the emails on his phone, keeping an eye on who was coming and going.

"Hello, Mr. Wood," a cheerful voice greeted him.

He looked up to see the thirty-something desk clerk—Paulie—standing in front of him. "Hi, Paulie," he said, and a full blush spread across her face.

She toyed with the pendant on her necklace as if she was nervous to be around him. All smiles and fluttery eyes. Irony at its finest. The woman he was interested in had taken off last night in a hurry, and a woman he wasn't interested in was practically begging him with her eyes to ask her out.

"How's your stay so far?" Paulie asked. She tilted her head, then rubbed her pink lipsticked lips together.

"Great so far," he said. "Went for a run this morning. The beaches are beautiful."

Paulie grinned. "We try."

Kevin laughed. "Hey, I wondered if you happen to know Raegan's schedule."

"Raegan in Events?" Paulie said, her brows drawing together.

How many Raegans were there at the hotel? "Yes, the woman who helped me yesterday."

Paulie's eyes widened, and then it was as if something clicked in her mind. Her smile was slow, knowing. "She'll be in today." Paulie looked toward the doors. "Probably soon. She's kind of a workaholic."

Kevin nodded, hoping he hadn't revealed his true interest. But it was too late now to take it back.

"She's a bit of a serious lady," Paulie said, her blue eyes assessing him. "Broke up with her longtime boyfriend a few months ago, and I don't think she's been dating since. Of course, anyone would be dumb to turn down a date from you." She laughed, and it ended in a high-pitched crescendo.

Kevin's mouth almost fell open. Apparently he was transparent.

"I think his name was Jack or Jordan, or something generic like that . . . Not that your name is totally unique. But KC is more unique than most, right?"

Before he could fathom a reply, Paulie barreled on. "Raegan is new at this job, you know, and she butted heads with a few of the staff when she came on. She's very organized, you know. I guess that could be a good thing or a bad thing, depending on how you want to look at it."

Keven realized Paulie wasn't going to hold anything back. An uncomfortable itch spread along the back of his neck. It was one thing asking when Raegan would be into work—quite another to be told her life history.

Paulie took a step closer and lowered her voice. "Probably not your type, if you were to ask me. She's a bit of a stiff, if you know what I mean. Gets caught up in the details, which is perfect for working in Events." She winked at Kevin. "She is pretty, though, I'll give you that. You're not the first man who's tried to pick up on her at the hotel."

He really didn't know what to think. Should he be offended? "I just wanted to ask her about something to do with the gala this weekend."

"Oh," Paulie said, her tone turning more businesslike. "Well, then. I suppose I can let her know you have a question." Her eyes narrowed, and a gleam crept into them. "I could give you her personal number, you know. If you call the events office, Jill might answer . . . unless you aren't particular."

Kevin exhaled. "I'll just call the events office." He rose to his feet, feeling like he needed to leave the lobby and Paulie behind as quickly as possible. "Thanks, Paulie."

She flashed him a smile and another blush.

Turning, Kevin headed back through the hotel. Instead of going back up to his room, where all he'd be greeted with was silence and emails about lawsuits, he headed toward the pool area. It was open, although no one was using it yet. Keeping vigilance in the lobby was no longer an option, not with Paulie on duty at the front desk.

He pushed open the glass door leading to the pool and found a chair beneath an umbrella table. In the cool shade of the warming day, he looked up the hotel directory on his phone. When he found the events number, he clicked CALL.

It rang three times, and then it went into voicemail. The woman's voice that came on wasn't Raegan's, but Kevin didn't let that deter him.

"Hi, this is KC Wood. I'm calling for Raegan. If you can return my call as soon as you can, that would be great," he said into his phone, then left his number.

He ended the call. There was nothing more he could really do. It was time to pull his head out of dreamland and get to work.

Seven

"There's a message for you on the main line," Jill called to Raegan as she entered her office.

Raegan paused, then stepped back into the corridor. Jill had come out of her office, a smile on her face.

"Who was it?"

"You'll just have to listen to it," Jill said. "And once you do, I want all the details from last night. You never sent me a picture."

Raegan's face flushed. "We'll talk in a minute." She returned to her desk and picked up the hotel phone, then dialed into the voicemail. When Kevin's voice came on the line, her heart thudded. *KC,* she told herself. *He's KC Wood.* Kevin, or KC, she wasn't sure what to call him now, was a slime ball. That's what she should call him.

What kind of guy was he—hitting on her when his twenty-something girlfriend-slash-assistant was arriving today? She supposed it was the Hollywood way, but she was not interested, at all. Mostly, she was upset that she'd even allowed herself to be tempted. She should have known a good-looking, charming, single guy like him was too good to be true.

"So?" Jill walked into her office, carrying a Dr. Pepper. She sat in the chair opposite of Raegan's desk.

Raegan didn't know how Jill could stand drinking soda so early in the morning. "Well..."

"Wait," Jill said, holding up her hand. "Before you tell me about last night, what's up with KC Wood calling you directly? Doesn't he have people to handle that for him?"

Raegan released a sigh. "He does. Specifically a blonde bombshell named Tiffany—at least, she sounds that way on the phone—no offense to any blondes out there." She looked away from Jill's confused gaze. "The guy I went to dinner with last night—Kevin—is actually KC Wood." She ignored Jill's gasp. "I didn't know who he really was until the waitress started acting all weird."

"Oh. My. Gosh," Jill said. "You're kidding!"

"No. Not at all." Raegan was well over the shock and dismay. Now she was just tired and wanted to get back to work. Stay as busy as possible.

"And he just called you on the main number, which means you didn't give him your cell." Jill leaned forward in her chair. "Raegan, you'd better tell me what happened."

"I left before we even ordered," Raegan said, moving her gaze toward the window to focus on something besides Jill's shocked expression. "I felt like an idiot. Here I was, having dinner with a major Hollywood producer, and I hadn't even realized it. I just thought he was generic Kevin."

"Wow," Jill said under her breath. "I need a moment to catch up."

"So did I, and that's why I left." Raegan shook her head. "I can't decide which I feel the most ridiculous about.

Flirting with a stranger whom I didn't recognize as an incredibly famous and well-known film producer. Or hours later, ditching him at a restaurant in front of a staff who all know me by name."

Jill was silent for a moment. "I see your dilemma. But I think you leaving him at the restaurant takes the cake."

Raegan groaned and let her head drop into her hands. "It's pretty awful, I know. And now he expects me to return his call—which will just bring me further humiliation."

"You sort of do owe him an explanation," Jill said, twisting open the soda cap and taking a drink of her Dr. Pepper. "I mean, he *will* be here all weekend. What if you run into him?"

Raegan raised her head. "I've thought of that, which is why I plan to stay in my office the whole time."

"You could never do that—not with your perfectionism. There's a major gala going on, remember?" Jill teased. "Who will double- and triple-check everything until the entire staff is annoyed?"

Raegan groaned again.

"Look, call him back, tell him the truth, and be done with it," Jill said, then narrowed her eyes. "By the way, what *is* the truth? Why can't you go out to dinner with a hot film producer?"

Raegan closed her eyes. "Tiffany."

"The blonde assistant? What does she have to do with you?"

"She's sharing his hotel room, so you know . . ."

Jill mouthed an O. "That makes things more complicated."

"That makes things nonexistent," Raegan corrected. She released a sigh. "But, you're right. I should at least call to explain. Not that the conversation will be a very pleasant one."

Jill was watching Raegan, a puzzled expression on her face.

"What?" Raegan said.

"I just . . . I thought I read an article recently about him," Jill said. "He and his former girlfriend have been broken up for a few months. I'm pretty sure her name wasn't Tiffany."

"Sounds like he moved on."

Jill nodded, then stood. "I'd better get back to work. Lots of stuff to do for the gala."

"Don't remind me," Raegan said.

"Call him and explain. Maybe it's not what you think," Jill said in a half whisper as she reached the office door.

"I wish," Raegan said with a sarcastic laugh. With Jill gone, she stared at the hotel phone for a moment, then picked it up and listened to Kevin's message again. Just the sound of his voice sent a ripple of warmth across her skin. Better to do this now than to let the stress build up.

She took a deep breath, then dialed. He answered on the first ring, and for a moment Raegan didn't say anything.

"Raegan?"

Why did she have to flirt with a stranger? Wasn't there some old-wives tale warning women against that? "Kevin— or KC. I don't know what to call you."

"Kevin," he said in that low voice of his. "KC is more of a work thing. Thanks for calling me back."

"You're welcome." She cringed. Now she was Miss Formal and Polite? "Hey, I'm really sorry about last night. I mean, it was really rude of me to hurry out like that. I can explain though."

She expected him to say it was no big deal, but he didn't

say anything. Only silence was on the other side of the line. Okay. She could do this. Truth. "I could give you a ton of excuses, I guess, that would make you feel a lot better than the truth."

Kevin chuckled softly, the sound of it warming her through. "Don't worry about my feelings, sweetheart."

She was speechless. *Sweetheart?* It wasn't sarcastic either. "I . . . Okay, I shouldn't have accepted a date with you. I'm more of a long-term-commitment type of girl, and although it was fun to talk to you, I'm not all that fun and easygoing."

"That's what Paulie said."

Raegan stopped. "What?"

"Front-desk-Paulie told me quite a bit about you—I wasn't trying to pry—but since you're being so open, I will be too." He paused, as if he expected her to respond, but Raegan hadn't been expecting the conversation to go this way. "I wasn't looking for a fling. And that's not what I intended when I asked you to dinner."

Raegan could buy that only *if* Tiffany wasn't in the picture. But she hadn't called him back to lecture him about his morals. The sooner she was off the phone with him the better. "I was really flattered you asked me out," Raegan said. "But I probably shouldn't have said yes."

"I'm sorry for the miscommunication about my name," Kevin said.

Raegan blew out a breath. "I could have asked you your last name," she said. "You don't even know mine."

"Are you a film producer too?" he asked.

She laughed, despite herself. "My last name is Stone."

"Even your name is rock-solid," he said, and she could tell he was smiling.

"That was really corny."

This time, he laughed. "Can we start over—have a redo, whatever they call it?"

Raegan's heart thumped . . . too good to be true . . . "You're an amazing, talented man."

Kevin groaned, and Raegan plowed on. "But I'm just not your type."

"What does that mean exactly?" Kevin asked. "I mean, what specific things do you have issues with in regards to me or my job?"

Raegan couldn't believe this. Did he like to be insulted? "I don't mean to be rude or offend you, and it's nothing that you or I can change. It's just that we're on opposites poles, and our lives are way too different." Before he could respond, she added, "I've really got to go. I hope your gala is a huge success."

She hung up before he could reply.

Eight

If Kevin had written the past ten minutes into a script, no director would find it believable. Talk about evasive. That was one description Paulie should have added to her assessment of Raegan Stone.

He dropped his phone onto the bed and crossed to his hotel bedroom windows overlooking the ocean. Opening the balcony door, he stepped out into the salty breeze. Even though he'd lived in California his whole life, there were few days in his adult years that he'd truly enjoyed his natural surroundings.

Raegan Stone. *Stone.* Yep, it was the perfect last name for her. Kevin braced his hands on the balcony rail and gazed at the undulating waves of the Pacific. She hadn't answered his question, and he wanted to know why. She'd practically hung up on him, and she'd walked out on him the night before. So why wasn't he just letting this go?

His phone rang, and for a second his heart skipped. Crossing back into the room, he picked it up from the bed, but instead of the hotel number—Raegan—it was Tiffany.

"Hey, Tiff," he answered. "Rita just called," Tiffany said, her voice shaky. "She said she's coming over to talk to me."

Kevin groaned. This was not good.

"What does she want, Kevin?" Tiffany asked. "I don't think I can handle her right now. It's been months since I last saw her, and it took me days to recover from that visit."

"I know," Kevin said in a calm voice. He'd even gone a couple of times to Tiffany's therapist with her. Kevin needed to tell her about the lawsuit, and then he had to prevent the meeting between them. "I'm not exactly sure why she wants to talk to you, but her lawyer emailed me this morning with a lawsuit notice."

Tiffany drew in her breath sharply. "She's suing you? For what?"

"Defamation of character," Kevin said, sitting on the edge of his bed. "She claims that the stories that you and I tell about your upbringing and how it's the whole reason for my charity all point back to her as a bad mother."

"She did that all herself," Tiffany said, her tone bitter.

"You're right," Kevin said. "And that's why I need you to listen to me. Throw your essentials into a bag, and start driving to Shell Beach. I'll have the security company send someone to your house so that when she shows up, he can turn her away politely."

"What if she gets here before I can leave?" Tiffany asked.

"She won't," he said. "It will take her an hour to get to you by bus. Tiffany, just come now. Start driving. I'll be here waiting."

She exhaled into the phone. "All right."

"See you soon."

Tiffany hung up, and Kevin stared at his phone for a moment. Why his sister had to wreak more havoc on his life and her daughter's was beyond him. She'd never taken care of Tiffany the years that she did have her. Kevin wouldn't be surprised if Rita had a new boyfriend who was trying to find a way to get money from him. It had happened before but had never gone so far as an actual lawsuit.

Two hours later, he was in the lobby. This time he wasn't trying to casually run into Raegan. Tiffany should have been here fifteen minutes ago. He'd already called to confirm that the security company was at her apartment and there had still been no sighting of Rita. Kevin didn't doubt she'd come, but he knew it would take her awhile to get to Tiffany's. Rita was dependent on public transportation, having had her driver's license suspended indefinitely.

With every car that pulled up in front of the hotel, his breathing stalled. He supposed Tiffany could have stopped to get something to eat. He'd called her a couple of times, but she hadn't answered.

Finally, her bright blue car pulled up to the hotel. Relief shuddered through Kevin as he strode to the car to meet her. Tiffany climbed out. Her eyes were puffy from crying, and streaked mascara ran down one cheek.

"You made it," Kevin said, then wrapped his arms around her.

She let out a single sob and laid her head against his chest and hugged him back. "I can't believe she's doing this to us." Her voice broke.

"I've already put in a call to my lawyer—our lawyer now."

"The timing couldn't be worse," Tiffany said with a sniffle. "I mean, it's like she knew this weekend was our grand gala."

Kevin clenched his jaw. Of course Rita knew. It wouldn't be hard to find out—the event was plastered all over their website. "We'll figure this out," he said, rubbing Tiffany's back for a moment, then drawing away.

She gave him a half-smile, but tears still budded in her eyes. "If I didn't have you, I don't know what I'd do." And then she was crying again.

Kevin put his arm around her. "Come on," he said. "Let's get you to the suite, and you can vent all you want."

She wiped at her eyes. "Good idea."

He handed her the room key. "You can head up. I'll park the car and bring up your things."

"Thanks, Kevin," she said, her tone sounding more cheerful now. She lifted up on her toes and kissed his cheek. "I feel better already."

Kevin watched her walk into the hotel, his heart hurting for his niece's pain. When would it end? As he turned back to the car, he caught a glimpse of a woman crossing the parking lot, walking away from him. *Raegan.* She must have walked right past them.

For a second, he thought about calling after her, to see if she'd tell him what was really bothering her. He felt he deserved an honest explanation.

No, he told himself firmly. Tiffany needed him now. The committee meeting was in a couple of hours, and he couldn't let himself get distracted. He walked back into the hotel, wishing his mother was still alive. She'd always been able to make Tiffany feel better whenever something difficult happened.

He hoped Tiffany's naturally bubbly personality would return soon. Even though she sometimes went overboard with her enthusiasm, he'd rather have that than the alternative.

When he reached the hotel room, he found that Tiffany had settled into the second bedroom. She stood on the balcony, looking out over the ocean.

As Kevin walked out to meet her, she said, "Everything seems more peaceful in a gorgeous place."

Kevin stopped next to her and leaned on the balcony rail. "Sorry about all of this."

She shook her head. "It's not your fault."

"You sound like your therapist," he said, and she smiled. He had spent years wondering if there was something more he could have done as a brother to prevent Rita's addictions. He knew the psychotherapy textbook answer was *no*, but that didn't always keep away the guilt. Rita was good at making him feel guilty. Even now.

Tiffany leaned her head on his shoulder, and they stood there for several moments, saying nothing. Sometimes just being with someone who understood what you were going through was as therapeutic as talking it over with a professional therapist.

"Oh, I almost forgot," Tiffany said, lifting her head. "I called the events lady at the hotel and chewed her out for not having everything ready for your arrival."

Kevin looked down at her with surprise. "What? Why? I said it was all right. I'm not some extravagant and spoiled celebrity."

"You are a celebrity, Kevin," Tiffany corrected. "Your name is on more credits than most Oscar-winning actors. And it's okay to demand some decent treatment once in a while."

Dread coursed through Kevin. "Who did you talk to? What was the lady's name?"

"Raegan Stone," Tiffany said, pulling out her phone. "I saved her contact information if you need to be more specific with her."

"No," Kevin said. "That's not what I want to do." He scrubbed his hand through his hair, knowing there was probably not going to be a good time to talk about this. Lawsuit or not. "Look, Tiffany, you're an amazing person. And I love having you helping me with my charity. After all, you're the inspiration behind all of this."

Tiffany's eyes pooled with tears. "You're firing me?"

"Not at all," Kevin said. "I'm just giving you some advice that will help both of us the long run. You can catch more flies with honey than with vinegar."

Tiffany wrinkled her nose. "That doesn't make sense."

Kevin smiled. "What if some guy told you that he loved your outfit, but you have a mascara smudge on your cheek?"

"No big deal. I'd check my face in the mirror."

"Right," Kevin said with a smile. "Now, what if that same guy told you that your makeup looked like a clown's?"

"I'd probably punch him," Tiffany said. "Or at least put him in his place."

"Yep, exactly. Honey versus vinegar."

Tiffany blew out a breath. "People like events managers are probably used to dealing with demanding customers."

"I'm sure they are, but I don't have to be one of them." He shoved his hands in his pockets and turned to look out over the ocean again. "Besides, I've met Raegan Stone, and she's a great lady."

Tiffany was silent for a moment. "You *met* her?"

"Yeah, I actually asked her out."

Tiffany stared at him, her eyes huge. "When did this happen? How?"

He explained their chance meetings, then her subsequent bailing on him, and now her refusal to explain what happened.

"Oh my gosh, Kevin. You like her, *really* like her. I mean, this is crazy." Tiffany gasped. "And I was rude to her—no wonder she got upset when she learned who you really were."

It was as if someone had hollowed out Kevin's stomach. "Were you that awful?"

She bit her lip, then nodded. "I'm calling her right now to apologize." She turned her phone on.

"Wait," Kevin said. "Don't say anything about me, okay?" It was all starting to make sense. Raegan had equivocated Kevin with Tiffany's outrageous demands. No wonder she was annoyed when she found out who he really was.

"Hello, is this Raegan Stone?" Tiffany said into her phone. She gave Kevin a thumbs up.

Kevin held his breath, trying to hear Raegan's voice through the phone. Her tone sounded business-like, polite, as Tiffany gushed an apology.

Kevin mouthed, *Don't say anything about me.*

Tiffany nodded, then continued to talk to Raegan. When Tiffany hung up, she smiled at him triumphantly. "There. You should be good to ask her out again."

"I'm not sure it's that easy, but thanks for doing that," Kevin said, his heart feeling tremendously lighter. He didn't know if Tiffany's phone call would soften Raegan's attitude toward him, but at least things had been made right. "If I do see her again, the air will hopefully be cleared between us."

"Are you still mad at me?" she asked.

"I wasn't mad," Kevin said. "Just wanted us to be on the same page."

"Sorry about everything," Tiffany said with a sheepish smile. "You're my hero."

"Talking about heroes, did you finish the agenda for the board meeting?"

"Almost," Tiffany said. "I'll get it finished up right now. Would it be too presumptuous to order room service for lunch? That way I can decompress for a while."

"Sure," Kevin said with a laugh.

Tiffany grinned. "What do you want?"

Kevin crossed to the mini kitchen and opened up the room service menu on the counter. "I'll take the salmon salad."

Tiffany was already dialing, still grinning.

"Behave yourself," Kevin said. He walked into the living room portion of the suite, where his laptop sat on the coffee table. He powered it on and opened up the document with the final guest list Tiffany had sent him a few days before. He was emailing each person a personal thank you. Saturday night would be a big night for the charity, and he wanted everyone who attended to feel as if they were a part of something big.

Nine

"Huh," Raegan said to herself. That was a strange phone call. She felt like she'd talked to two completely different people over the past couple of days: Tiffany 1 and Tiffany 2.

At least the woman had a conscience, but it still didn't really dismiss the fact that Tiffany was in a relationship with her boss. And her boss was a womanizer. Raegan didn't think it was a fling either... When Raegan had passed them in the parking lot on her way to lunch, she'd seen them hug.

It wasn't a casual hug either, but more intimate, tender even. It was actually quite sweet, which made Raegan feel even more awkward, yet glad she'd stopped the date when she did. Their age difference had to be ten to fifteen years apart.

Raegan blew out a breath. Why was she still thinking about Kevin? After this weekend, she was going to take a day off and drown herself in a mind-numbing movie marathon. She printed off the final gala menu, then went in search of the head chef. She wanted to double check that all of the food orders had arrived this morning. She left her office and walked along one of the back corridors toward the hotel kitchen.

"Hey there," Mari said, coming around the corner in front of Raegan.

"Mari, back to work so soon?" Raegan teased. Neither of them ever had weekends off. It was just part of the hotel business.

"Don't you know it," Mari said. "Where you headed?"

"To talk to the chef," Raegan said, coming to a stop. "Did you get any celebrity sightings yet?"

"One in particular," Mari said. "KC Wood. I think you know him?"

Raegan arched a brow. "*Know* him? Why would you say that?"

"Don't even try," Mari said with a laugh. She folded her arms. "I'm not moving until you tell me everything. Cathy from the restaurant said you ditched him at dinner."

"Oh, that."

"What I want to know first is how in the world you got invited to dinner by KC Wood."

"Kevin," Raegan corrected. "He goes by Kevin. KC is his media name."

"I think I read that somewhere once," Mari said. She grabbed Raegan's arm. "Okay. Spill what happened."

So Raegan told her. Everything from when she talked to him at the front desk to their meeting on the third floor to the moment she walked out on him at the restaurant. Then she ended with the message he left on the events' department answering service.

Mari listened with a frown on her face. "I still don't get why you left—I mean, I understand that dating someone famous might come with its own challenges."

"It's Tiffany—his assistant-aka-girlfriend," Raegan continued, filling Mari in on the demanding phone call, the shared suite, then the bizarre apology.

Mari's eyes narrowed. "Tiffany Wood? That's who's sharing his room—I assumed they were siblings or something."

Raegan froze. "They have the same last name?"

"Yeah," Mari said. "I was called up to deliver extra pillows, so I checked the guest list to see which celebrity was there."

"Maybe he's married," Raegan said, exhaling. This was even worse that she first thought.

"He's not married—it would have been all over the news," Mari said.

Raegan nodded, but she was still suspicious. "Maybe Tiffany used his last name as a cover. She seemed pretty paranoid about giving out certain information when I was on the phone with her." She stopped talking as another maid hurried past them down the hall.

When they were alone again, Mari said, "I don't know how they're related, or even if they are, but one thing is for certain, they aren't sleeping together."

Raegan stared at Mari. "Are you sure?"

"They were firmly settled into each of their rooms, and a maid knows."

Raegan's mind spun. Had she been mistaken all along? Was Tiffany related to Kevin? Would the information be online? "Oh wow, okay," Raegan said. "I may have been a complete idiot."

Mari tilted her head. "You can always call him and ask him."

"Funny," Raegan said. "I can just imagine how that conversation would go . . . 'Hi Kevin, just out of curiosity, are you related to the woman sharing your room?' He'd think I'm a crazy stalker."

"I don't know about that, Raegan," Mari said. "It sounds like from what you've told me, he's really interested in you. And maybe he's not the two-timer you think he is."

"Maybe," Raegan said, her voice faint. She didn't know what to think anymore. What if Tiffany was his sister or something? Would that change how she felt about Kevin? It wasn't like they were in any sort of relationship, but there was still the famous celebrity status. "Well, I'd better get to the kitchen and go over the orders with the chef."

"Raegan, do you want me to ask around about Kevin, or KC? I'm sure some of the employees keep up to date about Hollywood gossip."

"No," Raegan said. "I'm sure there's enough talk already going on about my restaurant fiasco." She released a sigh. "I'll figure it out."

Mari gave her a sympathetic smile. "Keep me posted. I'll be around all day."

Raegan nodded and watched Mari walk away. She looked down at the list in her hand but couldn't focus on the items. Now wasn't the time to talk to the hotel chef; she needed a few minutes by herself to think through things.

She walked to the elevators, deciding to go to one of the upper-floor lobbies and check on the flower arrangements. It would give her the time she needed before jumping back into business. She entered the elevator and hit the button for the fifth floor, then leaned back against the elevator wall and closed her eyes.

The elevator lifted, then slowed, and the doors dinged open. Raegan straightened and opened her eyes, but the elevator had stopped on the third floor, not the fifth. Two people were waiting, a tall man, and a blonde woman.

Kevin.

Raegan felt her heart stop. The moment their gazes connected, her face flushed hot.

The woman next to him had to be Tiffany—Raegan recognized her as the woman Kevin had hugged in the parking lot.

"Raegan," Kevin spoke first, his brows lifting in surprise.

"Hi," she said, her heart beating again. "I'm just going up to the fifth floor to check on the flower arrangements. I don't want to have any of the flowers wilting without me knowing it." Why was she blabbering?

Kevin just nodded, watching her closely. The elevators doors shut, and the elevator rose. "This is Tiffany, my niece. I think you've talked on the phone already."

Tiffany. His niece. Raegan wanted to be anywhere but confined to this five-by-five-foot elevator. *His niece.* They weren't in a relationship, and Kevin hadn't been two-timing... Yet, she'd walked out on a date.

But how could she truly apologize with Tiffany staring her down? Well, the woman wasn't really staring her down, but she was definitely looking—curiosity written all over her face.

Tiffany smiled and stuck out her hand. "Sorry about the rough start. It's great to meet you, Raegan Stone."

"You too, Tiffany. Welcome to our hotel." Raegan reverted to auto-pilot, which was the best she could do with her emotions and thoughts beating against each other. She felt as if she'd swallowed a rock—hard and heavy.

The elevator stopped on the fifth floor, and the door dinged open. Raegan was surprised when Kevin stepped off of the elevator.

"Where are you going?" Tiffany asked, apparently

surprised as well.

"I'll catch up with you in a few minutes," Kevin said to Tiffany. "Tell Preston that I want to review the PowerPoint for the gala first, so he can get it queued up while you wait for me."

Raegan's mind spun. She should have known—Kevin wasn't going to let her get away with her lame explanation on the phone earlier. He was a multi-million-dollar film producer, after all; it was clear he knew how to get answers and results.

His gaze cut to hers, and her heart thumped. He didn't seem mad or annoyed. In fact, he seemed to be teasing her.

Raegan released a silent breath and stepped off the elevator. She said something like "Nice to meet you" to Tiffany, although she couldn't be too sure. As the elevators closed on Tiffany's very curious expression, Raegan walked toward the lobby, intent on keeping busy.

Of course, Kevin didn't hesitate to follow her.

She could practically feel his gaze warming her back. For better or for worse, the lobby was empty. She spun around, folded her arms, and looked at Kevin, who came to a stop in front of her.

"Okay, so I admit that I owe you an apology," Raegan said. "A rather big apology."

One side of Kevin's mouth lifted into a smile.

"But it still doesn't mean that you and I are a good idea."

Kevin's mouth fell, and his brows drew together. "What exactly are you apologizing for? Walking out on me at the restaurant, or thinking that I'm a prima donna film producer?"

Raegan's mouth opened, then shut. "Well, both, but there's more." She looked away. She couldn't handle staring into his warm brown eyes right now. "I misjudged you."

"The prima donna part?" he asked.

She allowed herself a glance at him. "Not exactly." She let out a breath, then looked at him full-on. "It was Tiffany, at least who I thought Tiffany was at first."

"I know she can come off a bit over-zealous—"

"It wasn't that. I mean I work with a lot of different people, so those kinds of demands aren't such a big deal," Raegan said, clenching her hands together. *Here it goes.* She knew she had to say it all at once or she'd lose her nerve. "I thought she was your girlfriend, or KC Wood's girlfriend. So when I found out the Kevin I was out to dinner with was KC Wood, I just sort of lost it, I guess."

"Oh," he said, his gaze on her. "I wasn't expecting that."

Raegan looked down at her twisting hands. "It was all in my head, and I feel horrible that I was so judgmental."

"Hey," Kevin said in a soft voice, reaching for her hands. He separated them and linked his fingers through hers.

Raegan's heart rate sped up at his touch.

"Apology accepted," he said stepping closer to her.

She couldn't help laughing. He smiled down at her, and she suddenly realized how close they were standing, close enough to feel his warm breath against her skin and close enough to imagine what it might be like to feel his arms around her.

"Thank you," she said, stepping back, but his hand tightened around hers.

"I'm completely single, for the record," he said, amusement in his eyes. "I would have hoped that by asking you out, it was a big enough hint, but that's okay. All's well that ends well. Except I sincerely hope this isn't the end."

Raegan looked down at their interlaced hands, then

back up at him. "I don't want it to be the end either, and that's why I was so upset with myself . . . for liking you despite the fact that I thought you had a girlfriend."

"No girlfriend," Kevin said, leaning down slightly. Enough that Raegan wondered if he was going to kiss her, right here, in the fifth floor lobby.

Instead, he simply said, "Will you go out with me tonight—for real?"

"I will."

He squeezed her hands. "I'll be in the lobby at 6:00 after our board meetings wrap up. This time let's go someplace else. You choose."

Raegan nodded, having a hard time forming words. The last few minutes had upended all she'd thought of Kevin, and the thrill of actually going on a date with him shot through her. She could hardly believe this was happening. This guy was amazingly talented, and it seemed he was just as attracted to her as she was to him.

"I'll come up with the perfect place," Raegan said. "And I promise to not walk out on you."

He gave a soft laugh, then leaned down completely and kissed her cheek.

Heat rushed to Raegan's face, and she was sure he noticed as he drew away. He winked at her, then said he had to get going.

Raegan didn't know how long she stood at the edge of the lobby after he'd entered the elevator and disappeared. And she had no idea where the perfect place would be to eat.

Ten

Kevin nodded as Preston forwarded through the slideshow presentation. Preston volunteered on the board as their photographer, and even though, at first glance, his casual clothing and long, dark hair pulled into a ponytail made him look like a beach bum, he was one of the most sought-after photographers in LA.

The other board member was Samantha—she was everything finance. Just one look at her black-rimmed glasses and perfectly bobbed hair, and everyone knew she meant business. She was an expert on taxes and would rather add up columns of numbers than do almost anything else.

The next picture was of a young girl about nine years old on a swing. Her bright eyes held both hope and despair in them. Desperation, even. "Who's she?" Kevin asked.

"Bailey Richards," Preston filled in. "Her parents were both killed a couple of years ago, and the aunt she went to live with has a lot of addiction struggles. Bailey's been in foster care about six months now."

Kevin's heart went out to this little girl and all of the

girls in the slideshow presentation. Accompanying each picture was the girl's story, short and inspirational—all stories that would certainly touch the hearts of the attendees. Sometimes the weight of the girls' burdens was completely overwhelming, and he had to tell himself he *was* helping, although it seemed he was doing so little.

"She's a sweetie," Tiffany said. "She told me Elsa is her favorite princess."

Of course. Tiffany was lucky enough to travel with Preston, so she met most of the girls in the program.

"You've done a great job with these pictures," Kevin told Preston. "And the stories make me want to donate even more."

Preston smiled his lopsided grin. "That's the idea." Then his tone sobered. "This charity has been amazing to work with. It's probably the most important work I do."

Kevin nodded thoughtfully. The charity work was probably the most important work he did as well. His films brought in a lot of money, but what good was money if something great didn't come of it?

"I think the music needs to be slowed down," Samantha said. She tapped something on her iPad. "Like this." She played part of an instrumental song that had a strong melody, yet was soothing.

"What's the name of it?" Preston asked Samantha.

While the two of them talked music, Kevin checked the time on his cell again. He'd been checking it every few minutes, as if that would make the time move faster.

"It's only five minutes later than the last time you checked," Tiffany said.

Kevin snapped his head up to find that everyone was staring at him. "What?"

"He has a date," Tiffany stage-whispered to Samantha.

"Raegan Stone in the hotel events office."

Samantha's thin eyebrows arched. "Is Liz out of the picture, then?"

"She has been for a long time," Kevin said. "Whether she accepts it or not."

Preston chuckled. "I think this is about to get interesting."

Kevin shook his head. "It's just a date, and Liz is history no matter what." His board members continued to speculate and banter, but Kevin's mind was already elsewhere. He hadn't been this distracted in a meeting since, well, ever.

By 5:30, they'd reviewed all of the slides, made adjustments, gone over the budget, as well as the final guest list. Tiffany updated everyone on who'd RSVP'd and the security detail that would be present with so many *who's who* attending.

There was nothing more to cover, except wait for the inevitable last-minute crisis, which Tiffany was already braced for. Kevin just hoped his sister would stay quiet over the weekend.

"Thanks everyone," he said, rising to his feet. Everyone smiled as he stood up. "What?"

"Have a nice time tonight," Samantha said.

Preston just smirked, and Tiffany laughed. "I'll let you all know how it goes," she said. "Because we know he won't spill much information when he returns from his date."

"We'll see about that," Kevin said. He picked up his water bottle. "See you all tomorrow."

Once outside the conference room, Kevin exhaled. His heart drummed in his chest. Nervous. He was nervous. And he was early. He strode to the lobby area, knowing that if he went up to his room first, he'd have to put up with more ribbing from Tiffany.

He slowed his step as he entered the lobby. Raegan was already there, sitting on one of the couches, typing into her phone. He paused, noticing that she'd changed her clothing from what she'd been wearing earlier. Had she gone home to change? She wore a navy wrap-around dress that accentuated her curves—her real curves.

She looked up then and smiled when she saw him.

Kevin's heart soared. He exhaled carefully as he crossed toward her.

"You're early," she said, standing.

"You're early too." Her blue eyes seemed to melt right into him.

She lifted a shoulder. "Your car or mine?"

"I'll drive, and you can direct me."

Raegan smiled, and Kevin led the way out of the hotel. The sun topped the western horizon, splashing orange across the rows of cars in the parking lot. As they walked to his car, Raegan looked over at him. "How did your meeting go?"

"I think we're ready for tomorrow," Kevin said. "At least, as ready as we can be. With a bunch of celebrities, there will be a lot of unknowns."

"I'll bet," Raegan said. "You've probably met the most interesting people."

"True, but I think you're pretty interesting too."

Raegan gave a small smile. "You're a flirt."

"Not really," Kevin said, slowing as they neared his car. "You seem to bring it out in me." He used his key fob to unlock the car, then crossed to the passenger side and opened the door.

"I guess I can be your guinea pig, then," Raegan said, sliding into the front seat.

Kevin shut her door and hurried around to his side. As he sat down and started the car, she said, "I thought you'd have a fancier car than this."

Kevin drove a ten-year-old Mercedes, and the leather interior was showing some wear. "Don't let Beth hear you say that."

"Beth?"

Kevin put a finger to his lips, then pointed at the dash.

"You named your car?"

"We've been through a lot together."

Raegan ran her hand along the dash, and Kevin was glad he'd recently cleaned the car. "Sorry, Beth. You're a beautiful girl," she said.

Kevin laughed. "That's better."

"I like that you drive an older car," Raegan added in a soft voice.

He just smiled and drove to the end of the parking lot. "Which direction?"

Raegan guided him toward the downtown strip of beach shops that lined Tangerine Street. She pointed up ahead. "Park here, and we can walk to the restaurant."

Kevin parked and climbed out, then opened Raegan's car door. She climbed out, and said, "This way. I hope you like Chinese."

"What if I don't?"

"Too late, I've already made reservations," she said, smiling over at him. Twilight had descended, scattering the oranges and golds and replacing them with violet, which only made her eyes look bluer.

They stopped in front of a quaint restaurant called The Fortune Café. Kevin opened the door, and warm, heavenly smells poured out. "I think I might love Chinese food."

"Good," Raegan said with a laugh.

A waitress crossed toward them, and after introducing herself as Emma, she led them to a booth by a large window. Then she brought water and the menus over. After they ordered drinks, Raegan propped her elbows on the table, and said, "Since Paulie told you all about me, I think it's your turn."

"To tell you all about you?"

"No, tell me about *yourself*," Raegan said. "Besides the obvious."

"What's the obvious?" Kevin asked, taking a sip of his water.

"That you're some millionaire film producer."

Kevin nearly choked on his water. "Don't believe everything you read."

"So you're broke and make MTV videos?" Raegan said, lifting a corner of her mouth. A very kissable corner.

"Let me rephrase. You can believe some things you read, but not all of them." Kevin leaned forward, fiddling with the menu he had yet to look at. Raegan's eyes were much more interesting.

"So, tell me what to believe."

"I started acting as a kid—no, you wouldn't have seen me in anything. I was a professional extra. My claim to fame was a couple of Crest kids' commercials."

"You do have nice teeth."

"Thanks," Kevin said with a wink. "When it became clear that I wasn't going to be the next Hollywood sensation, my mom pulled me out of too-expensive acting classes, and I settled into middle school like any other kid. Playing baseball and teasing girls."

"Sounds like the American dream."

"Except I was fascinated by old films and documentaries. Watched them every chance I got. Some kids love to read; I loved to study films."

"College?"

"Film school."

"Of course."

"Produced my first film during school, wrote the screenplay and directed it, everything. Haven't looked back since."

"Would I know it?"

"Possibly."

"*Kevin.*"

"Okay, okay. It was called *Loved Like This*. Set records for bombing at all theaters nationwide. The DVD sales were decent."

Raegan narrowed her eyes. "Chick flick? You wrote and directed and produced a *chick flick*?" She pulled out her phone and started typing into it.

Kevin reached over and covered up her phone. "Don't look it up. It's not even on my IMDb profile. I pulled some strings to have it removed."

She looked up at him, her eyes gleaming. "I am *so* watching it tonight."

"If you do, don't tell me you did," Kevin said.

"Is it really that bad?"

"Not that bad . . . for a chick flick," he said, his face warming.

"Well, if it has your fingerprints on it, then I'm sure it's great," Raegan said.

The waitress was back, her eyes wide and appreciative. She set down a platter of wontons and dipping sauce. "Mr. Wood," the woman said. "I thought I recognized you. I hope you'll enjoy your visit to The Fortune Café."

"I'm sure I will," he said. "It smells great in here."

She looked over at Raegan, then back to Kevin. "Are you ready to order?"

Kevin looked down at the unopened menu. "What do you recommend?"

"The chicken cashew is great," Emma said.

"I'll take that," Raegan said.

"Me too," Kevin added.

"Great," Emma said. "I'll be back soon with your order."

"Do you ever get tired of being recognized?" Raegan said in a low voice after the waitress left.

"It doesn't happen that often," Kevin admitted. "Especially for women named Raegan Stone."

She pursed her lips, and her eyes filled with amusement. "At least I'm not a raving fan like Paulie—if I were, I'd probably be sitting on your lap right now and trying to get you to kiss me."

Kevin grinned. "This place is a little public . . . but if you're interested later . . ."

"Funny," Raegan said, her cheeks turned pink. "Tell me about Tiffany and how you are brave enough to have family work for you. My father and older brother, Jared, only lasted a couple of years trying to run a construction company together. It got pretty bad, and they had a falling out. In fact, they haven't communicated in a few years."

Kevin shook his head. "I'm sorry about that. I guess nothing in life is easy." He told her about his sister, Rita, how Tiffany came to live with them as a kid, and how his parents gained full custody. By the time he finished the short version, their food had arrived.

After Emma set down their plates and left, Kevin said, "I probably said too much for a first date."

"Second date," Raegan said, giving him a small smile. "Thanks for telling me." She picked up the chopsticks next to her plate. "I mean, it's incredibly sad, yet it just shows that angels are real." She pointed at him. "You and your parents are angels."

Kevin looked down at his plate and the steaming food,

trying to cover up how much her statement affected him. "I started the charity hoping to help more kids. But it seems like the more I learn, the more I realize how impossible the mountain is to climb."

Raegan's hand covered his, and he looked up. "You've already climbed at least a dozen mountains. Most people don't even climb one." She smiled at him encouragingly. "Come on, let's eat. This smells great."

They spent the next hour eating, talking, laughing, and Kevin found that he'd never enjoyed a first—or second—date more.

Eleven

Raegan didn't know whether to feel elated or guilty. What if she hadn't happened to run into Kevin and Tiffany in the elevator? She would have never known how wrongly she'd judged him, and she wouldn't have learned his amazing story. Everything about him was amazing. And more than once, sitting at dinner with him, she wondered what he saw in *her*.

When their fortune cookies had come, Kevin scooped them up and said they'd have dessert later. Then after he paid for the meal, he said, "Come on, let's go walk the beach. It's on my bucket list."

"You've never walked on a beach?" Raegan asked.

"Not with you."

She laughed. "Since when is walking on the beach with me on your bucket list?"

"Since now," he said, extending his hand toward her.

Her heart thumped at the gesture. She slipped her hand inside his and let him pull her to her feet. He didn't let go of her hand as he led her out of the restaurant and past his parked car. They walked toward the boardwalk, then crossed it and stepped onto the soft sand, still holding hands.

Raegan let herself get caught up in the warmth of his hand cocooned around hers, and for the time being, she pretended their lives weren't worlds apart. This night didn't have to end, did it? The sun had sunk below the horizon completely, and only scraps of color remained in the dark sky, soon to be pierced by thousands of stars.

"What else is on your bucket list?" she asked as they neared the water. She breathed in the fresh ocean air. The wind was gentle, cooling just a bit, blowing against the hem of her dress. The sand became cooler the closer they walked to the ocean.

Kevin stopped before they reached the wet stretch of sand. He turned toward her, still holding her hand, and Raegan's heart skittered at his nearness. "I'm adding to it as we go." The way he gazed at her made her feel breathless.

Raegan had to say something, or she'd get completely lost in his eyes. And that might lead to something too impulsive, like kissing. "Hike Mt. Everest? Deep sea dive? Jump out of a plane?"

His mouth lifted into a smile. "I've traveled the world and had remarkable experiences, but there was always something missing."

"What's that?" Raegan said just above a whisper.

"Someone to share it with," Kevin said, rubbing his thumb along the top of her hand.

His touch sent an army of shivers through her. She didn't know how to answer. They looked out over the ocean and were quiet for several moments. Raegan was sure he could hear her pounding heart above the sound of the waves.

Goose bumps broke out on her arms as a large wave crashed just beyond them, sending a fine spray in their direction. Another, larger ocean swell moved toward shore, and Kevin tugged her back. And then somehow, she was nestled against him, hiding her face against his chest as the next wave crashed, sending spray across both of them.

Kevin wrapped his arms about her with a laugh. "I think the ocean is trying to speak to us."

Raegan lifted her head, so close to Kevin now that the heat of his body blended with hers. "What's it trying to tell us? 'Get on with your bucket lists'?"

"Maybe." Kevin smiled, his gaze steady on hers, his eyes darkening with the night. Slowly, he lowered his head toward hers.

She knew he was going to kiss her, and she told herself she should step away from his embrace. They were on their first date, after all, and he was leaving after the weekend, and he existed in another world, and his life was leagues beyond hers...

His lips touched hers, gentle, and questioning. She couldn't move, couldn't respond. When he lifted his head a few inches and gazed at her, she whispered, "What are you doing?"

"Kissing you," he said, his voice husky.

"Is that on your bucket list too?"

He tilted his head. "Do you want it to be?"

"Not if it's going to be a one-time thing." Raegan wrapped her arms about his neck, drawing him closer. She hadn't kissed anyone since Brandon.

"I seriously doubt kissing you will be a one-time thing," Kevin whispered, his hands moving lower on her waist.

Raegan lifted up on her toes and pressed her mouth against his. His response was immediate, and he kissed her back, his lips no longer gentle or questioning. His kiss was demanding, yet caring, and she sighed beneath his touch. She felt like she was literally floating above the sand and that only his arms were keeping her grounded.

His hands slid up her back, cradling her against him. Every place he touched sent shivers of warmth through her, like the waves a few feet away, pulsing along her skin. She didn't remember being kissed like this by Brandon. Didn't remember shivers of warmth or her pounding pulse or her breath leaving her body.

She drew away, catching her breath, but Kevin didn't release her. He rested his forehead against hers, breathing equally hard. "Too fast?" he asked.

"Probably." But she didn't pull away either.

"Yeah," he said. "I should get you back to the hotel and your car."

Raegan shook her head, then wrapped her arms about his waist, resting her head against his chest. His arms held her close and secure.

"It's still early," she said. "And we're on a beach."

"Good points," Kevin said with a chuckle. Then he released a sigh.

"What's wrong?"

"Nothing at all," he said, his voice vibrating against her ear. "You're just unexpected."

"Is that a compliment?"

She sensed his smile.

"I haven't started on the compliments yet," he said.

She laughed and looked up at him. "Oh, really? Are you going to begin flirting again?"

"I think I've been doing that since I met you." He leaned down and kissed her again. This time shorter and sweeter. When he drew away, she wanted to pull him back.

"I need to know one thing," he said, his brown eyes capturing hers. "Why are you letting me kiss you? I mean, I know you aren't the type to mess around—according to Paulie."

Raegan let out a groan. "Remind me to kill Paulie later." She met his gaze and was struck with the openness there, the interest and curiosity. She didn't know if she could completely explain it. She hadn't ever kissed a man on the first date. "I think it's because you drive an older car and you didn't pay for dinner with a wad of cash."

Kevin's eyebrows shot up. "What's that supposed to mean?"

"That my first instinct about you when we met was correct," Raegan said, suddenly feeling awkward. Was she really being this blunt? "When I met you, I thought you were pretty amazing, even too good to be true. Then, when I found out your full name, all my prejudices came roaring in—even without the whole Tiffany thing. I couldn't let myself even consider going out with someone like you."

"And now? My kisses convinced you otherwise?" Kevin teased.

"You're unexpected as well," Raegan said, breathing in his spicy scent mixed with the salty ocean breeze.

"Hmmm." His hand trailed a path along her arm. "I guess that's good?"

"Very good," Raegan said, stepping away from him. She was getting too cozy, and she needed to keep a level head.

Kevin let her go but grasped her hand. They started to walk slowly along the beach, the sound of the waves a backdrop to their silence. Raegan reveled in the quiet moment, where she didn't feel like she needed to talk, just feeling his hand in hers and walking beside him was enough.

After a few moments, Kevin asked, "What's the craziest thing you've ever done?"

"Kissing on a first date," Raegan said.

"Are you serious?"

She nodded, then laughed.

"Okay, that's not really all that crazy," Kevin said, squeezing her hand.

"You're right. For some people, that would be normal." Raegan thought about all the changes she'd made over the past year. "I guess it was kind of crazy to change jobs, move cities, and break up with my boyfriend. It all happened at once, and I was a bit disoriented for a while."

"You went through a lot of change," Kevin said.

"What about you?" Raegan ventured. "I'm surprised you're single."

"Relationships don't last long in the world of Hollywood—too much make-believe, I guess. The last relationship I was in didn't go so well," Kevin said with a shrug. "Let's just say Liz was like a stick of dynamite, lit on one end, about ready to go off at any moment if she didn't get her way. She thinks I'm just waiting for her to come back into my life."

Raegan arched a brow, looking over at Kevin. He slowed to a stop, turning to face her. "How do you know I'm not like that?" she asked.

He stepped closer. "I just know. You're nothing like Liz, or any of those women I've dated off and on in the Hollywood scene. Why do you think I kissed you tonight? I'm pulling out all the stops to get you to go out with me again."

Her heart rate sped up. "It might be working."

"Oh yeah?" He leaned closer, and she leaned toward him as well. His brushed his lips against hers, then drew back with a smile. "I'm glad it's working."

She wanted to kiss him again, more fully, but she didn't want to be too forward. "You know we live more than a few miles apart. Going on another date might be hard."

"I'm hoping our next date will be the gala tomorrow night."

Raegan stared at him. "Won't all your friends and the media be there?"

"Some of my friends are coming, but it's closed to the media."

"Still, your friends are like... I don't know... famous?" Raegan spread her hands. "I mean, what will they think of me?"

"They'll think you're beautiful and I'm lucky."

"Flirt," Raegan said.

He laughed and wrapped an arm about her shoulders, and they started to walk again, Raegan leaning against him.

"So your turn now," she said. "Why did you ask me out?"

He was quiet for a minute, then he said, "You're going to think I watch too many movies."

Raegan arched a brow and waited.

"Okay, I do watch too many movies, but at least I've made a career from it." He was looking at her again. "I just had a strange feeling come over me when I first saw you—like I had to meet you. Like I was *meant* to meet you. I don't know if I can explain it."

They reached the boardwalk and stepped onto the wooden slats.

"Like being struck by lightning?" Raegan teased, although her pulse was racing. She'd had the same feeling when she met him. Intense interest, almost unreasonable. "Maybe I've watched too many movies too."

He laughed. "That's a compliment in my book." The stars were out in full force now, and the foot traffic had thinned. He reached into his pocket and pulled out the two fortune cookies from the restaurant. "Time to read our fortunes." He handed one over to Raegan.

She cracked hers open first. "*You're starting on a new adventure.*"

"Sounds pretty accurate to me . . . Tonight has been an adventure," Kevin said with a smile. He opened his and read, "*Your past is about to catch up with your present.*"

"Hmmm. Not sure if that sounds ominous or not."

Kevin shrugged. "It's not like these really come true anyway." They reached the car, and he opened the passenger door for Raegan.

Once inside the car, Kevin started the engine, then looked over at her and said, "Tell me about Brandon."

She drew in a breath, surprised at his direct question. Looking out the window at the passing shops and their glowing displays, she said, "We dated for six years. On and off, but it seemed that he was more interested in the *idea* of a girlfriend than being a boyfriend back. I never met his family until about two years into our relationship, and I barely knew any of his friends."

Kevin let out a low whistle. "Why did you stay with him for that long? Why not two or three years?"

That was the exact question Raegan had asked herself many times. They pulled into The Mariposa parking lot, and Kevin turned into a parking space, then killed the engine.

"Honestly," Raegan started, "I think I liked the convenience as well. Brandon was a nice guy—nothing to swoon over, but no drama either. Unless I considered my feelings and the fact that he never seemed interested in proposing."

Kevin leaned his head back on his seat and looked over at her. "So he was boring?"

"Not *boring*." *Maybe boring.* Brandon was comfortable. "Just not . . . you."

"You don't find me boring?" Kevin asked.

Raegan laughed. "Hardly." She looked away from his intense gaze. And, she didn't mention that the thought of his kisses still made her body feel warm.

He was still looking at her. "So, would you like to go to the gala tomorrow night with me?"

She exhaled and glanced over at him. The light from the streetlamp cast shadows throughout the car, and the darkness seemed to bring a new intimacy. "I will," she said.

Twelve

Kevin checked the incoming text on his cell phone. *Good morning.* He smiled. Raegan had responded, and it was only 8:00 a.m. He'd sent his first text a few minutes ago, not knowing if it was too early, even though she was working today at the hotel. He crossed to the balcony doors and opened them, letting in the ocean breeze.

He hadn't been able to stop thinking about her last night after they'd said goodbye in the parking lot, and this morning was no different. If he thought maybe he'd have an altered perspective about Raegan Stone in the morning light, he'd been wrong. She was still consuming his thoughts.

Sleep well? He texted back.

Off and on.

He didn't ask what that might mean, he just wrote. *Me too. Are you at the hotel yet?*

Will be there soon. Can't figure out what to wear to the gala tonight. You might want to rethink the invite.

Kevin exhaled, then dialed her number. She picked up on the second ring.

"Hi," she said, and Kevin found himself smiling at the sound of her voice.

"Hey, so I thought instead of texting, I could tell you that I can get a dress delivered to you. There's this online catalog that Tiffany has used—"

"Wait," Raegan interrupted with a laugh. "You aren't going *Pretty Woman* on me, are you?"

Kevin felt his face redden. He lowered his voice. "Not unless you're going to stay with me for a week."

Raegan exhaled. "When I said I can't figure out what to wear, that didn't mean that I needed you to rescue me."

Kevin wasn't sure how to read her tone. "Sorry?"

Her laughter eased his worries. "I won't be as fancy as some of your friends, but I won't disappoint, Mr. Wood."

"I don't think you could ever disappoint," he said.

"I'm glad you think so," her voice was soft, with a serious edge.

"So when do I get to see you?"

"5:30 tonight?" she suggested.

"Breakfast?"

"Kevin . . ." Her voice washed over him. He decided he loved her saying his name. "I have work," she continued, "and I'm sure you do too. Don't you have a script to review or a gala to host?"

"Humans still need to eat," Kevin said, wondering if he could set the world record for early morning flirting. "Why not eat together?"

"I already ate," she said, her tone light.

"Maybe you could check your email or something while I eat."

Her laughter warmed him through, and he found himself grinning while standing on the hotel balcony.

"Thirty minutes?" he said. "I'll order breakfast to be delivered by the pool."

She didn't hesitate this time. "All right. I'll take a bagel and juice."

"Perfect."

Twenty minutes later, Kevin was sitting by a glass-like pool as a pair of starlings perched on the nearby gate. He had slept little the night before, but he wasn't tired at all. He'd started to scroll through emails when Tiffany called.

"Hi, Tiff," he said, answering.

"Kevin, where are you?" she asked, her voice sounding odd.

"I'm—"

"I just turned on my phone and found a message from my mom," Tiffany said. "She said she's coming to the hotel to talk to me."

The breath left his body. "When? How did she know you're here?" He stood and walked around the pool until he was at the far side by an overhang of palm trees.

"It's on the website," Tiffany said in a shaky voice.

Of course it was. Kevin knew that, but his mind was spinning. "When?" he repeated. He turned, looking back at the hotel. It would be impossible to change the location of the gala. But he couldn't have his sister showing up—that would attract the media.

"I don't know," Tiffany said. "The message was sent at six in the morning."

6:00 a.m. If she had a car, Rita could be here by now. "Check the bus schedules from LA," he said. "We need to know how much time we have."

"What if she has a ride?"

Kevin heard the fear in her voice. "Come down to the pool area. I'll make some calls while I wait for you." He hung up, then scrolled through his contacts to find Preston's number. The more people who could be on the lookout for Rita, the better.

The door leading from the hotel to the pool area opened, and Raegan stepped through. Kevin's heart thumped as she walked toward him. She wore a white blouse and black trousers, with strappy sandals. Not much different than all the other hotel employees, but Raegan looked classy.

Her deep blue eyes were focused on him, and for a moment Kevin wished there was no gala this weekend, no lawsuit from his sister, no hundred people showing up to listen to him speak tonight.

"What's wrong?" Raegan asked, reaching his side and looking up at him.

"I—It's a long story," he said. Rita's timing couldn't be worse.

"Can I help?"

Kevin debated in his mind and was about to tell her *no*, something he would have told Liz, or any other woman he was dating. He'd keep the serious family business personal. But Raegan was different. "My sister, Rita, has filed a lawsuit for defamation of character," he said. "Rita claims that with Tiffany telling her story, and me broadcasting her story through my charity, it's causing her financial hardship."

Raegan held his gaze, questioning, yet steady.

"Tiffany has only told the truth, and it's her story to tell," Kevin said. "No one forced her to tell about her childhood, and no one is making money off of it. She has gone through so much with her mother that it's better if they don't talk in person. It's hard to explain without getting into the psychological impact of what's it's like for Tiffany to face her mother.

"Rita left a message on Tiffany's phone that she's

coming to the hotel," he continued. He scrubbed a hand through his hair. "My sister will turn the gala into a media circus."

"When is she coming?" Raegan said in a quiet voice.

"She doesn't have a car, so that's what we're trying to work out," Kevin said. "The closer it is to the gala, the harder it will be to get her to leave before it starts."

Raegan grasped Kevin's hand. "We have plenty of time between now and the gala. I'll talk to our security and those at the front desk. When she comes, we'll be notified right away."

"No cops?" Kevin asked.

"Is she violent?"

"No," he said.

"Is she clean?" Raegan asked.

"As far as I know." Kevin squeezed her hand.

"Let me do this for you," she said. "Worse case, we can forbid her from staying on the property."

Relief rushed through Kevin, although a part of him didn't dare hope. His sister could be a very determined woman. But as he looked into Raegan's eyes, he decided to trust her offer to help.

"Thank you," he said, pulling her toward him and kissing her cheek.

"I'll call you when I have news." She released his hand. "And let me know if you find out anything more."

"I will," Kevin said and watched her walk away.

Moments later, Tiffany came through the door, eyes wide, sweats pulled on, and hair in a sloppy ponytail. Had her mother already arrived? Kevin's heart stilled, until Tiffany reached him and said, "The first bus she could've taken was at 7:30."

Kevin checked the time on his phone. "So she could be

here in about an hour . . . at the earliest." He pulled Tiffany into a hug. "Raegan is talking to security and the desk clerks. Do you want to go stay at another hotel?"

Tiffany pulled back and blinked up at him. "No, I want to be wherever you are."

He nodded.

She turned to gaze over the pool. "Do you think she's right? That I shouldn't tell my story?"

Kevin moved to her side and put an arm around her. "You've never named her, and the media has never pinpointed who she is. I think you should keep telling your story. You change lives every time you do."

Tiffany sniffled. "I worked so hard to forgive her and to move on, but when something like this happens, the hardness returns."

"I know, and I'm sorry," Kevin said. He kissed the top of her head. "Whenever she shows up, I'll talk to her, and if necessary, we'll take extra measures to make sure she doesn't upset you."

Tiffany exhaled. "If only I could be sure she's changed, I wouldn't mind trying to build a relationship with her."

Kevin had always known Tiffany's heart was too soft, sometimes too soft for her own good. This was just one example. "You're one in a million, Tiff."

The door from the hotel opened, and a waiter came out, pushing a cart.

"Breakfast?" Tiffany said.

Kevin had almost forgotten. "I invited Raegan, but she already left, and I won't be able to eat it all."

Tiffany watched as the waiter set out the plates and arranged the food and drinks.

Kevin thanked and tipped the waiter, then said to Tiffany, "Hungry?"

"Yes, but I don't think I can eat," she said. She sat down with a sigh, and when Kevin lifted the metal lids of the food, Tiffany's eyes lit up.

"All right, I guess I can eat." She dished scrambled eggs and fruit onto her place.

Kevin texted Raegan. *Breakfast is here if you have time. Tiffany's eating with me too.*

Thirteen

Raegan read the text from Kevin and smiled. She'd just hung up with hotel security, and they were on the lookout for Kevin's sister. She wasn't worried about the woman creating a huge scene, especially if Rita was aware of the security. But she was worried about Kevin and Tiffany and this constant angst in their lives.

She understood it—maybe she hadn't experienced it to the extreme Tiffany had, but her father and older brother Jared had always been at odds with each other. Ever since he was a teen, it seemed Jared did things just to anger her father. Why they went into business together, she never did completely understand—aside from the money matter. But when they finally blew up for the last time, and their partnership dissolved, everything just became sad. A sad waste. The two men hadn't talked for three years.

Her brother's kids hardly knew their grandparents, and holidays felt bereft without Jared around. Raegan hated it. Why couldn't they see past each other's mistakes and stubbornness and forgive each other—bring the family back together?

Raegan left the office and headed for the pool area. She had an idea for Tiffany, and Kevin, and just hoped it would help. When she stepped out onto the pool patio, both of them looked over at her. Despite the turmoil of the morning, Raegan's heart thumped at the sight of Kevin smiling at her in greeting. After they'd shared family stories the night before, and she'd told him about her ex-boyfriend, she felt even more connected to him.

She crossed to the table, and Kevin stood and pulled out a chair for her. Raegan updated them on the calls she'd made while she put food on her plate. Then she told Tiffany the story she'd told Kevin about the falling out between her father and brother.

Tiffany listened closely, then said, "It took me a lot of years and therapy to really forgive my mother, but I agree that I'd love a relationship with her. I just don't know if that's possible."

Raegan was quiet for a moment, then said, "I have something to show you. Not a lot of hotel guests get to see it, especially if they're only staying one night." She rose from the table and led Tiffany and Kevin into the hotel, then down a long corridor until they reached an outside door that led to the atrium.

The air was moist and fragrant inside the atrium, and flowers bloomed plentifully, competing for color.

"This is beautiful," Tiffany said as they stepped inside.

Raegan smiled over at her. "There's sort of a secret garden beyond it. Come on, I'll show you." She led them through an archway of rose bushes thick with pink and red blooms. The cobblestone path wound its way through several gardens until the path opened up to display a stone well. The larger stones glinted bronze and copper in the morning light, and set among the larger stones were collections of smaller colorful stones.

"Oh," Tiffany said. "Butterflies."

Raegan nodded. "We call it the Butterfly Wishing Well." She crossed to it and leaned over, looking down inside the darkness for a moment. "The well was transported from a small town in Mexico, where it was originally built hundreds of years ago. Legend is that any coin dropped inside will lead to your heart's wish coming true."

She turned back to Tiffany, who was wiping tears from her cheeks. Kevin had put his arm around her shoulders.

"How does it work?" Tiffany asked.

"The village legend was that the butterflies carry the wishes to heaven, where only the most sincere wishes are granted."

"My grandparents are in heaven," Tiffany said in a quiet voice.

Raegan met her gaze and felt her own eyes tear up. She held out a coin from the few she'd slipped into her pocket earlier. Tiffany stepped forward and took the coin. She walked to the edge of the well and stood there for a moment, her eyes closed. Then she dropped the coin inside.

Everyone was so still that Raegan heard the faint sound the coin made when it hit the water. Tiffany exhaled, then she turned to Raegan and hugged her.

Next she hugged Kevin. "Thank you both," she said when she released him. "I'm going to get ready for the day. And, Raegan? When my mother comes, tell her I'd like to speak to her."

Raegan couldn't have been more surprised, and Kevin opened his mouth as if he was about to protest; but then he said nothing and watched Tiffany walk away.

He crossed to Raegan and grasped her hand. "I don't even know how to thank you," he said. "This place is perfect. Healing."

Raegan looked up at him and saw the gratitude in his brown eyes. "It is pretty much perfect." She moved closer to him. "I'm sorry all of this is happening on the day of your gala."

Kevin pulled her into his arms and rested his head on top of hers. "I think it will turn out fine. If Tiffany is willing to speak with her mother, that is a really good step. Up until now, she's been very anxious about it."

Raegan leaned into him, enjoyed the strength and warmth of his arms. "And what about you? Will you speak with her?"

He exhaled, his breath warm against her cheek and neck. "I'm going to try, and I'm hoping to talk her out of the lawsuit." He drew away slightly, looking into her eyes. "If we can repair our relationships instead of resorting to threats and lawsuits, this world will be a much better place."

"Agreed," Raegan said, smiling up at him. "Do you have a wish to make?"

He grinned. "I do."

She fished another coin out of her pocket and handed it to him. He took it with one hand, and with his other hand, he interlocked their fingers. Then he led her the few steps to the well.

"What are you going to wish for?"

He cast her a sideways glance. "Will the wish be granted if I tell you?"

"If you whisper it," she said, trying to hold back a laugh.

He leaned down, his lips right next to her ear as he whispered. "I wish I could kiss you again."

Tingles danced along her skin. "You don't need to toss a coin in a well for that wish to come true."

His lips pressed against her cheek. "That's good to know." And then his mouth was on hers, kissing her. She lifted up on her toes and wrapped her arms around his neck. Pulling him closer, she kissed him back and let herself melt into his touch.

His fingers tangled in her hair as he intensified his kiss. Raegan simply breathed him in, letting any past or future concerns fade for a short time. For now, it was just Kevin and her in a garden by a wishing well.

Kevin moved his hands down her back, and a warm shiver ran through her. How was it possible that their bodies seemed to fit so perfectly together? The more she kissed him, the more she didn't want to be separated from him.

"Raegan," Kevin whispered between kisses. "Your phone keeps buzzing."

Raegan only pulled him closer. "It can wait."

"Mmmm," Kevin mumbled, kissing her again.

But the phone started buzzing anew seconds later.

She drew away from Kevin, disoriented and light-headed. Inhaling, she pulled her cell out of her pocket. "It's security." She answered immediately, still trying to catch her breath.

After she listened to the man on the other end of the line, she said, "Thank you, I'm on my way." She hung up and met Kevin's gaze. "She's at the front desk."

"So soon?"

"It looks like someone else is with her—a man who probably gave her a ride."

"Let's go," Kevin said, setting his mouth into a firm line. He took her hand, and they walked back through the garden, then through the atrium. Once inside the hotel, he let go of her hand and straightened the collar of his shirt.

"I'll text Tiffany," Raegan said. "We can bring your sister to the Pebble Conference Room, and Tiffany can meet us there."

Kevin just nodded, and Raegan hoped that the situation wouldn't escalate and that Tiffany could have a cleansing discussion with her mother.

They reached the lobby, and a woman standing in front of the reception desk turned and peered over at them. Raegan immediately noticed the resemblance, although Kevin's sister had obviously lived a harsh life. Lines on her face pulled against her eyes and mouth, and her body was stick-thin beneath her baggy t-shirt and worn jeans.

Her dark hair was pulled into a sloppy ponytail, and she wore no makeup except for garish red lipstick. Her eyes widened when she saw Kevin striding toward her, and her gaze flicked between Kevin and Raegan.

"Rita." Kevin stopped in front of his sister. "Who's this?"

Kevin obviously meant the short, bald guy next to Rita. He looked to be in his mid-thirties, but premature balding had caused him to shave his hair off.

Raegan knew right away that she didn't trust whoever this guy was, and it was easy enough to assume he was Rita's boyfriend.

"Jerry, this is my hotshot brother, Kevin," Rita said in a raspy voice, probably marred by years of smoking.

Jerry wiped his thick palm on his seen-better-days khakis, then stuck out his hand. Kevin grasped it for a second, then let go, keeping his steely gaze on Jerry as if he was trying to see into his mind. Raegan was impressed Kevin had even shaken the man's hand.

Rita didn't miss one bit of the unspoken exchange between the men. She also didn't miss the fact that three security officers were standing nearby. "Where's Tiffany?" she asked, her eyes boring into Kevin.

"We're meeting her in one of the hotel's conference rooms," Kevin said.

Raegan could practically see the tension radiating from him. She stepped forward and stuck out her hand to Rita. "I'm Raegan Stone, events coordinator for the hotel. I'm also a friend of Kevin's and Tiffany's. If you'll follow me, I'll take you and your brother to the conference room."

Rita's dark gaze settled on Raegan, and she lifted her hand to reluctantly shake Raegan's. Her hand was cool and dry, with little grip.

"This way please," Raegan said, releasing Rita's hand. As Jerry stepped forward to follow, Raegan said, "You'll be more comfortable waiting in the lobby, Jerry."

"No," Rita said. "He's coming with us."

"Unfortunately, he's not on our guest list," Raegan said. "Only pre-arranged guests can meet in our conference rooms." She kept her gaze steady on Rita. "If you want to meet your daughter, then Jerry has to wait here."

Rita's eyes narrowed, and she looked from Jerry, to Kevin, to Raegan. "All right," she finally said. "But you'd better not bully me about anything else."

Kevin tensed, but Raegan shot him a look that everything would be okay. The group walked along the corridor, with two of the security officers following.

"Who are those guys?" Rita hissed to Kevin.

"Insurance that the meeting will be peaceful," Kevin said in a calm voice.

"What? You think I'm going to freak out or something?"

Kevin met her gaze full-on. "I honestly don't know what your motivations are, Rita. First you file a lawsuit, then you insist on driving two hours to confront Tiffany. My job as her uncle and employer is to make sure she feels safe, and I'll do whatever that takes."

Rita folded her arms and stared straight ahead. But Raegan noticed her expression had softened.

Tiffany was standing just inside the door to the conference room. Rita's step slowed when she saw her daughter.

Tiffany gave a small nod, her expression unreadable, then moved into the room and took a seat at the table. Kevin walked into the room next, then Rita. She sat across from Tiffany and placed her hands on the table and clenched them together.

Kevin moved back toward the door and told the security officers they could wait outside. "Are you sure?" Raegan asked him in a quiet voice.

"Yes," he said. "Thanks for making Jerry stay in the lobby. I think we'll have a decent discussion now." He reached for her hand. "Do you want to come in?"

"I'll let you have your privacy," Raegan said. "But I'll wait in the hallway for you if you want."

His gaze held hers. "Definitely. And thank you again."

Raegan watched him go inside the room and shut the door. Then she crossed to the other side of the hall and leaned against the wall.

Fourteen

Kevin decided to let Tiffany steer the conversation. He was there in a supportive role and wouldn't intervene unless necessary. He thought back to the wishing well in the hotel's garden and marveled at how such a simple thing could turn Tiffany's heart toward her mother. Especially since her mother wasn't entirely deserving of Tiffany's kindness.

But the woman who sat across from Kevin now was not the sister of a few years ago. Kevin had sensed the change in Rita the moment he saw her in the lobby. Yes, her words had been sharp and defiant, but it was almost as if she was acting in front of her friend Jerry. Kevin sensed that his first impression was right that his sister had a boyfriend who was trying to take advantage of her.

"Rita," Tiffany began. Her therapist had counseled her to call her mother by her first name as a way of disassociating herself from the deep pain of neglect. "I'm glad you made it here safe."

Rita's thin brows shot up, and she said, "I wanted to talk to you alone." She threw Kevin a significant glance.

Tiffany exhaled slowly. "Let's take things one step at a time. For now, I'm more comfortable with Kevin with us when we get together. And I'd like to spend more time with you."

"Oh." Rita looked down at her hands, her mouth trembling. "I'd like to spend more time with you, too."

"Kevin told me about the lawsuit," Tiffany said.

Kevin snapped his head to look at Tiffany, surprised that she'd be so direct.

"Tell me why you're so upset," Tiffany said.

Rita gave a slight shake of her head, then brought her hands to her face. She took several breaths, as if to steady her emotion. Then she fumbled in the bag she had over her shoulder, and Kevin tensed, watching her every movement. She took out a cigarette, then dropped it back in her bag. "I guess I can't smoke in here."

Neither Kevin nor Tiffany said anything. Rita rubbed her face, closing her eyes for a moment, then looked at Tiffany, eyes rimmed in red. "I read your story on Kevin's website, and it tore my heart out."

Kevin placed a hand over Tiffany's.

"I know . . . I know that things aren't good between us," Rita said. "And I know I've made terrible mistakes, but I'm trying to get everything together as best as I can." She looked down at her hands again.

"What about Jerry?" Tiffany asked. "Did he ask you to file a lawsuit against your own brother?"

Rita shook her head, then stopped. "Yes, he did. I agreed with him at the time." She looked from Tiffany to Kevin. "But I didn't expect to see you both. I thought you'd try to kick me out of the hotel."

"My greatest wish is to move past all the bad stuff we

went through," Tiffany said. "To forgive each other and start over."

Tears filled Rita's eyes. "You . . . *forgive* me?" she whispered.

"I do," Tiffany said, her eyes tearing up as well. She turned her hand over and squeezed Kevin's hand. "But your lawsuit is preventing us from healing our relationship."

Rita sniffed and wiped at the moisture on her face. "I'm sorry for that. I'm sorry for everything." She covered her mouth with her hand and choked back a sob. "I don't want to sue you, Kevin," she said, looking at him. "I don't want to make another mistake."

Kevin's heart swelled. He'd heard words of apology and manipulation from his sister before, but the atmosphere in the room was different this time. Her tears or her sorrowful tone didn't convince him. It was his intuition—Rita was sincere this time.

He reached across the table with his other hand and grasped hers. He hadn't had any physical contact with his sister in years. Her hand was thin and fragile. "Tell your story, Rita. Tonight, at the gala, tell your story."

She stared at him in stunned silence. Then Tiffany took her other hand, and their intertwined hands made a complete circle. A broken family becoming whole again.

"What do I say?" she asked in a small voice.

"The truth," he said. "If they hear the truth from a woman who fought her way back again, hearts will change tonight."

She looked over at Tiffany, tears dripping down her face. Then she said in the softest whisper, "I'll do it."

It was as if all sound and breathing had stopped in the room, giving way to an utter stillness. Kevin blinked back the tears forming in his own eyes.

Rita exhaled. "I need some paper," she continued in a quiet voice. "I need to organize my thoughts, and I don't want to leave out the important things."

Kevin squeezed his sister's hand. "We can get some paper."

She nodded. "And Kevin? Can you tell Jerry I won't need him to take me back home? I'll find a bus after the gala."

"It will be too late for a bus when the gala gets over," Kevin said. "Stay at the hotel tonight, and I'll drive you back in the morning."

"Really?" Rita said.

"Of course." He looked over at Tiffany. "She'll need a dress. Do you have something?"

"There's a row of shops on Tangerine Street. I'm sure we could find something."

"All right," Kevin said, rising to his feet. "Shopping it is. But first, I'll find some paper."

He opened the door and saw Raegan still waiting with the two security guards. He shut the door behind him and told the guards that everything was fine and they were no longer needed.

Raegan was watching with curiosity. He crossed to her and said, "She's going to tell her story at the gala. I don't know what else will happen, but at least we have that. I'm going to find Jerry and send him home, then apparently I'm shopping for a dress with Tiffany and Rita."

"Wow," Raegan said, then wrapped her arms about his waist. Kevin pulled her tightly against him. "I'm so glad," she said. "But let me go with them shopping. You probably have a lot to do."

"I do, but this is more important." Kevin slipped his hand into hers. "We'll all go."

Raegan smiled up at him. "All right. I can play hooky for a bit."

He leaned down and kissed her cheek, lingering. "How can I thank you for everything?"

"I'm sure something will come to mind."

He was about to kiss her for real when the conference room door opened. Tiffany came out with Rita, who gave a small smile to Raegan.

Rita looked at Raegan and said, "I'm sorry about all of this—bringing drama to your hotel."

Raegan touched Rita's arm. "Don't worry about it. Kevin told me what you want to do tonight. You're a courageous woman."

Rita's eyes filled with tears. "Thank you," she whispered.

"Kevin will go talk to Jerry," Raegan said. "And while he's doing that, I want to show you a special place in the hotel garden."

Kevin grinned, knowing what Raegan had planned. It seemed that wishes, and dreams, could very well come true. He left the women heading in the other direction, and he walked to the lobby.

Jerry was leaning on the reception counter talking to Paulie. He was obviously flirting, but Paulie looked quite horrified.

"Jerry," Kevin said, and the man whirled around. His expression filled with all kinds of guilt when he saw who'd called his name. "Good news," Kevin continued. "Rita will be staying at the hotel with us tonight, so she doesn't need a ride home."

Jerry's brows shot up. "I—what do you mean? What happened?" His eyes narrowed. "What did you tell her this time?"

"This time?" Kevin said. "I don't know what you're talking about. But Rita wanted me to pass on the message. Thanks for bringing her out." He folded his arms and kept his gaze steady on Jerry.

"But—I—Where is Rita?"

"She's with her daughter, and they'll be together for the rest of the day," Kevin said, leaning in and saying in a quiet voice, "I think your plans have been derailed. It's best you get out of here quickly."

Jerry's round face reddened. He stared at Kevin for a moment, then finally turned. Kevin watched as the man walked out the hotel. When he was confident Jerry had truly left, Kevin went to find Raegan and his sister and niece.

By the time he reached the atrium, the women were already coming out. Rita looked as if she'd found an instant best friend in Raegan.

As soon as Rita saw Kevin, she slowed. "Did Jerry leave?" she asked.

"He did," Kevin said. "He wasn't too happy about it though."

Rita pursed her lips and looked away for a moment. When she met Kevin's gaze again, her eyes were watery. "I'm breaking up with Jerry, and I'm dropping the lawsuit." She looked over at Tiffany. "You're the most important thing in my life, and I don't ever want to jeopardize that."

Tiffany nodded, then whispered. "Thanks, Mom." She pulled Rita into a hug, and Kevin felt his heart swell until his throat was thick with emotion.

Raegan came to stand beside Kevin. She leaned against him, and he wrapped an arm about her. Having Raegan nestled against him and watching his sister and niece getting along was beyond anything he could have ever dreamed up this weekend.

DREAMS COME TRUE

When Rita and Tiffany drew apart, both wiping their eyes, Tiffany said, "Let's go shopping."

Kevin laughed, his heart feeling lighter than it had in years.

Fifteen

The gala was a whirlwind of introductions to Kevin's friends and associates. And the armor Raegan had built up—assuming everyone would be assessing her—melted away in minutes. She had no idea the rich and famous could be so absolutely genuine. No one seemed to look down on her for being an average, everyday woman; in fact, she felt she was being admired by both the men and women.

She'd worn a simple navy gown that reached to the floor and was accompanied by a black sequined shrug. Her hair was pulled up off her neck and twisted into a simple up-do. Raegan guessed her dress cost a fraction of what the other women were wearing.

Kevin kept a hold of her hand through the first part of the evening during the cocktail reception. Raegan was sure she should know more people than she recognized, and all of their names sounded familiar as well. She'd have to do a lot of Googling later on. It was sweet to see Tiffany lead her mother around and introduce her to the guests.

DREAMS COME TRUE

Rita was welcomed with no questions or raised eyebrows. Raegan could almost see the woman grow in stature with each passing minute.

"How are you doing?" Kevin whispered in her ear when the two women they were talking to turned their attention to a man who entered their conversation circle.

"I'm amazed," Raegan said truthfully. "You're amazing."

He smiled, then kissed her cheek, and Raegan felt the warmth buzz through her.

"I think you're the amazing one," Kevin said.

She wished all of the people in the room could melt away for a few moments. Instead, she settled for a shared smile.

"Our table is over here," Kevin said, leading her through a series of tables. He stopped to greet several people along the way.

"Of course it's up front," Raegan commented with a laugh as they arrived at their table. Tiffany and Rita were already seated at the table, and Raegan was glad that at least they were familiar.

Kevin pulled out the chair for her, then leaned down. "I'll be right back. Someone's got to get this thing started."

He strode away, leaving all kinds of tingles in his wake. Up on the small stage, he adjusted the microphone, then said, "Welcome to the Dreams Come True Gala. I'm so pleased to see all of you here. Please take your seats and enjoy the meal. In about half an hour we'll start the program, with Preston McNeil as our host."

Raegan's heart thumped as Kevin's eyes met hers several times while he addressed the crowd. And when he stepped off the stage and walked directly toward her, she was glad she was sitting down. He looked more than fabulous in a tuxedo, and Raegan felt as if she was in a dream herself.

Dinner went by quickly, and it was a new experience being treated as a guest at the hotel. Jill and Mari had both texted Raegan multiple times, each wanting reports of the evening. When Preston got up to begin the program, Raegan saw Tiffany smile at Rita and pat her hand. Raegan's heart expanded just watching the healing that was taking place between the two women.

Preston called Kevin up to introduce his sister, and it seemed that everyone in the crowd was sitting on the edge of their chairs. He'd explained to Raegan earlier that they'd never had a speaker who was a rehabilitated parent.

Kevin welcomed Rita onto the stage, then took his place at the table again, next to Raegan. They held hands, and Raegan could practically feel the nervous thump of his heart. They needn't have worried. Rita's speech was heartfelt and sincere, and Raegan didn't think there was a dry eye in the room, including the servers'. It was clear that her regrets were profound, but she had been able to move forward by keeping her focus on healing her relationship with her family.

When Rita finished, everyone stood and clapped. Tiffany and Kevin went to meet Rita, and both of them hugged her. Raegan couldn't stop smiling through her tears. The crowd quieted as the lights lowered and Preston started a slideshow presentation of children who were recipients of the Dreams Come True charity.

"Let's get out of here," Kevin whispered in her ear.

"Can we leave?" Raegan said. "What about the rest of the program?"

"Preston has it covered, and we won't be gone too long." Kevin stood, then pulled Raegan to her feet. They exited out of the nearest side door.

Once in the corridor, Raegan said, "Where are we going?"

"It's a surprise." Kevin led her toward the atrium.

"What? You want to make a wish now?" Raegan teased.

He flashed her a smile; then they stepped into the atrium. The velvety darkness of the evening was broken up by hundreds of tiny white lights interspersed among the climbing ivy. The place was empty, and soft music was playing.

Kevin stopped and drew her toward him. "I don't need a wishing well."

She wrapped her arms about his neck. "You sound pretty confident, Mr. Wood."

"I hope my assumptions aren't wrong," he said, his breath touching her face.

"What assumptions?"

"That you like me," he said in a near whisper. "I know I like you."

"I think you can assume that I like you," Raegan said, her heart rate speeding up.

He kissed her, softly at first, then heating up as he pulled her closer.

Raegan felt herself drowning in everything that was Kevin—his kissing, the strength of his body, the way he teased her, and how comfortable she felt around him.

Kevin buried his face against her neck and started to sway, dancing slowly. They rotated, becoming immersed in the ambience of sweet-smelling flowers and soft music.

"I think dreams do come true," Raegan said, not really meaning to speak it out loud. Being here, alone with Kevin, she felt as if anything was possible. Yet . . . he was leaving tomorrow, and the thought made her feel like a vast stretch of empty days lay before her. "What happens tomorrow?" she asked.

Kevin kept dancing with her for a few more moments;

then he slowed and lifted his head, looking into her eyes. "What do you want to happen, Raegan?"

The way he was looking at her made her toes curl and her heart thump. "I don't know—I don't want you to leave though. Maybe you could extend your stay?"

One side of his mouth lifted. "I don't think hotel living would be very convenient after a while, even if I could see you more. I'd probably become a stalker, and you wouldn't get much work done."

Raegan laughed, although inside she wondered how they could possibly make a long-distance relationship work.

"Raegan," he said, his hands moving to her face. "Do you know what else is on my bucket list?"

She shook her head.

"I've always wanted to buy a beach house."

Raegan stared at him. "What are you saying?"

"That I don't want this to end—*us* to end," he said, his hands sliding along her neck, then resting on her shoulders. "Tomorrow I have an appointment with a realtor named Paul Studly . . . don't laugh about his name. He's going to show me some available properties. Do you want to come?"

Raegan's heart about flipped over. "Yes," was all she could manage; then she was lifting up on her toes and pulling his face toward hers.

Kevin grinned right before kissing her again. "Good. I don't think I could have wished for anything better."

Dear Reader,

We hoped you enjoyed *The Mariposa Hotel*! This has been a fun project, and reviews help us spread the word. Please consider reviewing *Mariposa* on Amazon, Goodreads, Barnes & Noble, GooglePlay, Kobo, or iTunes. Or if you'd like to contact one of us personally, our websites are listed in our author bios.

Sincerely,
Julie, Melanie & Heather

then he slowed and lifted his head, looking into her eyes. "What do you want to happen, Raegan?"

The way he was looking at her made her toes curl and her heart thump. "I don't know—I don't want you to leave though. Maybe you could extend your stay?"

One side of his mouth lifted. "I don't think hotel living would be very convenient after a while, even if I could see you more. I'd probably become a stalker, and you wouldn't get much work done."

Raegan laughed, although inside she wondered how they could possibly make a long-distance relationship work.

"Raegan," he said, his hands moving to her face. "Do you know what else is on my bucket list?"

She shook her head.

"I've always wanted to buy a beach house."

Raegan stared at him. "What are you saying?"

"That I don't want this to end—*us* to end," he said, his hands sliding along her neck, then resting on her shoulders. "Tomorrow I have an appointment with a realtor named Paul Studly . . . don't laugh about his name. He's going to show me some available properties. Do you want to come?"

Raegan's heart about flipped over. "Yes," was all she could manage; then she was lifting up on her toes and pulling his face toward hers.

Kevin grinned right before kissing her again. "Good. I don't think I could have wished for anything better."

Dear Reader,

We hoped you enjoyed *The Mariposa Hotel*! This has been a fun project, and reviews help us spread the word. Please consider reviewing *Mariposa* on Amazon, Goodreads, Barnes & Noble, GooglePlay, Kobo, or iTunes. Or if you'd like to contact one of us personally, our websites are listed in our author bios.

Sincerely,
Julie, Melanie & Heather

The Tangerine Street Romance series:

Julie Wright

Julie Wright started her first book when she was fifteen. She's written over a dozen books since then, is a Whitney Award winner, and feels she's finally getting the hang of this writing gig. She enjoys speaking to writing groups, youth groups, and schools. She loves reading, eating, writing, hiking, playing on the beach with her kids, and snuggling with her husband to watch movies. Julie's favorite thing to do is watch her husband make dinner. She hates mayonnaise but has a healthy respect for ice cream.

Visit her website: JulieWright.com
Twitter: @scatteredjules

Melanie Jacobson

Melanie Bennett Jacobson is an avid reader, amateur cook, and champion shopper. She consumes astonishing amounts of chocolate, chick flicks, and romance novels. After meeting her husband online, she is now living happily married in Southern California with her growing family and a series of doomed houseplants. Melanie is a former English teacher and a sometime blogger who loves to laugh and make others laugh. In her downtime (ha!), she writes romantic comedies and pines after beautiful shoes.

Visit her website: MelanieJacobson.net
Twitter: @Writestuff_Mel

Heather B. Moore

Heather B. Moore is a *USA Today* bestselling author of more than a dozen historical novels and thrillers, written under the pen name H.B. Moore. She writes women's fiction, romance and inspirational nonfiction under Heather B. Moore. This can all be confusing, so her kids just call her Mom. Heather attended Cairo American College in Egypt, the Anglican School of Jerusalem in Israel, and earned a Bachelor of Science degree from Brigham Young University in Utah.

Heather's email list at: HBMoore.com/contact/
Blog: MyWritersLair.blogspot.com
Website: HBMoore.com
Twitter: @heatherbmoore

www.ingramcontent.com/pod-product-compliance
Lightning Source LLC
LaVergne TN
LVHW021232080526
838199LV00088B/4323